A Stitch in Crime

A STITCH IN CRIME

BETTY HECHTMAN

WHEELER
CHIVERS

This Large Print edition is published by Wheeler Publishing, Waterville, Maine, USA and by BBC Audiobooks Ltd, Bath, England.
Wheeler Publishing, a part of Gale, Cengage Learning.
Copyright © 2010 by Betty Hechtman.
The moral right of the author has been asserted.
A Crochet Mystery.

LIBRARY OF CONGRESS CATALOGING-IN-PUBLICATION DATA

Hechtman, Betty, 1947–
   A stitch in crime / by Betty Hechtman. — Large print ed.
     p. cm. — (A crochet mystery) (Wheeler publishing large print cozy mystery)
     Originally published: New York : Berkley Prime Crime, 2010.
     ISBN-13: 978-1-4104-2685-7
     ISBN-10: 1-4104-2685-8
     1. Crocheting—Fiction. 2. Murder—Investigation—Fiction. 3. Large type books. I. Title.
PS3608.E288S75 2010
813'.6—dc22
                                      2010007320

BRITISH LIBRARY CATALOGUING-IN-PUBLICATION DATA AVAILABLE

Published in 2010 in the U.S. by arrangement with The Berkley Publishing Group, a member of Penguin Group (USA) Inc.
Published in 2010 in the U.K. by arrangement with the author.

U.K. Hardcover: 978 1 408 49138 6 (Chivers Large Print)
U.K. Softcover: 978 1 408 49139 3 (Camden Large Print)

Printed in the United States of America
1 2 3 4 5 6 7 14 13 12 11 10

ACKNOWLEDGMENTS

I'd like to thank Sandy Harding for her continued enthusiasm and great editing. Thanks to everyone at Berkley Prime Crime for the great cover and all their efforts on my behalf. None of this would have happened without my agent, Jessica Faust.

Thank you, Howard Marx, M.D., for the quick answers to all my medical questions. Appellate Defender Judy Libby keeps the lawyer information coming. Roberta Martia is my crochet tester and chief cheerleader.

And Burl and Max — you guys are still the best. Thanks for being such devoted recipe testers.

CHAPTER 1

"Molly, please try to get through the weekend without any dead bodies," Mrs. Shedd
said, pushing the rhinestone-encrusted
clipboard across her desk to me. "And take
good care of this. It's the first time I've
turned it over to anyone." I could see why
she made the dead body comment. After
forty-seven years of not one dead body
showing up in my life, there had been a
plethora of them in the past couple of years.

"Don't worry," I said. "No murder or
mayhem, I promise." I completely meant it
when I said it. Too bad it turned out not to
be true.

I stared at the fancy clipboard for a mo-
ment as what it meant sank in. Every
September the bookstore where I worked,
Shedd & Royal Books and More, put on
the Get Out of the Heat and Light Your
Creative Fire retreat on the Monterey
Peninsula. The "getting out of the heat"

referred to the September weather in Tarzana, California, which was always hot and dry. In contrast, the Monterey area was cool and damp year round. I'd never been on one of the retreats, but I knew Mrs. Shedd chose four or five creative pursuits, such as writing or candle making, and lined up local people to put on the workshops. The retreaters committed to a topic and went to a number of sessions over the long weekend. At the end there was a gathering and everyone got to show off what they'd done.

"This retreat is your baby. Are you sure you want to do this?" I asked, expecting some kind of explanation.

Mrs. Shedd shook her head, making her perfect blond pageboy swing. "I'm more than sure. It's your baby now, Molly. Something's come up and I can't go," she said cryptically.

Pamela Shedd was the co-owner of Shedd & Royal Books and More, which made her my boss. I was surprised she didn't give me any more details of why she suddenly couldn't go on the retreat, but it wasn't my place to ask. Since I was the community relations–event coordinator for the bookstore, it made sense that she was putting me in charge. But no way was it going to sit well with my co-worker Adele Abrams.

My boss picked up a box from the floor next to her and handed it to me, saying it held the folders for the presenters along with the schedule for the weekend. Later I could pick up the larger boxes with the folders for the retreaters and the other supplies. She seemed relieved to have passed everything off to me. "Oh, and be sure to have fun."

I put the clipboard on top of the box and took it with me as I headed across the bookstore to the event area, where my crochet group, the Tarzana Hookers, was already assembled. Morning sunlight streamed in the window that faced Ventura Boulevard. The long table was strewn with balls of yarn, coffee cups and some completed projects the members had brought in to show off to the group. The crochet group met regularly at Shedd & Royal. Adele Abrams, who along with being my coworker, was coleader of the group and a crochet fanatic, was waving around her hook, which had something white and fuzzy hanging from it. As I got closer, she began to pass around what she was working on.

"Pink, you missed it," Adele said, her voice full of excitement. I had gotten past being upset about her insistence on calling me by my last name. "I just created a stitch." She pointed toward what looked like a row of fuzzy, white yarn bumps in Eduardo's hand. Eduardo Linnares was our only male member. I doubt most people would pick him out as a crocheter. In his other life he was a cover model, and he definitely looked the part. He was tall with long, shiny black hair, handsome, even features and a muscular body that must have required long hours at the gym. But he fit into the group very nicely thanks to his pleasant disposition and his skill with a hook. His grandmother had taught him well.

"Creating stitches is something we crochet divas do," Adele said, crowing with pride. "I'm thinking of calling it the marshmallow stitch."

At the word "marshmallow," CeeCee Collins looked up. She was the host of the reality show *Making Amends* and had a legendary sweet tooth; hence her interest at the mention of a sweet. When she realized what Adele was talking about, she seemed momentarily disappointed before taking the piece of yarn from Eduardo and examining it.

CeeCee's acting career had recently had a resurgence, and she'd gone from occasional cameos to being in the limelight. The best thing about her was that she could be a celebrity and a regular person at the same time. Well, sort of a regular person. She was the only one of us who had to be concerned about being caught by the paparazzi with soup dripping down her chin.

"I can't say it looks good enough to eat, but you're right — the way it puffs up with the halo of white, bulky yarn does make it look like a marshmallow, dear. What are you going to do with it?"

"I used that baby yarn we made the cuddle blankets with," Adele said, referring to a group project in which we made soft blankets for traumatized children. She took the strip and held it on her wrist. "I could make a bracelet." Then she held it across her chest. "Or keep going and make a vest." Adele was amply built and had an eye for the outrageous when it came to clothes. Knowing her, she'd probably go for the vest.

Sheila Altman put down her hook and looked at Adele's creation. She was dressed in a black suit, which was her uniform for her job as the receptionist at the local women's gym. For once she seemed relatively anxiety free. Just hearing about all she had on her plate made me nervous. Along with juggling several jobs, she was going to school to become a costume designer, and lived in a rented room partially paid for by babysitting the homeowner's kids. "I think you should use it for trim," Sheila said, taking the strip and holding it at the bottom of the blue scarf she was working on.

Then Sheila handed the piece to me. As Adele's gaze turned my way, she saw the box with the clipboard on top that I had set on the table. I prepared myself for the onslaught.

"What are you doing with the rhinestone clipboard?" Adele demanded. Was there a little quiver in her lip? When I didn't answer immediately, she stood up. "Well, Pink, what's the story?"

Even after several years, Adele had still not gotten over the fact I'd been hired as the event coordinator at Shedd & Royal Books and More. It didn't matter that I had a background in public relations thanks to my late husband Charlie's business; Adele still thought she should have gotten the position. To soothe her hurt feelings, she had gotten the children's story time. And over time, Adele had managed to work her way into handling some events with me.

"Mrs. Shedd told me she isn't going to the Get Out of the Heat and Light Your Creative Fire weekend. She put me in charge and turned over the rhinestone clipboard," I said finally.

"That's ridiculous! You're not qualified. How many of the retreats have you gone on?" Adele said. Without waiting for an answer, she continued. "I've been on every one since I started working here, which was years before you started."

Adele was right on that point — I had never been on one of the retreats. I had been left in charge of the bookstore while Mrs. Shedd and Adele went. But I had already arranged to go this year as a participant and to help Mrs. Shedd. Why should it matter that I hadn't gone before, anyway? I had put on countless author events. Yes, there had been a few problems, like the smoke alarm going off during a cookbook demo and the fire department showing up. Another time the men's bathroom flooded when it turned out a fixit book author didn't know quite how to fix it. But the sense of not knowing what was going to happen had turned out to be a benefit, and was attracting more and more people to the bookstore's events.

It occurred to me that that sort of unpredictability might not transfer well to the retreat. But certainly I could get through four days without anything terrible happening. I was in my late forties, mature and able to handle things, right? Okay, I'd gotten involved in a few murders, but I'd managed to solve them, hadn't I? Besides, there weren't going to be any murders during the weekend. I simply wouldn't allow it to happen.

"I'm sorry you feel that way, Adele, but it's a done deal," I said, trying to end the discussion. I knew there was nothing I could say that could smooth things over. At least I now understood Adele's over-the-top behavior. Once, when we had sat crocheting together in the kids' department, she had opened up and told me her life story. It was kind of like Cinderella without Prince Charming, the fairy godmother, or the happy ending. All she'd gotten were the nasty stepmother and stepsisters.

But understanding her history didn't mean her personality was always easy to take.

I sensed someone come up behind me. "Excuse me, ladies," a female voice said. "Which one of you is Molly Pink?"

Before I could volunteer the information, several fingers were pointing toward me.

A woman with shoulder-length champagne blond hair and Angelina Jolie–quality puffy lips stepped into my line of vision. Before I could speak, Adele stood up so quickly her chair fell over, and she rushed up to the new arrival.

"I know who you are. You're Izabelle Landers." Then Adele did something I never thought I would see. She raised her arms in a worshipful position and bowed to the newcomer. "I'm awed by your crochet work." Adele turned to the rest of the table. "She's the author of *A Subtle Touch of Crochet.*" All of our gazes moved back to Izabelle, who appeared uncomfortable at Adele's antics.

"Mrs. Shedd said to see you," Izabelle said to me. "She said you had the folders for the weekend." Then I put it all together. "You're doing the crochet workshops, right?" Of course, I recognized her now from the photo on the back of her book, though her green eyes were much more startling in person.

Adele stepped in front of me. "Did I mention that your book on crochet embellishments has been an inspiration? I love embellishments." As if to illustrate, Adele turned around in model fashion. There was nothing subtle about her embellishments. She wiggled her behind to show off the trim she'd added to the back pockets of her jeans and then kicked her leg out to show off the line of what looked like coasters she'd attached to the bottom of her pants. She pulled her bag off the table and swung it in

Izabelle's face. "I got this flower pattern from your book," she said, pointing out the felted fuchsia flowers clustered around the handles of the black fabric tote bag.

Izabelle nodded uncomfortably at the fashion show and at the first chance turned back to me, saying she was going up to the retreat a day early and wanted to pick up her folder.

"You'll find all the information in here," I said, handing Izabelle a thick packet.

"I'll be going to your workshops, though obviously I'm a very experienced crocheter," Adele said, grabbing the white puffy piece and holding it out. "I'm a crochet designer, too. I just invented a stitch."

Izabelle barely looked at Adele's offering. My bookstore associate didn't seem to have any radar to detect how people were reacting to her. Instead of picking up on Izabelle's dismissal, Adele put her crochet creation on the table and hung close to the weekend presenter, prattling on about how she'd be glad to help out with the workshop. Izabelle thumbed through the folder.

"Before you leave, would you sign the copies we have of your book?" Adele didn't wait for an answer, she just ran off toward the craft books. Izabelle definitely heard that question and looked over everyone's works-in-progress as she waited for Adele's return.

"Sorry I'm late," Dinah Lyons said, arriving in a burst of energy. She's my best friend and a freshman English instructor at Beasley Community College. She wore her salt-and-pepper hair short, which, along with her scarf wardrobe, gave her an arty, offbeat look. I was surprised at the flowing piece of white chiffon she was wearing, since she usually went for a couple of scarves in unusual color combinations. Dinah looked at Izabelle, assumed she was a new member of the group, and started to introduce herself, but she was stopped by Izabelle's condescending smile — as if it was ridiculous to think she'd be one of us.

Izabelle set Dinah straight about who she was and why she was there. Then she spoke to the rest of us. "I don't usually put on retreat workshops. The only reason I agreed to do the crochet session was Mrs. Shedd said I could demonstrate the fusion craft featured in my upcoming book. I want to practice it in front of a live audience before I go on the road with it. When my new book comes out, I'm going to be doing a major tour with stops at *The Today Show, Martha Stewart,* and some others." Izabelle waited for the expected oohs and aahs, the loudest of which came from Adele as she returned, holding several of the large hardbound copies of Izabelle's current release.

CeeCee took advantage of the lull in conversation. "Molly, if you're in charge, then I guess you're the one I have to break the bad news to. You know I committed to running the acting workshop at the retreat, but I'm not going to make it until the last day." Izabelle looked at our resident celebrity and seemed to just get who she was as CeeCee explained that the Hearts and Barks charity we'd helped before was having its yearly luncheon and that the entertainment was scenes from some current musicals. "The headliner, Helen Jones, had an emergency appendectomy, and you know the show has to go on, particularly when you've sold lots and lots of tickets and you don't want to cancel and refund all that money meant to help the free pet clinic." CeeCee paused to see if I was getting it. "I'm not sure you girls know, but I've done my share of singing and dancing, and my name means something. I couldn't say no."

Not a good sign. I'd barely been in charge of the weekend for an hour and Adele was practically smothering the crochet workshop leader, and now CeeCee was telling me she was going to be a no-show. I opened my mouth to object, but CeeCee turned on her

18

magnetic smile.

"Now, dear, just because I can't make it doesn't mean I'm leaving you in the lurch. I found a replacement. He'll probably do even better than I would have. He not only acts, but is the director of his own little theater. He knows how to work with actors, or people who want to be actors, better than I do."

Izabelle had signed the books and set them on the table, and was now intently looking at CeeCee. "I thought it was you, but then I wasn't sure. But it really is you, isn't it?"

CeeCee was used to those kinds of comments and smiled, even though she'd been interrupted. Instinctively she touched the beret she wore over her highlighted brown hair to make sure it was straight. She always dressed to be seen even when she was just coming to lead the crochet group. Izabelle said how much she'd liked CeeCee's old sitcom. "With all your years in the business, you've probably done tons of promotion on TV shows. I bet you could give me some pointers. You know how it is — nobody wants to fluff an interview with Matt Lauer."

"I don't know if I can help you, but if you're going to the retreat, I bet my replacement could." CeeCee turned to me. "Bennett Franklyn is an actor's actor. He'll do great." CeeCee looked over the group to see our reaction. She seemed disconcerted when Izabelle was the only one who recognized the name. "He's on *Raf Gibraltar.* You know — the main character is some kind of science teacher–secret agent who saves the free world every week by using everyday items to stop the bad guys. There's lots of duct tape and coat hangers. Once he used a kid's pencil to stop a fuel leak." There was a chorus of recognition.

"Then Bennett plays Raf Gibraltar?" Dinah asked.

CeeCee seemed perturbed by our ignorance of acting professionals. "No, no. He plays his older brother. You'll recognize him when you see him. People always think they know him from somewhere. He has those everyman looks. His wife is his manager. She'll be coming as well."

Izabelle was listening, at least until Adele interrupted, asking Izabelle about the fusion craft.

"You'll have to wait until I do my demonstration." Izabelle pushed the signed books toward Adele and said she had to go. Adele squeezed her hand and said she couldn't wait to hear about the fusion craft before

Izabelle picked up her things and left.

Dinah was the next to notice the rhine-stone clipboard on top of the box. She picked it up and looked at me. "What's this?" CeeCee, Sheila, Eduardo, and I all rolled our eyes as Adele told her in full detail what it was, what it meant and, most of all, that once again she hadn't gotten her due.

In a huff, Adele went off to the bookstore café to see what kind of cookies Bob, our barista-cookie baker, had made. As soon as she was gone, Dinah came over and hugged me. "How wonderful that you're going to be in charge."

I smiled weakly. "Yes, this is my big chance to show off my leadership qualities, but what if I screw up? I was just planning to be a participant at the retreat, and help Mrs. Shedd. 'Help' is the important word here. Help isn't the buck stopping with me."

"Don't worry," Dinah said, releasing me and going back to her seat. "Look at all those author events you've put on. They've all been fine." She winced and then went on.

"Okay, maybe there were a few mishaps, like the stink bomb." Dinah caught herself again and put on her inspirational tone. "But even with the mishaps, everything always turned out well and you sold a lot of books. You'll do fine this weekend. I personally promise not to be a problem."

Dinah was leading a memoir-writing workshop.

Sheila chimed in and reminded me that she was going to be there, too. "You can count on me if you need any help," she said.

Eduardo and CeeCee both voiced their confidence, and apologized for not being able to offer any support because they weren't getting there until the last day.

"You're not coming?" I said to Eduardo. He explained that he had a photo shoot for a cover that was big time. "It's a Roberta Iron book," he said, referring to the romance novel superstar.

Adele returned with a snickerdoodle and a latte. "Why, exactly, isn't Mrs. Shedd coming?"

"All she said was that something had come up," I said.

CeeCee cocked her head. "I bet it has something to do with Joshua Royal. Things have sure changed since he came back. Pamela Shedd must be well into her sixties, and Joshua, too, but they're acting like a couple of teenagers."

That was true. When Mrs. Shedd hired me as the event coordinator, Mr. Royal was such a silent partner that I didn't think he existed. And then one day he'd just shown up. It was obvious they had some kind of history and were picking up its threads.

With all this talk about the fancy clipboard, I finally had a look at it and thumbed through the pages it held. "Mrs. Shedd said the crochet group would make afghans over the weekend and donate them to a homeless shelter up there," I said, my voice rising in concern.

"It's obvious she doesn't crochet," CeeCee said with a sigh. "Even if we weren't going to do a crochet-along project, it would be impossible except for the speediest of crocheters to make an afghan that fast."

There was something else on the page in front of me. Another little plan of Mrs. Shedd's that she hadn't mentioned. She had crossed out candle making and written in knitting. "When did she add a knitting workshop?" I blurted out. If Adele was upset about me getting the rhinestone clipboard, it was nothing compared to her reaction to the word *knitting.*

She smacked her fist on the table. "I can't believe she betrayed us like that."

All of the Tarzana Hookers agreed that crochet was better than knitting, but we weren't militant like Adele. Before I could calm her, she launched into her tirade.

"We crocheters are not going to be the stepsisters of knitting anymore. Why does everyone insist on saying 'knitting and crocheting'? Why not the other way around? 'Crocheting and knitting' is alphabetical."

We all just listened as Adele went on. We'd heard it many times before.

Half an hour later, the group broke up. CeeCee left in a hurry to get to a production meeting for her show. Sheila had to get to one of her several jobs. Dinah had to get to class. Adele and I were left to put away the table. As Adele was packing away her hooks, she looked around the table. "Pink, where is it?"

"Where's what?" I asked, looking at the cleared table. Adele stuck her head under the table and checked the floor. She seemed a little panicky.

"The piece with the marshmallow stitch I created is missing."

CHAPTER 2

It had taken a while, but I'd finally calmed Adele down by convincing her someone in the group must have scooped up her work when they were packing up their own.

Adele stopped the frantic search and flopped into one of the chairs we hadn't folded up. "You're probably right."

Typical Adele. She could call me by my last name and hassle me every chance she got, but she forgot it all and expected me to help her when she had some kind of trouble. Dinah had asked me why I didn't just tell Adele to back off when she got annoying or demanding, and I had explained that I looked at Adele like that cousin everyone has who annoys you no end, but you put up with her because she's family. Okay, Adele wasn't family in the real sense of the word, but in a looser sense she was.

I gave Adele a sympathetic smile and went to touch her shoulder. "Pink, just because you helped me look for my marshmallow stitch doesn't mean I've forgotten about the rhinestone clipboard," she said. "I'm going to talk to Mrs. Shedd. I've worked at the bookstore longer. I've gone to three of the workshop weekends, and you've gone to . . . ?"

Adele didn't let up until I repeated that I had never been to one. After that she tilted her head with a knowing look. "And Pink, just to let you know, if you have any expectations of having a good time, you might as well cancel them. The rhinestone clipboard comes with twenty-four-hour responsibility."

I tried to dismiss Adele's warning. I knew about putting on events. Hadn't I handled countless book signings? Then I started to think about it. I never sat in the audience at events. I was always keyed up and standing just out of sight. And there was the setting up and tearing down. Oh, dear, I hated to admit it, but Adele was right. The rhinestone clipboard came with a definite downside. I would be so busy making sure everything went right, I wouldn't get to take part in the crochet workshop or have any time for fun.

As I put the table back in the storage room, I realized I'd never gotten a chance to take out the lightweight bubble gum pink scarf I was working on. Was this a preview of the weekend?

Suddenly, another problem surfaced. Barry Greenberg.

Barry Greenberg was my boyfriend, though I thought that title sounded stupid for a homicide detective in his early fifties. I also thought the term *dating* sounded too giggly and high schoolish. For a long time I had fought the idea of any title connected with our relationship, even though he was definitely woven into the fabric of my life. Barry had wanted us to move on and get engaged or married, but I had resisted. I'd been Mrs. Pink for a lot of years, and I wasn't ready to be Mrs. Somebody Else yet. So, we basically settled on being just . . . a couple.

Barry was supposed to come on the retreat with me. He wasn't going to take part in the workshops, but it had seemed like there would be plenty of time for us to do things together.

It had taken a lot of juggling for him to get the weekend off and make arrangements for his son, Jeffrey, to spend the time at a friend's house, and we were looking forward to this time away together. Even if I had to help Mrs. Shedd, I was sure I'd be free for moonlight walks along the beach that was supposed to be across the street from the conference center where the retreat was being held. Meals were included, but we figured we'd slip away for dinners on our own. Barry had already made reservations at several restaurants that he promised were heavy on romance. Now that the bucks were going to be stopping with me, there was no way I could slip away for dinner and moonlit strolls. Adele was right. I might as well forget about having a good time.

This was certainly a different turn of events. How many plans had been broken because Barry picked up a homicide? Or he had to fly off somewhere to follow a suspect? Or an important lead came up just as our salad arrived? Sometimes I felt like Barry was married to his job and I was the other woman. Now that the shoe was on the other foot, I was sure he would understand. At least I hoped so.

I took out my cell phone and called. "Greenberg," Barry said tersely. His tone softened when he heard my voice, but barely. I could hear the adrenaline flowing in his voice, making it high-pitched and choppy as he said something to his partner about making a right turn at the next street. The trouble with cell phones is you never know what somebody is doing when you reach them, or where they are. And I always seem to get Barry at the wrong place.

"What?" he said abruptly, then apologized for being short.

"Maybe this isn't the best time," I said.

Barry is not one to put things off, and once he realized I had called for a reason, he insisted on knowing why, even if he was on the way to a situation that was probably dangerous. I gave him the short version. "Basically, I'm calling off our weekend because I have to work."

"What?" He choked. It wasn't the kind of *what* that meant he didn't hear. It was the kind of *what* that meant he didn't understand. Sure, he could always understand his work interrupting everything, but not mine. "But I rearranged everyone's schedule to get the time off," he argued. "This is so last-minute. We were leaving tomorrow. C'mon, Molly, how much do you really have to do?"

Then suddenly he said he had to hang up, and I heard a lot of sirens in the background.

Apparently the shoe on the other foot didn't fit so well.

As I was leaving the bookstore café with a red-eye in hand, Mrs. Shedd stopped. She had her purse and was obviously on her way out. Mr. Royal was waiting outside and seemed to be waving at her to hurry up.

"That man is so impatient. I guess we have a lot of time to make up for," she said, referring to all the years Mr. Royal had been traveling the world. She leaned close and handed me a piece of paper. "I'm sure you won't need this — it's only for emergencies." I glanced down at the elaborate directions on how to reach her. "Joshua surprised me with tickets for a cruise. You know, one of those last-minute deals. We're off to Mexico." Her smile suddenly dimmed. "I've never done anything like this before. I've always been the responsible good soldier. But I thought it was time I did something impulsive and let someone else be the responsible one." She nodded toward me. "I guess that's it. Rayaad will be handling things here. And you've got the weekend covered." Her expression focused. "Oh, there was just one more little snafu. The tai chi master I'd lined up canceled at the last minute." Mrs. Shedd shook her head. "Don't you just hate it when people are undependable?" She pointed toward the box of packets still in the event area. "Don't worry, I already found somebody. I put a blank name tag in the box for him and relabeled the folder. You'll do fine." And then she was gone. So CeeCee was right. Mrs. Shedd was doing something with Mr. Royal.

Before I could finish my coffee with a shot of espresso, a black Crown Victoria stopped in the red zone in front of the bookstore. Barry got out and rushed inside.

As always when he was working, he wore a nicely fitting dark suit and a subdued tie, but whatever he'd been in the middle of had left him looking frazzled. He ran his hand through his neatly cut dark hair, and for a moment emotion cut into his expressionless cop face. He didn't look happy.

He crossed the space between us in a few steps. His dark eyes were flaring by the time he reached me.

"Babe, you can't just dump our plans." He glanced around and, seeing that no one was looking, put his arms around me. Generally, when he was working, he was completely hands free. "C'mon. I won't be in the way. How much time can it really take? You have to eat and you have to sleep and you have to get some kind of breaks. I had big plans," he said, his voice heavy with suggestion.

His proximity was giving a lot of weight to his argument, and the thought of his plans made me a little rubbery in the knees.

It wasn't that I didn't want to spend time with him, it was just that I now had more responsibility. For a moment I started to weaken. Was I really listening to Adele and her warning? Hadn't Mrs. Shedd told me to have fun? What better way to have fun than to spend some quality time with Barry? But then my good sense kicked in. I had the rhinestone clipboard and the responsibility that went with it. I didn't want to be thinking of how I could slip away every minute. I wanted my mind focused on the job at hand. And that meant no distractions. No Barry.

When he finally accepted that he couldn't change my mind, Barry double-timed it outside, and a moment later the car pulled away. I packed up the box of presenters' packets along with the rhinestone clipboard and headed for home. This weekend was not going to be a vacation.

CHAPTER 3

"You should look at this as an opportunity," Dinah said. "You said yourself that Mrs. Shedd is spending less and less time at the bookstore, and to back out of this weekend at the last minute —" Dinah looked me in the eye. "I'd say it's only a matter of time until she turns over running the whole place to someone. And I'd guess you're at the top of her list."

My son Samuel had just dropped us at LAX, and we were walking into the terminal along with throngs of early afternoon travelers. Samuel had assured me I didn't have to worry; he would take care of the dogs, get the mail, and water my flowers. I wasn't worried because my older son, Peter, had assured me he would take care of the dogs, mail, and plants. Barry had promised to do the same. What can I say? I had asked all three to take care of things in my absence. Each of them was busy and not used to having a couple of dogs depending solely on him. I figured the worst that would happen was the dogs and plants would get too much care.

"You could be right. But she could turn over the bookstore to someone else. Or she and Mr. Royal could decide to shut the place down altogether," I said as we stopped at one of the self-service kiosks and got our boarding passes before heading up the escalator to security.

The line snaked around, and as people moved forward, they were already removing their computers from their bags, kicking off shoes, and sliding off belts.

"Rats," Dinah said, looking at the line.

"I know what you mean. It's such a hassle going through security."

"No," Dinah said. "Well, yes, it is a hassle, but that isn't what my comment was about. I saw all the laptops and realized I didn't bring mine. You didn't bring yours, by chance?"

Dinah reconsidered her comment almost before the last of it left her mouth as she remembered I got along with only a desktop model.

"It'll be okay. I'm sure you can live for a weekend without checking your e-mail or going on the Internet." We had reached the conveyer belt and were loading our shoes, purses, tote bags, scarves and sweaters into plastic trays.

Once we were through the checkpoint and had ourselves back together, Dinah followed me toward the escalators that led to a waiting area level with the tarmac.

Adele and Sheila had left early in the morning because they were driving up. I still had the rhinestone clipboard, but they had taken the box of folders for the workshop leaders along with the packets for the retreaters. One of the workshop leaders had left a box of supplies for them to bring up, too. I had already heard from Adele that they had arrived.

Dinah noticed the furrow in my brow. "You're still worried about the weekend, aren't you? I'm telling you, you'll do fine."

"I just keep thinking if this weekend goes badly, it might be the thing that pushes Mrs. Shedd and Mr. Royal to close down." Dinah knew how much the job meant to me. I loved going to work and putting on the events.

After my husband, Charlie, passed away, working at the bookstore had been a whole new beginning for me. I finally had an identity. For so long I had been known only in relation to someone else. I was Samuel and Peter's mother. I was Charlie's wife. Or the She La La's Liza Aronson's daughter. At the bookstore I was just Molly.

Dinah tried to calm my concern. "It's going to be great. I'm looking forward to working with my memoir writers. We'll be out of the heat for a few days, and no matter what Adele says, I bet even with your responsibilities, you'll have some time to crochet and enjoy yourself. Nothing bad is going to happen."

Dinah's last statement made me uneasy. It sounded like she was tempting fate. We took the escalator down and walked into the waiting area.

"But they assured me there would be no problem." A woman's shrill voice rose above the din of conversation, and I looked toward the commotion. She was talking to the airline employee who was checking in passengers.

"I don't know who you talked to, but here's our policy. We can't guarantee anything," the uniformed employee said in a restrained tone.

"Do you know who he is?" the woman demanded in a loud voice, pointing at a man standing off to the side.

He had nondescript looks with close-cropped, frizzy light hair and a benign expression. I looked at him — and then looked again. An "Oh no" escaped my lips, and Dinah gave me a funny look. The man was Bennett Franklyn. I absolutely recognized him from the rerun of the *Raf Gibraltar* show I'd watched on a cable channel the night before.

CeeCee's description of him floated through my mind. "People always think they know him from somewhere, but they can never place where. Usually they think they went to school with him."

Apparently the airline employee didn't recognize him, though, and this set the woman off even more. By now I had figured the plain woman in the denim pantsuit must be the wife/manager, Nora, CeeCee had mentioned. Dinah noticed me staring.

"Obnoxious isn't she?" Dinah said, jutting her chin toward the confrontation. "But not our problem."

I smiled weakly. "Maybe it is. I'm pretty sure that's our substitute acting instructor, Bennett Franklyn, and his wife, Nora. Since they're on the way to the workshop, they're kind of my responsibility. Maybe I should step in."

Dinah grabbed my arm to keep me from moving. "Your watch starts when the retreat does."

Finally the airline employee handed Nora Franklyn two boarding passes and said it was the best she could do, and let them board the plane first.

"See, they worked out their own problem," Dinah said as we boarded the small plane. Bennett and Nora were seated in the first row, and I noticed her talking to the people in the seats behind them. No matter what Dinah said, I had the feeling the peace with the Franklyns was only temporary.

A little over an hour later, the tiny plane landed at the equally tiny Monterey airport. Nora and Bennett had deplaned quickly, and I saw them entering the terminal building as we came down the stairway from the plane. I was right about the peace only being temporary. As soon as Dinah and I walked into the miniature terminal, I heard myself being paged over the loudspeaker. Well, I figured it was me, even though the page was for Polly Mink.

If the Franklyns noticed we'd been on the plane with them, they didn't show it as I approached and introduced myself with the correct name.

"You can tell the driver to pick up our bags. We'll just go directly to the car," Nora said, glancing around. I had to explain there wasn't a driver, and said I'd help them get a cab. Nora appeared exasperated at my suggestion. "I don't suppose you arranged for a rental car, either?" As soon as she saw the negative shake of my head, she let out a hopeless groan and gestured for Bennett to follow her as they headed toward the rental car counter.

"That went well," Dinah said with a roll of her eyes.

"Too bad CeeCee had to cancel. She would have gone along with us in a cab," I said, my shoulders sagging. "What have I gotten myself into?"

Dinah tried to reassure me. "Once they get to the conference center, they'll be fine. You'll see."

We got our bags and headed through the door to the short line of cabs that stood waiting. A fellow passenger followed us outside. "Did I hear someone call you Polly Pink?" the silver-haired man asked me. I nodded with an uncertain smile. Now what, I wondered as he held out his hand.

"Commander Blaine," he said in an upbeat voice, introducing himself as he shook my hand. He'd caught me off guard, and I struggled to place the name.

"Pamela Shedd called me and told me you'd be taking over for her," he said to me, but his gaze kept darting toward Dinah and

I wondered if he even heard me give my correct name. "And you are?" he said to her. He couldn't have been more obvious with his interest. If I was a person who believed in love at first sight, that would have been it.

Dinah was divorced and had been trying to meet someone forever. So far she'd met nothing but duds. I wasn't sure if Commander was his first name, a nickname, or his title, but he appeared a lot more promising than any of the guys she'd described to me. I expected her to pick up on the way his gaze stayed on her and at least smile. Instead, she looked away in a dismissive manner.

Dinah was somewhere in her fifties, though the exact place was a deeply held secret even I, her best friend, didn't know. After all the wild-goose chases and murder investigations we'd been through, you'd think she would have trusted that I wouldn't judge her by her age, but she still wouldn't tell. Dinah is a bundle of energy, and even though I'd just met Commander Blaine, he seemed to have a similar enthusiastic attitude. So why did she seem to be ignoring him?

Not that Dinah's reaction dampened Commander Blaine's enthusiasm as he suggested we share a cab. He seemed to pick up on my confusion of how to address him. "You can just call me Commander," he said, "and I'll call you Molly." He turned toward Dinah, and for a moment I thought he was going to say he'd call her Sweetheart or something like it, which I knew wouldn't have gone over well with her. Luckily, he used her first name and said everyone was informal at the retreats. Apparently even Mrs. Shedd had always gone by her first name. He looked up at the blue sky. "Beautiful here, isn't it? Smell that air."

Actually I was a little surprised at the bright sun and warm temperature, but he told me the airport was inland and to wait until we got on the other side of the mountains. "You'll get plenty of misty, cool air then."

We caught our cab and in a few moments were on our way. Whoever said men don't talk much apparently hadn't met Commander Blaine. He leaned over the front seat and for the whole ride kept a running commentary about the workshop he was responsible for.

"I've been coming to the creative weekend for the past three years," he said as we drove along the twisty road that led between the mountains. "Pamela saw the column I write

41

in the *Tarzana Gazette* about entertaining."
His tone made it sound like the paper was
the *New York Times* instead of a local
freebie. "And she asked me if I'd be interested in doing a workshop." His expression
brightened as he apparently relived the moment. "Would I? But of course. I love
entertaining and teaching people how to
coordinate activities, decorations, and food.
I think a theme really pulls things together.
I'd like to talk to your crochet group. I could
use the yarn to thread an event together."
He made a face at the lameness of his pun.
Good! At least he didn't take himself too
seriously.

Though Dinah was looking out the window, I knew she was listening as he continued. "You can thank your lucky stars I'm
not a prima donna like that other couple. I
don't know if Pamela Shedd told you, but I
always handle the extra weekend social
activities in addition to putting on my
workshop. Just say the word and I'll put
together a murder mystery event."

I thanked him but said no. My plan was
to stay as far away as possible from murder,
even a fictional one.

Dinah couldn't stand it anymore and
turned toward him. She asked him if he
made his living putting on parties. His smile

deepened when she spoke, and he explained that he had a day job. He owned the Tarzana Mail and Office Center. He conveniently had several coupons available and gave them to us.

As the road began to go through a forest of giant pine trees, the sun disappeared and a silvery mist blew in through the driver's open window. The temperature dropped, and I pulled on the thick black cardigan I'd brought.

We entered the small town of Pacific Grove, which Commander said was referred to as PG by people in the know. "Too bad the butterflies aren't here," he said as we turned off the highway onto a street that seemed to be on the edge of a forest.

"Butterflies?" I said.

"Every year between October and February thousands of monarch butterflies flock to Pacific Grove. There's a sanctuary over there," he said, pointing in the distance. There's something about the microclimate of the area, with its Monterey pines and eucalyptus trees, that makes it perfect for the creatures." He directed his comment at Dinah. "You really ought to come up when they're here. It's magical the way they cluster in the trees."

Why was Dinah pretending not to be interested?

"Here we are," Commander Blaine said as the cab slid between two tall stone markers with "Asilomar" emblazoned on them. It felt like we were entering another world. On either side of the driveway there were tall trees with tangled growth below them. The cab stopped next to a low building, and we all got out.

"I thought you said this was a resort," Dinah said, looking at the rustic building and the forest and ground below that had been left wild. I knew what Dinah meant. I'd been expecting something different, too — something along the lines of manicured lawns, luxurious spa amenities, and maybe high tea served at umbrella-shaded tables. None of that seemed likely here. Commander unloaded our bags from the cab and held the door as the three of us went into what he called the administration building but what the name plate referred to as the Phoebe Apperson Hearst Social Hall. Inside was a huge, airy room with an open ceiling and exposed beams. A sitting area with a small TV was adjacent to a large stone fireplace complete with an inviting fire. A piano, a pool table, and a Ping-Pong table filled the back area, and the other end was given over to the registration desk. It felt like something between the lobby of a hotel and the gathering room of a camp.

Unfortunately, Nora and Bennett were already at the registration desk. Nora looked stunned and marched over to me. "This isn't a hotel," she sputtered. She pointed to a freestanding board that listed the day's menu. "Look at this. There's not even a restaurant. It's a dining hall. I can't eat here." She let out a big sigh. "If CeeCee Collins had talked to me, I never would have agreed to let Bennett step in for her, but she went directly to him."

I covered up my own surprise at the place and tried to smooth things over. "Maybe it isn't what you expected, but why not give it some time? Even the food might turn out better than you expect." It didn't work, and she walked off with an exasperated huff sound.

While we waited to check in, Adele Abrams walked in. *Walked* isn't quite the right word. *Marched* is better. With her khaki culottes, matching camp shirt, and brown ankle boots she looked like Smokey Bear's sister. She had finished off the outfit with a wide-brimmed ranger hat that she said was authentic, proudly showing us the crease on the top that was meant to let falling acorns roll off. Sheila Altman was with her and had a stunned look. Who could blame her? She had just spent six hours or more driving with Adele.

Once we all had our keys, Adele wanted to show us around. "Pink, if you're going to be in charge, you ought to know what's what." She turned back and looked at our feet. "I hope you all have good walking shoes." Adele walked backward, facing the three of us, as she gave the background of the place.

The layout and camplike feeling began to make sense when she explained that Asilomar was originally built as a YWCA camp. "The grounds are spread over a hundred acres," she said, turning before leading us up a hilly walkway bordered by golden wild grass. "The area we're staying in and using for the retreat is part of the historic core." Adele pointed to several two-story buildings with weathered wooden shingles that had large nameplates identifying them as Lodge and Scripps, and said that was where our group was being housed.

The air was certainly bracing, and I'd read somewhere that this kind of climate was conducive to creative thoughts, but something about the place seemed moody and brooding. Maybe it was the gloomy sky and the fog drifting in. Or all the brown wooden buildings that seemed dark and forbidding. It didn't help that Commander Blaine kept repeating that we were on a little piece of land at the end of the continent jutting out into the ocean, and the waves were huge and rough.

Even the stately Monterey pines were a scruffy dark green. And the cypress trees with their gnarled trunks and horizontal foliage reminded me of bent old men with windblown hair, trying to run away. I looked at Dinah and had the feeling she shared my reaction.

"Maybe when there are more people here, it'll seem a little more cheerful," she said, then leaned closer. "I bet if you sat around telling ghost stories, a real one might show up."

"I heard that," Adele said. "You two are nuts. Asilomar is wonderful."

By now we'd made a full circle and were back at the administration building. Commander turned toward the plant-covered sand dunes nestled against the property and was about to say something, but Adele beat him to the punch.

"There's a boardwalk over there that goes through the dunes to the street. The beach is across the street."

"Maybe we should show it to them now,"

Commander suggested.

"No," Adele said firmly. "Pink needs to know where the locations for the retreat are, like the Crocker Dining Hall." Adele indicated a building with a covered entryway and lots of tall windows that was just down the walkway.

"They ring the bell on top of the administration building to announce mealtimes," Commander added. Adele pointed out a few other small buildings where our workshops were going to be held, and then it seemed like the end of our tour. As Dinah and I left them, Commander added that Asilomar meant *refuge by the sea.*

Dinah and I picked up our bags in the administration building and headed outside. Commander said he would catch up with us — I think he really meant Dinah — later, and went with Adele to get some things she'd brought for his workshop.

We pulled our bags up the steep path, past the golden grass-covered hill, toward the weathered building Adele had pointed out as Lodge. Just inside we passed through a communal living room with overstuffed chairs and a fireplace. We determined our rooms were on the second floor, and we went up the stairs.

As we looked down the dark corridor, Izabelle Landers stepped out of one of the rooms and walked toward us. True to the title of her book, Izabelle wore only a subtle touch of crochet in the form of tiny rose pink flowers around the neck and sleeves of her black wool jacket. When she got closer, I saw there were pearls in the centers of the flowers.

"Your jacket is exquisite," I said, fighting the desire to touch the flowers and examine the stitches.

Izabelle thanked me. With the puffed-up lips, her smile looked almost painful. Dinah and I had already decided there was maybe a ten percent chance she was born with those lips.

"I'm going to sit by the fire in the administration building and finish crocheting a shrug," Izabelle said, holding out a small tote bag with her supplies. "It'll be nice against the chill up here." I sighed at the mental image. Sitting in front of a roaring fireplace and crocheting sounded very appealing. Maybe, if I was lucky, there would be some time during the weekend when I'd get a chance to do it, too. Izabelle looked at the cards our keys were attached to and pointed toward the front of the building. "Those room numbers are up there."

We were still on the landing at the top of

the stairs when we heard some noise down below. We all looked over the railing. Nora and Bennett had walked into the living room and were looking around. More correctly, she was looking around and he'd dropped into one of the overstuffed chairs.

Izabelle seemed to stare at him.

"I'll save you the trouble of wracking your brain where you know him from. That's Bennett Franklyn. He plays the older brother on that *Raf Gibraltar* show."

"I know who he is," Izabelle said, still looking over the railing at him. "It's just different seeing him in person."

"He may look like the guy next door, but he has charisma at the same time," I said. "And he's certainly the peacock of the family." I caught sight of Nora's face. She might make lots of noise, but her appearance was surprisingly drab. She had brown hair you couldn't attach a fancy adjective to, like mink or chestnut. It was cut in a short, no-fuss, kind of style. She definitely had a light touch when it came to makeup, and though I wouldn't call her fat by any means, in the size zero world of Hollywood, others probably would.

Nora paced in front of the fireplace, appearing agitated. "This won't do."

Bennett stood and touched her arm with

50

tenderness. "Don't fret so, hon. It won't kill us to spend a weekend here. And the payoff is worth it."

Payoff? I wondered what he meant.

Izabelle pushed the tote bag on her arm. "Well, ladies, see you later."

"I thought we'd all meet up at dinner," I said. "It'll give all the workshop leaders a chance to get to know each other."

"Right," Izabelle said before going downstairs. She walked up to the Hollywood couple and introduced herself. I heard her tell Bennett that she liked his show.

"Let's find our rooms," I said as we left our post and went down a dark, wood-paneled hallway. Our rooms were adjacent in the front corner of the building. Just before I went inside mine, I glanced down the corridor. A short man with a head shaped like a brick was walking down the hallway looking at room numbers. He stopped in front of a door and rapped impatiently, but no one answered. Dinah noticed him, too. He must have felt he was being watched, because he looked up abruptly and stared back at us. The anger in his expression sent a shiver up my spine.

"Is he one of our people?" she asked.

"I hope not," I said, opening my door. My cell began to ring as I went inside.

CHAPTER 4

"Babe, we would have worked something out," Barry said. He'd called to make sure I arrived okay and to let me know he had gone over to take care of the dogs. I had just finished giving him the rundown on my accommodations, which would have been our accommodations, had Mrs. Shedd not dropped the weekend in my lap.

"You're saying that because you're not here looking at this room." I let my eyes sweep it again. "Did I mention no TV or telephone, though since everybody has a cell these days, that's neither here nor there."

Barry laughed. "I had planned to do much better things in the room than watch TV."

"Okay, but the twin beds are the narrowest twin beds I've ever seen. One is under the windows on the side wall and the other is on the back wall."

"I'm good at moving furniture," Barry said.

"Not in this room. It's way too small. And it's kind of cold in here." I looked around for a heat source, which there wasn't.

"I would have kept you warm," Barry said in a low voice. "I can still come up there."

I hesitated, but only for a second. "No, let's leave it as it is. I can tell this is going to be a no-fun weekend." He accepted what I said but didn't sound happy as he signed off.

I unpacked and did a little damage control to my appearance. I had just put down my hairbrush when I heard the dinner bell ring. Dinah heard it too and we met in the hall. I looked upon dinner as the official beginning of the retreat. The air was heavy with moisture and seemed to be getting more opaque and colder as Dinah and I headed to the dining hall. It was hard to believe it was hot and clear in Tarzana. I had forsaken my usual khaki slacks and shirt for the jeans, black turtleneck, and black corduroy blazer Dinah had suggested as the perfect casual, yet with a touch of authority, look. I was glad I'd added the long, red wool scarf. It was one of my earliest crochet creations, and wearing it wound around my neck added a nice touch of warmth.

The cavernous dining room was almost empty, and there was no problem snagging a couple of the large round tables for our group. Across the room a group of birders from Arizona were having their farewell dinner, and a sprinkling of guests not connected with any group were scattered around some tables in another corner.

I clutched the rhinestone clipboard for courage and straightened the pile of packets I'd brought to give out. Bennett Franklyn was the first to arrive — alone.

"Where's Nora?" Dinah asked.

"She brought some food to our room," he said with a friendly smile. "It's been a tough day for her. I hope it isn't a problem, but we changed our accommodations. We're in Long View now." He vaguely pointed off in the distance.

Thanks to Adele and Commander's tour, I knew Long View was on the edge of Asilomar, and though the long building had a weathered look similar to Lodge, it was actually much newer. The rooms were a little larger and the wide windows had a view of the ocean. If it kept the peace, it was fine with me.

As our group began to filter in, I handed out packets and pointed out the cafeteria line in the back. Commander and Bennett headed for the line together. Dinah offered to get food for both of us, and Izabelle said

54

she'd already eaten. She sat down and helped herself to the pitcher of iced tea in the center of the table.

I glanced at the rhinestone clipboard. I had placed check marks next to Bennett Franklyn for the acting workshop, Commander Blaine for entertaining, Dinah for memoirs and Izabelle Landers for crochet and fusion. I was still looking for Jeen Wolf and her husband. She was doing the knitting workshop, and I guessed he was along for the ride. Mrs. Shedd hadn't given me the name of the tai chi replacement teacher; she'd just crossed out Master Riki and written in TBA.

Bennett and Commander were talking about parties when they returned carrying plates of steaming food. "Personally, I find all those black-tie events boring, but my wife likes them," Bennett said, setting his plate on the table before pulling out a chair. Apparently dinner consisted of meat loaf, mashed potatoes, and succotash. There was a thick layer of gravy over everything.

Commander was listening, but his eyes were on Dinah as she set down two plates of food and pulled out a chair. He nodded toward the spot next to her.

"Is this seat taken?" he asked in a hopeful voice. I knew Dinah well enough to read her expression. She wanted to say it was, but she also didn't want to make problems. She pulled out the chair and invited him to sit. I had forgotten to ask her about her earlier reaction to him. It certainly mystified me.

Dinah announced she was going back for rolls. Commander urged her to sit, and took off to get them. She rolled her eyes. Somebody needed to tell him not to try so hard.

Izabelle moved until she was next to Bennett. Commander came back with the rolls, and Izabelle glanced up at him. Commander's reaction surprised me. I thought he would smile at her in acknowledgment, but instead his eyes narrowed. In turn she gave a little toss of her head, which I took to indicate that she knew him but dismissed him as unimportant.

"I bet you could give me some pointers," she said to Bennett, explaining her upcoming tour and TV appearances.

"Sure," he said in a friendly voice. I let out a sigh of relief. So far, so good. Or maybe not.

Adele sailed into the dining hall with Sheila trailing behind her. Adele had changed out of her forest ranger look and was in full crochet embellishment mode down to the cloche hat with the two-tone flower. She flipped her mohair shawl over her shoulder as she put dibs on the chair on the other side of Izabelle. Sheila stopped next to me, looking pale and tense. With her nerves, it was no wonder. Sharing a tiny room with Adele couldn't be fun. I handed her a name tag. Technically Adele and Sheila weren't workshop leaders, but I looked upon them as support staff. Adele picked up her name tag and the two of them went off to get food.

A couple hesitated at the entrance to the dining hall. Even if they hadn't been together, I would have known they were a couple. They were both tall and lanky, and had the same very straight posture. Both had neatly trimmed hair, though the colors were very different. Hers was such a dark brown, it was almost black, and was perfectly straight except for slightly turning under as it grazed the bottoms of her ears. She had thick, straight-across bangs. His hair and close-cropped beard were wheat colored.

They were dressed alike, too. Both wore classic waist-high jeans that hung loosely over their slender frames, and topped them with heavy, gray cable-knit cardigans. I could just make out the writing on their tucked-in tee shirts: *Knitters Make the Best*

Lovers. I thought the shirts were kind of funny since they both looked so prim.

Adele was already on the way back with her dinner. In hopes of avoiding a war between the knitters and her, I steered them toward the empty table and introduced myself.

"Jeen Wolf," the woman said, holding out her hand.

"And I'm Jym," the man said, standing next to her. "Or as we like to call ourselves —"

"A couple of knitters," they said in unison with a flourish. Adele was within earshot, and I thought she was going to choke.

"So you're both knitters. My list only had Jeen," I said, holding out one packet.

"I like to think I'm the bonus," Jym said with a wink, and added that one packet would be fine for both of them. They glanced at the other presenters. Jeen's expression changed when her gaze reached Izabelle. "Izabelle Pilsen?" Jeen said. Izabelle seemed startled as she turned toward the voice.

"It's Izabelle Landers now," she said once she'd seen who'd spoken.

"I barely recognized you," Jeen said. "You must have lost, what, twenty pounds?"

Was it my imagination, or was there an

edge in Jeen's voice?

"Give or take a few pounds," Izabelle said, trying to shrug off the comment. "It's been a long time. I was just showing off my crochet book," Isabelle said, picking up the copy and handing it to Jeen. "What about you? What have you been up to?" I was just guessing, but I thought Izabelle already knew the answer to her question, and whatever Jeen had been doing, it didn't measure up to Izabelle's achievements. Jeen muttered something about having to catch up later. After taking the book from his wife, Jym nodded a greeting to Izabelle and handed the book back to her. She gave him a knowing smile, and he looked away quickly. I hoped that didn't mean there was going to be some kind of drama involving the three of them.

The awkward moment was made even more awkward as Adele stepped in the couple's faces. "I just want you to know that for this weekend, crocheters rule. None of that 'knitting and crochet.' Any references will be to 'crochet and knitting.' Okay?"

The Wolfs seemed taken aback by Adele's pronouncement and watched her flounce back to her seat. "She's a little intense," Jeen said.

I tried to smooth things over by introducing the new arrivals to the rest of the group. Jym knew who Bennett was right away. He was a fan of the show and started reeling off all the clever devices that had been on the show lately. I didn't have to introduce Commander Blaine.

"You have the copy shop, right?" Jym said, extending his hand.

Commander's cheerful expression wavered and recovered. "It's a complete office and mailing center. But my workshop is all about entertaining."

The rest of the introductions went without incident, and the Wolfs got their food and joined the others. A short time later one of the kitchen employees came from the other side of the room with a cart of vacuum pots of coffee and slabs of candy-bar-topped cheesecake.

My plate of food was still untouched, and I left it on a tray stand. The woman made the rounds with her cart, leaving everyone but Izabelle with a piece of the cheesecake.

"She probably heard how many calories and almost fainted," Dinah said when she accepted a piece. She took one for me as well and set it on the table, even though I hadn't eaten my dinner. I glanced over the rhinestone clipboard. All the presenters were accounted for except the tai chi person.

When everyone had finished dessert and coffee, I stood up and gave my little welcoming speech. I said the retreaters would be arriving throughout the next morning, and the workshops would begin after lunch. Commander Blaine raised his hand, and when I gestured for him to speak, he stood.

"I just wanted to add that in addition to my workshops on entertaining, I'll be putting on little events during the weekend. The first is the campfire and s'mores reception."

As he continued, describing how most people just thought of the regular ingredients of milk chocolate, marshmallows, and graham crackers, he took the concept to a new gourmet level. I tuned out, as I imagined everyone else did, as he ran through the different variations on the common camping treat. When he finished, I took the floor again. I'd been dreading dropping the bomb, but there was no choice. I broke the news that Mrs. Shedd had promised a local shelter that the retreat would donate handmade afghans. Izabelle and the Wolfs responded as I'd expected. They already had plans for their workshops, and there wasn't enough time over the weekend.

Adele stepped in — or, more correctly — overstepped her boundaries. "I'm sure the crocheters will figure out a way to come up with something." Izabelle and the Wolfs glared at her. I quickly asked if anyone else had any announcements, and when there were none, the group broke up. Dinah and I hung behind to finish our coffee and cake. At least, she ate cake. I just had coffee.

"You did great," she said in a true best-friend encouraging voice. "No disasters, no dead bodies."

"Just a few bumps in the road, thanks to Adele," I replied. The kitchen crew was clearing the tables, and I was about to suggest that Dinah and I leave when someone else came into the dining hall. My mouth fell open when I realized who Mrs. Shedd had gotten to teach tai chi.

CHAPTER 5

"Hi, Sunshine," Mason Fields said as he crossed the empty dining hall to our table. "I'm guessing by your open mouth that you weren't expecting me."

The cleaning crew was beginning to put the chairs on the tables and sweep the floor. Mason's expression clouded over. "Looks like I missed dinner, huh?"

"You're right on both counts," I said, still looking at him with disbelief. Dinah greeted him with a nod and a smile, and he gave her a wave.

"How come you never told me you do tai chi?" I asked, feeling a little unsettled.

Mason laughed. "You never asked. Sunshine, there's a lot you don't know about me. Tai chi brings balance to my life, though I'm not quite a master at it. Your boss made me sound better than I am. My teacher, Master Riki, was supposed to do the weekend, but he broke his leg. Nothing to do

63

with tai chi, something about a slippery waxed floor. I was already coming up to Santa Cruz this weekend for my aunt's eightieth birthday. I heard you were going to be running this workshop weekend, and I didn't want to leave you hanging." He glanced at Dinah and me and the empty table around us. "Where's the detective?"

"Barry didn't come," I said. We were getting looks from the two men doing the chair moving and sweeping. Who could blame them? They wanted to be done and go home. "Maybe we ought to take it outside," I said.

Besides his apparent skill at tai chi, Mason was a well-known criminal lawyer. Well-known because he was the one celebrities in trouble turned to. He was known for keeping them out of jail. He also had a self-deprecating sense of humor that was endearing.

We had sort of a flirty friendship. Mason had wanted it to become something more, and during the time Barry and I had broken up, it almost had. Mason and I seemed to be on the same page relationship-wise. We both wanted something casual. Only his definition of casual turned out to be too no-strings for me. Even so, we had stayed friends. And since I seemed to find myself mixed up in murders, it was handy to have a criminal attorney around just in case.

Outside, the air was so thick with moisture that it had a texture. And it was dark. I asked Mason if he'd checked in; he nodded and mentioned his room was in Lodge. "I think my room is right down the hall from yours," he said with a devilish smile. Did I mention that Mason was still hoping for more than friendship?

"Sorry I'm so late, but my flight got diverted to San Jose because of the fog, and then I had to drive from there. Are there any restaurants in this place?" He gestured toward the grounds that were mostly invisible thanks to the fact we seemed to be in the middle of a cloud.

"No, and there's no room service. Have you been to your room yet?" I asked.

"Yes. I noticed there was no television, no telephone, and not much in the way of luxurious amenities. Personally, I like it for a change. When I come here, I usually stay at one of the resorts in Pebble Beach," he said. "Now, there must be some place to eat in the area."

I suggested we check with the registration desk, and we headed up the walkway to the administration building. As we were climbing the stairs to the deck, Nora Franklyn appeared out of the darkness, pulling a white windbreaker around her.

"Have you seen Bennett?" she said with an edge in her voice. She glanced past us toward the empty dining hall.

"Last time I saw him, he was walking out with the others. Why don't you call his cell phone?"

Nora appeared dismayed. "I would, but he left his cell in the room." She looked around the dark area. "This place is impossible at night with all those winding paths."

I wanted to say it was her idea to move to a building at the edge of the grounds. I wanted to, but didn't. It would only irritate her more.

Instead, I tried acting sympathetic. "I'm sure he'll show up. Maybe you just missed him." I gestured toward the path ahead that disappeared into the fog. "If we see him, I'll tell him you're looking for him." Nora didn't fly into a tirade, but she didn't seem pacified either, and I thought I heard her mutter something about leaving in the morning.

"She doesn't seem happy," Mason said, watching her go.

"I hope she's not serious about leaving in the morning. What am I going to do if they go? I have people arriving who're expecting an acting workshop with a known actor."

"It'll be okay," Mason said. "She's just upset. I've had clients like Bennett. You see these people on TV shows acting like they can run the world, but in real life they're clueless. She probably has to take care of everything all the time. He gets to be the nice guy and she has to be the hammer."

"Do you think I should help her look for him?" She was almost out of sight. Dinah grabbed my arm.

"Snap out of it," she said. "He's not that helpless. He'll find his way back to their room even without his phone and in the fog. And she won't leave in the morning. It seems to me she's been threatening something since the moment we first saw her."

"Dinah's right, Sunshine," Mason said. "Let's get back to finding some food."

We went inside the administration building and Mason talked to the redheaded clerk. Meanwhile, Dinah and I checked out the long table set up for morning registration. Sheila and Adele had left the boxes of folders under the table along with a check-in list. I opened a random folder and was glad to see it had a schedule, map, name tag, and meal ticket.

"Apparently there's only one option," Mason said, leaning against the pool table as I put the folder back and pushed the box under the table. "The nearby restaurants are already closed, but there's a market still open." As we headed toward Mason's rental car, which was parked near the gate, Commander Blaine caught up with us, and when he heard where we were going, he asked if he could tag along.

"I need to get some things for my session tomorrow," Commander said. Dinah didn't join in as Mason and I invited him along. I was really going to have to find out what was up with her. The street outside was very dark, and we followed the clerk's directions. A few blocks up, we passed some businesses and a restaurant. All closed for the night. I was relieved to see cars in the grocery store parking lot. At dinner I had been too busy being concerned about everybody to eat, and I was very hungry.

We each got a basket and started going through the aisles. Mason headed off to the prepared foods, Dinah and I went on a cookie hunt, and Commander headed for parts unknown.

I pulled Dinah into the aisle with the toothpaste and cat food. "Okay, what's with you and Commander Blaine? He brightens up like a three-hundred-watt halogen bulb every time he sees you, and you look at him like he's dust. What's the problem?"

Dinah shook her head so vehemently that her dangle earrings began to jangle. "There's no point in encouraging him. He's not my type. Did you look at his jeans? And the shoes! And did you listen to him?"

I had to admit I hadn't been paying attention to his pants or footwear. We slipped around the aisles until we looked down and saw Commander reading the labels on the olive jars. At first I thought Dinah had lost her mind, then I got it. His jeans had creases so sharp you could probably cut butter with them. The shoes were tasseled loafers that were polished to perfection. The kind I called party shoes.

"Too fussy," Dinah said, coming up behind me. "I bet he wears boxers, and they're probably starched and ironed."

Down the aisle out of earshot, Commander looked up from an olive jar and waved us over to ask our opinion on whether to get the plain olives or the pimento ones. I wasn't sure what the olives were for.

"Sorry," he said, "I should explain. I had a few boxes of things shipped up here for the workshop, but I always forget some things and I also always like to add some fresh things."

I looked at the jar of olives again. "Are

those for your gourmet s'mores?"

Commander's eyes lit up as he laughed. "No. I don't go that far outside the box with the s'mores. Olives and chocolate. Even for the most adventuresome palate that sounds like a bad combo. Part of my workshop is teaching people how to use vegetables to make amusing table decorations. It's along the line of radish roses, but a step up. I make palm trees out of crookneck squash and cucumber peel, and stick olives on as coconuts."

While he was talking, Dinah was behind him, rolling her eyes. Maybe he was a little too excited about the details of his workshop. Actually, until that moment I hadn't really thought about the content of his workshop.

"So, your workshop group puts together the s'mores?" I asked.

"No, no. The s'mores I do personally. The group will be helping set up some of the other activities. And my people will be doing the food and decorations for the final party. The rest of the workshops provide the entertainment."

At the moment the closing party seemed a long way off, but I was glad he had it covered.

Mason showed up carrying some kind of

70

sandwich and a container of lemonade. Commander glanced from Mason's dinner option to our empty baskets. "Are you gals hungry, too?"

Dinah and I said something about dinner being a little heavy for our liking but we were thinking about a snack.

"You can just pick up some food and go back and eat it in your room, or we can make something out of it. My personal philosophy is to make an event out of everything. I love impromptu get-togethers. How about it?"

"I'm in," Mason said. "The sandwich would have been okay, but your idea sounds much better."

I looked toward Dinah, expecting something negative after what she'd said about Commander.

"You know, I feel that way, too. Why not have some fun?" Dinah actually smiled at him, and they all turned toward me. I got it. As the holder of the rhinestone clipboard, I was the decision maker.

"Go for it," I said, catching some of Commander's enthusiasm. Mason replaced his sandwich and drink and came back with a cart. Dinah and I abandoned the baskets, and we began to follow our party leader through the store.

"I've got a perfect idea," the silver-haired man said as he headed for the bakery. He picked up a long French baguette and put it in the cart. He kept going, stopping along the way to add more items. By the time we headed for the checkout, we had bread, sliced cheese, cartons of soup, and a flourless chocolate cake for our late-night meal, and trail mix and cookies to keep for snacks in our rooms.

We paid, then headed out into the darkness, already having fun. Even the fog made our excursion more exciting. By the time we went back through the gates of Asilomar, we were all laughing. I didn't even realize how tense I'd been until the tension fell away.

"C'mon, let's go to the fire circle," Commander said as we passed the administration building. I didn't know what he was referring to until we got to an area on the edge of the grounds. I had passed it before, but it had been empty and plain, and hadn't made any impression on me. Now there was a fire in the pit in the center, though no one was sitting around it.

"They built the fire for the bird group's farewell," Commander explained. A low wall with a glass layer on top formed the enclosure and protected it from the constant

72

wind. We put our packages on the benches and sat around the fire. The warmth felt good and the brightness was reassuring. Commander said he had to get some equipment from his room.

The man might have too-sharp creases in his jeans, but he knew how to pull together a last-minute meal. He came back with a box of supplies, and within a few minutes he was holding some kind of contraption with the bread and cheese inside over the fire. Dinah was holding the long wire handle of the pot the soup was heating in.

"Still think he's too fussy?" I said under my breath to Dinah after the food had been served. She was too busy eating one of the chewy toasted sandwiches to speak. The nod of her head said he'd definitely earned some points.

"This is going to be a great weekend," Mason said, smiling at me as he toasted everyone with a mug of the hot soup.

Mason, Dinah, and I ate the chocolate cake with our hands, a messy choice that gave me a case of the giggles. I don't know if it was because of our sticky fingers or it was just the final release of all the tension I'd built up in the day. Our party organizer would have earned more points with Dinah if he hadn't eaten his cake with a plastic fork and a napkin.

I jumped when my cell phone began to vibrate, then ring, and tried to swallow my laughter, but that only made it worse.

I answered, trying to keep the chocolate crumbs off the phone and the giggle out of my voice. I failed at both.

"Hi. I called to say good night," Barry said. I managed to get out what I thought was a serious sounding hello as I stood to collect myself. Then I took a few steps away for privacy. Commander had produced some marshmallows and long forks, and the rest of the group had started roasting the white puffs over the fire.

"You sound funny. Is everything all right?" Barry said. I swallowed a few times and tried to think of something serious to get the giggles to stop, but I couldn't keep the laughter out of my voice as I attempted to tell him everything was fine.

"Where are you? I hear voices in the background." Barry never turned off his detective skills. I moved farther away, hoping to muffle the sounds, but it was too late. I heard Commander call Mason by name and comment on his marshmallow roasting technique. Barry heard it, too.

Barry had a basic animosity toward Mason Fields based on their work. In Barry's mind, lawyers like Mason helped criminals run free. Barry didn't like it that Mason and I were friends, either. I suppose his guy radar saw a threat. I could see his point.

"What's Mason doing there?" Barry demanded. I could picture him suddenly sitting upright and then standing and pacing, probably running his hand through his short, dark hair. And his usual hooded expression was probably blown.

The giggles finally went away. "Mason is one of the presenters," I began, and then carefully explained that Mrs. Shedd had merely told me she got a replacement tai chi teacher, but not who. "I didn't know he was coming when I told you to stay home," I said, wincing. I hoped Barry would leave it at that, but Mr. Detective had picked up on the fact that there was some kind of fun going on. He wanted details. It was useless to try to gloss over it. Barry is very good at interrogation.

"I promise this was just accidental fun," I said, hoping to pacify him.

"Okay, then," he said at last. "So, you'll be too busy with your rhinestone clipboard to spend any more time with him this weekend, right?"

I uh-huhed in answer, and he said there was another reason for the call. "Were you expecting any deliveries?" When I said I wasn't, he mentioned some sealed boxes on my front porch. "Are you involved in something you haven't told me about?" he asked in his interrogation voice. I knew he was referring to a special delivery I'd gotten in the past — a dead mackerel with a marzipan apple in its mouth, meant as a warning.

"My life is an open book. No murders. No dead bodies. No warnings," I said, pleased that it was true. Barry still wasn't sold on the idea of putting the boxes in the house and wanted to open them, but I convinced him to leave them shut and put them in the garage until I got back. Just before he signed off, his voice softened. "Miss you, babe."

"Me, too," I said, and meant it.

The phone call put a damper on things for me. I felt guilty about having a good time and uncomfortable that I'd been caught. I didn't want to ruin the rest of our little group's picnic, so I said I wanted to get back to my room and go over the schedule again. Both Mason and Dinah offered to go with me, but I told them to stay and enjoy the fire. It was hard to shake my feeling of responsibility for everything and everyone. It didn't seem right that I should be giggling around a campfire.

After I had gone only a few steps, the fire pit area slipped into oblivion thanks to the cloud sitting on the ground. All my worry over being in charge had already come back with a vengeance, and I almost walked into the figure ahead of me on the path.

"Bennett," I said with surprise. "Nora is looking for you."

I couldn't see his expression, but it seemed like he was rolling his eyes and shrugging. I took it as a so-what-else-is-new kind of gesture.

"I was playing a solo game of pool." He gestured in the direction of the administration building.

"Then everything is okay," I said, putting on my leader-of-the-pack voice.

"Was she giving you a hard time?" he asked.

Why not clear things up? I mentioned her talking about leaving in the morning and being less than thrilled with everything.

"Don't worry, we're not leaving in the morning. You have to understand: Nora's a great manager. She's always looking out for my best interest and wants me to be treated like a star." He let out a chuckle. "I, however, know I'm just an actor." His self-deprecating manner won me over, and we walked the rest of the way to Lodge together. I started to go in, and he continued on the path toward their accommodations. Yes, Bennett was pleasant and reassuring, but I couldn't help thinking of what Mason had said about actor clients he'd had. They played the nice guy and let their spouse be the hammer.

CHAPTER 6

The loud, insistent knock at my door made me sit up suddenly. The rhinestone clipboard fell off the bed, hitting the floor with a loud clatter. Had I really slept with it? I looked around, trying to orient myself. After a moment I recognized the dark wood-paneled walls and ceiling of my Asilomar room. I'd left the curtains open, and the dim light filtering in implied that it was very early morning. The window was open a crack, and the room had filled with chilly, damp air. More noise came from the door. This time it was closer to pounding. My stomach did a flip-flop. It sounded like trouble.

The floor was icy on my bare feet as I got out of bed. Maybe icy was a bit of a stretch, but it was certainly very cold. The red readout on the clock radio said six thirty. I regretted not having brought a robe and slippers, and pulled the dusty rose shawl I'd crocheted over my nightgown. My shoulders felt warm, but it didn't do much for the rest of me as I crossed to the door.

Adele was tapping her foot when I opened the door. "It's about time," she said, shaking her head. My groggy feeling was instantly gone with one glance at Adele's outfit. The fuchsia of her sweat outfit hit my eyes with a jolt — and who knew they made chartreuse sneakers? She completed the look with a backward baseball cap and a scarf of coaster-size doilies strung together and wrapped around her neck. "Pink, you've got a problem. No, it's more than a problem. It's a disaster." She took in my outfit. "You better put on some clothes. You're going to have to do something. You're in charge, remember? The big cheese with the rhinestone clipboard. The buck stops with you."

Adele's rant was interrupted by a door opening. Dinah stuck her head out. "What's all the commotion about?"

I pulled Adele into my room, and Dinah followed. No need to alert the whole floor that something bad had happened before I had the details.

"So, what is it?" I asked.

"I can't tell you. I have to show you. Downstairs."

Adele tends toward drama, but I couldn't take a chance. I threw on yesterday's clothes and shoved my sleep-shaped hair under a beige beanie I'd crocheted recently, figuring I'd deal with the disaster and come back for a shower before breakfast.

Okay, there are some things that can't be fixed. And for once Adele hadn't gone for hyperbole. As soon as we stepped outside, I got it. It was like stepping inside a marshmallow. All I could see was white. Even though we'd gone only a few steps from the entrance to Lodge, the building was already disappearing in the white air swirling around it.

Dinah came down the steps a few minutes later, glanced around, and rushed to join us. She'd pulled on some red sweats and covered the wilted spikes of her hair with a black baseball cap.

"Wait for me," a voice called from behind us. When I turned back, I saw that Sheila had just tumbled out the door. She screeched to a stop, reacting to the opaque air. I couldn't make out her expression, but I could hear her breath become shallow and ragged. I got it right away. She was feeling panicky, and I could relate. There was something claustrophobic about a fog this thick.

She took a tentative step toward us, eyeing the sky nervously.

"It's okay, honey," Dinah said, putting her arm around Sheila when she finally reached us. We all urged Sheila to take some deep breaths, and gradually her features lost their frantic expression. Adele started to reel off information about how bad it was as she dragged us all to the administration building, where the lone TV was tuned to a live report.

A newscaster was standing at a police roadblock. Behind her it looked as if a white curtain had been pulled across the road. "It's a complete whiteout and has been named the Pacific Grove Fogout," she said, gesturing to the road behind her.

The redheaded guy at the registration desk began to talk. "It's a complete whiteout. All the roads are closed around here. You can't see past the hood of your car." He shook his head. "We get fog all the time around here, but never like this. I bet it's because of global warming."

He pushed a pile of phone messages across the counter. "These are for you — from your retreat people. They're all stuck, and won't be able to get here until the fog lifts. Everything — and I mean everything — is shut down, not moving, nothing going

82

anywhere. Not even the park ranger or the security guy could make it in." He mumbled something about having worked all night, and his replacement couldn't make it in, either. Then he stared at us, looking a little crazed and his voice verging on hysterical. "We're stranded, ladies. It's like we're on an island with no boat." He leaned across the counter. "Be careful."

We went back outside, and when I held my arm out, I could barely see my hand. As we walked down the path, a deer rushed in front of us, appearing as confused as we were.

"Pink, what are you going to do?" Adele said.

I had considered lots of things that might happen during the weekend, but being caught inside a cloud wasn't one of them. I gave up hope for a hot shower and a change of clothes. Maybe after breakfast. I suggested we move on to the dining hall.

"What are you going to do, Pink?" Adele said again, walking on one side of me.

"Molly will come up with something," Dinah said from the other side. Sheila appeared overwhelmed by the fog and stayed close to Dinah.

"The obvious thing is to postpone everything until the campers get here," I said as the bell began to ring, announcing break-fast.

"Good morning, ladies," an all-too-cheerful male voice said from behind us. Dinah stiffened and moved closer to Sheila. As Commander Blaine caught up with us, I began to see Dinah's point. He was too eager, too cheerful, and his cargo pants too wrinkle-free. He rushed ahead as we walked up the stairs to the dining hall, grabbed the door, and held it open for us. Did he even notice the fog?

Two women and a man were standing in the entrance, blocking our way as we came inside.

"Are any of you with the Shedd & Royal creative weekend?" a woman in lavender pants and a white sweatshirt with lavender trim asked.

Adele gave me a nudge to the front. "She's the one you want to talk to."

The woman said they had arrived late the night before. "It was terrible finding this place in the dark and with the fog coming in." Then she brightened. "But we're here now, and we can't wait for the workshops to begin. Where do we register?"

Adele nudged me again. "Pink, you better break the news to them."

"News?" the other woman said.

"Have you looked outside?" I mentioned the fog, the messages from the other campers, and finally my plan to postpone the start of the activities until everyone could get there.

The woman in the lavender pants appeared displeased with what I said. "So the workshop presenters can't get here?" she said.

"No, they're all here," I said.

She seemed upset with my answer and turned to the man. "Edward, do something."

Edward straightened and cleared his throat. It turned out he was a lawyer, and he gave me some legal mumbo jumbo about implied contracts and we had to perform or we'd be in breach. He threw the word *sue* around a few times. I knew it was probably just hot air, and that even though Mason didn't practice that kind of law, he could still probably outlawyer Edward. But did I want three unhappy campers? Three unhappy campers who might spread the word around Tarzana that I had ruined their weekend?

"Well, of course you're right." I explained that I'd made the plan to postpone when I thought no campers had arrived. "But now that I know you're here, we'll have some workshops today." They seemed satisfied and hadn't picked up on my mention of *some* workshops. I said I would get them their orientation packets after breakfast and sent them over to tables by the window.

Izabelle came in on a cloud of floral perfume. Before I could mention the table for our group, Adele had already stepped in and was guiding Izabelle to our corner. I heard a snippet of conversation as Adele moved her head around to show off her earrings. Something about their being made with double picot stitches.

"We might as well sit down," I said, stepping in from the entrance.

"Who are they?" Sheila said. She started to point, then caught herself and gestured with her chin. *They* were a man and woman at a table in the far corner of the room.

"That's the guy I saw in the hall when we first got here. He looked so angry, all I could think of was that if looks could kill, I would have been dead," I said. Sheila sucked in her breath, and I said I was just trying to be clever. "I don't think he was angry with me. He just glanced my way. I don't even know who he is."

I hadn't noticed that Commander had left us until he rejoined us and grabbed my arm.

"We've got a problem," he said, leading

me toward the kitchen. I knew Dinah wanted to stay at the table, but true-blue friend that she is, she followed along.

When we got to the kitchen, Commander pointed to two women sitting by a counter, leaning on their elbows. Only now did I realize that there had been no food smells when we walked in. One of the women explained they worked cleanup and knew nothing about cooking. They lived nearby and had been able to walk to Asilomar. None of the cook staff could get there.

"I have an idea," Commander began. "I just wanted to get your okay first."

When I heard it involved his getting breakfast, I couldn't say yes fast enough.

I stepped back into the dining room and announced there would be a delay of breakfast, then went back to the kitchen to help.

A short time later, I returned and invited our group to get their food. It turned out the two employees were good at helping once they were told what to do. Commander had a wonderful recipe for a breakfast casserole. It was amazing what he'd done with some eggs, bread, green onions and shredded cheese. Dinah and I had found fruit to cut up for salad and made pots of coffee. There was orange juice, too. We'd set up the food buffet style on the stainless steel counter.

Everything smelled delicious, and the small group began to help themselves.

"Well, Sunshine, good job with breakfast," Mason said as he picked up a plate. I was still getting used to his outfit. I was accustomed to seeing him in finely tailored suits or high-end casual wear. The white cotton pants and kimono jacket over a long-sleeve knit shirt seemed out of place on him along with the black cotton shoes. As usual, a lock of his warm brown hair had fallen across his forehead, giving him an earnest look as he put some food on his plate.

"Commander deserves the credit. He pulled it all together. We just did the grunt work."

Mason picked up a mug for coffee. "Is there any milk?"

One of the Asilomar employees got a carton of milk from the refrigerator and started to put it on the counter, but Commander wanted her to pour it into a small pitcher. I noticed a photo of a little girl on the carton. Dinah did, too.

"I didn't know they were still running those pictures of missing kids," she said. "That little girl looks like Ashley-Angela." For a moment Dinah sounded wistful, then she straightened up. "Just tell me to shut up," she said with a laugh. Ashley-Angela and her fraternal twin brother, E. Conner, were the children of Dinah's ex and his second wife, who was now an ex, too. In some bizarre twist of fate, Dinah had ended up caring for the kids and had gotten attached to them. She was truly sorry to see them go when their father finally came for them. But she was glad to get her freedom back, too. Sometimes when she saw a kid who resembled one of the twins, she still got sad and missed them.

"This girl is older than Ashley-Angela," I said, looking at the carton.

"They just made the picture look that way. The girl has probably been missing for a couple of years. Kids change a lot, and somehow they fix the picture so it shows how she would look." Dinah poured some milk in a little pitcher and handed it to Mason.

Some more people came in, and I noticed Adele talking to the woman I'd seen sitting in the dining room. I caught a snippet of the conversation and was surprised to hear Adele doing her spiel about knitters trying to take over the world. The angry man came across the room to me.

"Hi, I'm Spenser Futterman," he said, putting out his hand. "And that's my niece

Marni." He gestured toward the woman talking to Adele. "We're not part of your group, but we were supposed to get breakfast . . ."

He let his voice trail off, and I got the message. They were hungry and wanted to join us. When I looked at him close up, he had a rather pleasant face now that he wasn't angry.

"We all have to stick together," I said, inviting them to help themselves. As Spenser poured two glasses of juice, Izabelle came in. Spenser looked up, and their eyes met.

"You're here?" she said. She sounded surprised and anything but happy to see him.

"I need to talk to you." He stepped closer to her, and she moved away.

"There's nothing to say," Izabelle said, taking a plate of fruit and going back to the dining hall. She walked past Marni without any sign of recognition.

"What was that about?" Dinah asked, coming up next to me.

"Why do I think it's trouble?" I replied.

CHAPTER 7

I waited until everyone was eating and then dashed back to my room for a shower. While helping serve breakfast, I'd come up with a solution that would pacify Miss Lavender Pants and her crew. The hot shower felt good until I stepped out into the cold room. So cold that steam rose off my hot body. Great! Just what I needed! Fog inside, too. I threw on fresh clothes and got back to the dining hall just as everyone was having their second cup of coffee.

I stood between the tables to make my announcement. "Even though most of the retreaters aren't here, we're going to have some workshop sessions after lunch." At the word *lunch* Commander Blaine popped out of his seat.

"Don't worry about lunch," he said. "I'm setting up a do-it-yourself sandwich bar." I waited until he sat down to continue.

"Dinah Lyons will be putting on a writing

workshop, followed by a crochet class with Izabelle Landers. Since there are so few retreaters, I'm hoping all of you will support Dinah and Izabelle and come to both sessions."

I was relieved when I got a round of affirmative nods. However, Bennett said not to count on his wife participating. As the meal broke up, Miss Lavender Pants went over to Commander Blaine to shower him with praise about breakfast and his plan for lunch. I had to laugh at Dinah. She kept trying to ignore Commander, but when Miss Lavender Pants explained that Edward, the lawyer, was her brother and made the point that she was unattached, the spark in Dinah's eyes gave her away. She was interested, even if she wouldn't admit it.

I headed over to the administration building to check on the fog news. The redheaded desk clerk had his head down on the counter. When I woke him, he said nothing had changed.

Commander Blaine came in behind me, carrying a large box. He put it down on the long table set up for our campers' registration.

"Mind if I put these underneath?" he asked, pulling the boxes of folders to the edge of the table.

"It looks like no one is going to be coming until this fog lifts, so why not?" I said, wondering what he was doing. He had my boxes out of the way in a flash and flipped the lid off the box he'd brought. It took me a moment to figure out what was in it, and then I recognized rows of gift-size shopping bags. "What are those for?" I asked as he began to put them in rows on the table.

He took the rhinestone clipboard off the table where I'd put it and flipped to the schedule. "It's the first activity I have planned. After the afternoon workshops, there's a s'mores break."

"Right," I said, remembering his s'more discussion earlier. "But are you sure you want to do that with so few people here?"

"Yes. I think it's even more important to do something special." He took out a pile of long wire forks and stuck them in a metal container, then picked up one of the treat bags to show me its contents. There was a packet of marshmallows, four graham crackers, and four pieces of chocolate. "This is your basic everyday variety, but I have also made up gourmet versions." He showed me the stickers on the fronts of the bags. He was a little over the top, insisting on listing the different fillings. Did I really need to know there was a choice of dark chocolate, white chocolate, plain milk chocolate, milk chocolate with peanut butter, chocolate with almonds, and chocolate with coconut?

"I thought I would put the things out now, so I could go to the workshops like you asked." Commander Blaine didn't say it, but by the way his eyes brightened, I imagined he was thinking about Dinah's workshop in particular. I helped him set up the rest of the bags. There were far more bags than people, but he wanted to make sure everyone could have their choice. By the time we finished, it was noon. Commander rushed ahead to make the final arrangements for lunch while I looked for Dinah.

"All I can say is your fussy friend is a gem," I said as Dinah and I walked into the dining hall.

"He's not my friend," Dinah protested, "though he deserves points for breakfast and lunch."

The lights were on in the dining hall and something smelled good. Commander came out from the kitchen and said he'd set up the sandwich bar and hot soup.

Everyone seemed satisfied with lunch. Mason had brought me some tomato soup and a Swiss cheese sandwich, but I was too keyed up about the afternoon to eat.

I was glad I'd picked Dinah's workshop to

kick off with. Her years of teaching English to reluctant freshmen had made her a master at handling any kind of group. This crowd would be a snap. Right after lunch, I led the group to a small building that housed meeting rooms. A long table was at the front along with several rows of school chairs with table arms. From inside, the trees just a few feet away melted into the thick white. The bonus was that all the white reflected back into the room, making it seem brighter.

Dinah set down her supplies while everyone but Commander found a seat. He hung around the front, offering to help. She gave him a stack of small notebooks and pens to hand out. Dinah leaned against the front of the table and began to talk memoir writing.

I had never seen my friend in action, so I took a seat at the back of the room.

"Anything can get you started," Dinah began. "I'm going to give you what may seem like a silly assignment, but when we read what you've written, you'll see how your take on it is unique and shows who you are." She paused to build up the suspense. "I want you to write about orange soda for ten minutes." I heard a collective *huh,* and for a moment I wondered if she knew what she was doing. She seemed to expect the panicky stares, and told them just to put their pens on the paper and write anything that came to mind. She set a timer, and surprisingly, after a few moments everyone began to write. When the bell went off, Dinah told them to stop.

"Okay, let's see what you wrote. Anyone want to start?" Miss Lavender Pants's attorney brother raised his hand first. His piece had something to do with a client who claimed to have found a dead roach in a bottle of the bright soda. "My client took the settlement they offered before we went to court. I know I would have won if she had just agreed to let me go to trial. Like everything else, I just didn't get my fair chance."

There was a smattering of applause as he sat down. Now I got what Dinah had said. Edward had certainly tipped his hand that he felt like a victim.

Izabelle volunteered next. Edward had just read his piece — she presented hers.

"Orange soda," she said, making eye contact with members of the group. "Personally, I don't like it. I think it looks like paint and tastes like carbonated candy." Izabelle must have had very good recall of what she wrote as she glanced only occasionally at her paper as she spoke. No wonder she volunteered. She had said something about wanting as much opportunity as possible to be in front of a group before she went out on the road with her mystery craft presentations.

"I was going to say I never drink it, but then I remembered there was one time. My sister and I went to Tina Geyser's birthday party. It was in her backyard, and so hot I could feel the sweat drip down my sides. Some of the kids turned on the sprinklers and started running through the spray. Mrs. Geyser came out and yelled at them. I always thought she looked like the evil queen in *Snow White.* She said unless we all sat down at the picnic table, we would have to go home without having cake."

Izabelle made sure she still had everyone's attention. Nobody could accuse her of having writer's block.

"Tina's mother brought out plastic glasses of soda on a hammered aluminum tray. There were two glasses of orange soda, and the rest were lemon-lime. My sister got all upset when Mrs. Geyser started at the other end of the table and Billy Palmer took one of the glasses of orange soda.

" 'I have dibs on the other,' she called out, but Mrs. Geyser said there would be no dibs, and she would have to wait her turn like everybody else. Each time somebody reached for a glass, my sister moaned because she thought they were going to take the orange. But nobody did. Mrs. Geyser got to me, and my sister started to relax. I pretended to reach for a glass of lemon-lime, but at the last second, I took the orange instead. I drank the whole glass while my sister cried. I guess she didn't get it was a joke."

And neither did the rest of us. There was a moment of dead air, and then a hesitant trickle of applause as Dinah stepped in and commented on Izabelle's good use of story-telling. That was how Dinah won over all those unruly freshmen. She knew how to find the positive.

Dinah glanced at her watch and said there was time for one more person to read. Adele was out of her chair before Dinah finished the sentence. Adele's piece detailed how she had played orange soda in a modern dance recital and described being dressed in yards and yards of orange gauze.

While Dinah gave them the next writing assignment, I left to get some soft drinks ready for the break. I hoped that after all the attention orange soda had just gotten, nobody asked for any, since all we had was cola and lemon-lime. I came back at the end of the allotted time and announced that the next workshop would begin in twenty minutes.

Bennett stopped on his way to the door. "Sorry, here's where I draw the line about being a good sport. I'm probably doing you a favor. My attempt at crocheting would give you nightmares." Commander excused himself as well, saying he had to make sure the fire pit was ready for the next activity. I thought Miss Lavender Pants's brother and Mason might make some excuses, too, but they both surprised me by saying they'd be back. Izabelle pointed to a large plastic box under the table and asked if I would set up her supplies before she rushed out.

Sheila stopped at the front and offered to help me. Dinah pulled out the box and put it on the table. Adele joined us and assisted in laying out hooks and balls of yarn, along with some samples and several copies of *A Subtle Touch of Crochet* with notes attached saying they were for sale.

I put a pile of printed directions with the other things. Much as I would have liked to participate in the crochet workshop, I felt obligated to act as an observer. Just looking at the hooks on the table made my hands long to crochet. Later, when I was alone, I'd have some time. With everything set up,

Dinah, Sheila, and I took seats in the back. Adele stayed in the front, patrolling the teacher zone. As usual she was a walking advertisement for her craft. Over her black turtleneck and black leggings, she wore a long vest made out of classic granny squares done in ruby red, creamy white, and black edging. I always said Adele and I had our differences, but I would never dispute her crochet ability. If only she hadn't worn the hat, she would have looked fine. It was newsboy style, and even if it was masterfully crocheted, the way she had it pulled low on her forehead just looked silly.

Miss Lavender Pants, Edward, and his wife, along with the knitting couple, came back in and took their seats. When Mason arrived, I realized that was everybody — everybody but Izabelle.

"As soon as Izabelle returns, we'll begin, people," Adele said. She had put on her authority voice and was beginning to strut across the front. The door opened, and Izabelle came in, carrying a shopping bag. She'd added a few touches to her outfit, all crocheted. I saw her do a double take at Adele's position. She made a face and stepped in front of her, putting some sample scarves and baby blankets on the table. "I just want you to get an idea of some of the possibilities."

Izabelle turned back toward the group and took off her black wool jacket. As she stepped closer to the class, I saw Adele look up. Her gaze stopped on Izabelle's neck, and her mouth opened into a troubled expression. "What's that?" she said, pointing at Izabelle's neck.

"This?" the crochet presenter said, touching the fuzzy white puffs. "It's just something I made with this stitch I came up with. I'll be demonstrating it in a later session. I call it Izabelle's Cloud."

"But that's my work," Adele said, stepping close to her. "I invented that stitch. You just figured out my stitch and then added on to the piece I started."

Before Izabelle could respond, Adele looked frantically from me to Sheila to Dinah. "You saw it. Remember I called it the marshmallow stitch? And then my work disappeared." Adele's gaze stuck on me. "You said somebody in our group probably picked it up by mistake."

Neither Sheila nor Dinah had much recollection; I, however, did remember Adele saying something about her work disappearing.

Izabelle looked at Adele with a condescending smile. "I'm sure you're mistaken. I came up with this stitch eons ago." She lifted her shoulder-length hair to show the choker that consisted of four white, fuzzy puffs with spaces in between. It appeared to tie at the back.

Adele was not to be dissuaded. "I know that's my work. It disappeared the other day when you came by the Hookers meeting. I can prove it, too. I spilled a little pink pearl nail polish on the back of it." She reached toward Izabelle. "Take it off and let me have a look."

Izabelle was no longer smiling. She glared at Adele. "Don't be ridiculous. I don't have to prove anything." She picked up one of the hooks and shoved it toward Adele. "If this is your work, let's see you do a sample of your marshmallow stitch."

"I can't repeat it. I was just experimenting when I made the stitch. I was going to undo my stitches and write down what I'd done, but my work disappeared first." Adele's voice cracked. She must have realized she was losing ground.

Izabelle glanced toward the crowd. "Sometimes people want to be crochet designers so badly, they imagine they've come up with something fresh." She pulled out a printed sheet and said it was really an advanced stitch, but she had directions in case anyone was interested.

Her words were like lighter fluid on a campfire. Adele lost it and went to grab Izabelle. I stepped in to block Adele before she made contact, and put my arm around her. I started to usher her toward the door while whispering that she was making a scene.

"Pink, I am not making a scene," she said. "She is." She pointed at Izabelle. Just before I got Adele out the door, she stomped her foot and turned back one last time.

"Don't think this is over. You're not going to get away with this."

CHAPTER 8

"Adele sure blows hot and cold. One minute she's practically kissing the ground Izabelle walks on, and the next she's threatening her," Dinah said. I had done my best to save the situation after I got Adele out the door, but the damage was done. Nobody could concentrate on crochet. Even those of us who knew how couldn't do a foundation chain without screwing up. I did the only things I could do. I ended it, and hoped Commander's s'mores interlude would sweeten up the atmosphere. Izabelle had taken off with the rest of the group, leaving Dinah, Sheila, and me to gather up her things.

"This fog *is* getting tiresome," I said with a sigh. We were walking down the path toward the administration building, not that we could see it. The walkway disappeared into the ether up ahead. We were walking slowly when Bennett suddenly appeared from the whiteout behind us, and after greeting us he disappeared again as he moved a little bit ahead. It was no wonder the roads had been shut down.

"What if Adele is waiting for Izabelle to show up in the administration building?" Dinah said, trying to peer into the distance.

"Good point. Adele was really over the top, and she's not one to give up." I picked up speed, picturing Adele jumping out from behind a curtain and pulling the choker off of Izabelle's neck.

The administration building suddenly appeared out of the fog. When we reached the door, I pulled it open quickly and looked around inside. To my relief, all was peaceful. Commander was hovering over the long table, pointing out bags of s'mores ingredients to the knitting couple. Miss Lavender Pants seemed to be having a hard time choosing and was easing her way around to Commander's side of the table.

I almost laughed when I caught sight of Dinah's expression. It was amazing how someone else wanting Commander had changed her opinion. With a swirl of her long, rust-colored scarf, she crossed the space to the table. Commander Blaine's eyes lit up when he saw her. At the same time Miss Lavender Pants's lips twisted in annoyance.

"Hey, Sunshine." I recognized Mason's voice. I hadn't noticed him playing a solo game of pool. I was still surprised by the white outfit and the soft shoes. He put down his pool cue and joined me. "You look tense. But then you had quite an afternoon. I bet you didn't know that on top of everything else, you'd end up having to be a bouncer," he said with a chuckle before giving my shoulders a quick therapeutic massage. "What you need is to sit around the campfire and have some s'mores."

We walked up to the table and I let Mason take over the s'mores selection. Commander made a point of telling me he thought the s'mores were a crowd pleaser and asked that I mention it to Mrs. Shedd. "She tried to talk me out of doing them, but I fought to keep them in."

Mason took my arm and we walked out on the deck side of the administration building and headed down the walkway to the fire circle. Commander might have been raving about the popularity of his treat event, but for now we had the area to ourselves. Mason picked a bench and I reached for one of the bags.

"Molly, I have it covered." He gestured for me to sit down, and when I seemed surprised, he chuckled. "I guess you don't know that I've done my share of camping and know my way around making a s'more."

"You're right, I didn't know. You're full of surprises. First the tai chi, and now you turn out to be a whiz at campfire treats." I sighed, and he looked up from skewering the sweet white puffs on two of the long forks.

"You're still upset about the fracas in your crochet workshop. You did the best you could under the circumstances." He got ready to put the marshmallows over the fire.

"Do you think Izabelle Landers stole your fellow Hooker's work?" He tried not to, but he laughed over the word *Hooker.*

"It's hard to say if Izabelle was so insulted by the accusation that she wouldn't take off the choker and let Adele look at it, or if she was hiding something. I know Adele did misplace her work, and it was the day Izabelle stopped by our group meeting. But Izabelle Landers is a well-known crochet designer, and Adele is starved for attention and always trying to get herself into the spotlight." I put my chin in my hands and slumped. "I don't know what I'm going to do."

"The best advice I can offer is to keep them apart."

I let out a mirthless laugh. "Like that's going to work. We eat together. Their rooms are probably down the hall from each other. And that's not even considering the workshop sessions."

Mason kept turning the marshmallows until they were a perfect golden brown while he pondered my problem. The patience was typical of him.

"Give yourself a few minutes off," he said. "And taste this." He had put all the pieces together, and as he held out the sweet treat, my mouth watered. Who knew he'd turn out to be a killer s'more maker on top of everything else? I took a bite. The marshmallows were perfectly toasted on the outside and molten on the inside. Everyone else I knew was always in a hurry and ended up with black, blistered marshmallows that tasted like ashes. Mason's creation worked together. The heat melted the chocolate and the graham crackers held it all together.

Mason had made a s'more for himself as well. When he tried to eat it, it broke and he ended up with marshmallow on his nose. He looked funny, and I started to laugh. He pretended to be upset and then stuck a blob of marshmallow on my nose. Now it was his turn to laugh. All the tension flooded out. Something about the way Mason never seemed to take anything too seriously made him fun to be with. The treat and the fire began to work their magic, and I sighed as relaxation kicked in. That is, until my cell phone went off.

"Just checking in, babe," Barry's voice said. "I wanted to make sure you were all right with the fog emergency."

"So far, so good," I said with a crack in my voice. There was no reason for me to feel guilty. All I was doing was sharing a s'more with a friend.

"Is that Barry?" Mason said. "Tell him I'm looking out for you." I threw him a dark look and he responded with an innocent shrug. As if I believed he didn't know what he was doing. Of course it worked. Barry started interrogating me on where I was and what I was doing and where was everybody else.

"Every time I talk to you, you seem to be with Mason. And campfires and making s'mores sound like fun to me. I can roast marshmallows, too." He sounded hurt, so I got up and walked away for some privacy while I explained I wasn't really having fun. I told him about Adele and the blowup.

"Babe, I'm sure you'll figure out something. I hate to add to your concerns, but remember the boxes I put in the garage yesterday? When I came by today, they'd been moved to your front hall." I told him to leave them where they were, and after we clicked off, I called my sons. Peter was at work and didn't know anything about the boxes. I got Samuel's voice mail and left a message. When I clicked off, Mason was holding out another perfectly executed s'more. I felt another wave of guilt, but took the oozing graham crackers anyway. I saw Commander's point; the s'mores were absolutely delicious.

Some more of our group showed up with bags of supplies, and suddenly I was back to being the holder of the rhinestone clipboard. Mason and I traded looks. He got it — fun time was over. We left the fire circle and he announced he was going back to his room to practice his tai chi routine. "You're welcome to come. I'll throw in a private lesson." His tone was genuine, no smarmy innuendo. I gave him a nice thank you, but no thank you. Besides, I needed to figure out what I was going to do about Adele and Izabella.

Mason disappeared in the fog and I went to the gift shop, hoping to snag a red-eye. The coffee wagon person was a no-show along with the rest of the staff, but the desk clerk let me make my own. While I was sip-ping the strong brew, I went to check out the social hall. Dinah grabbed me. "Stay here," she commanded.

Dinah was my best friend and she had always come through for me, so if she needed me to stay somewhere, I did it without question. A lot of the bags were gone from the table. I noticed Commander Blaine wasn't there, nor was Miss Lavender Pants. Just as I was going to ask what had happened to them, Commander Blaine came through the door in a burst of enthusiasm.

"I got my jacket, so now we can go," he said, stopping next to Dinah.

"Good," Dinah said with a pasted-on smile. "Won't it be nice to take a walk and look for driftwood to use for Commander's workshop?" she added, grabbing my arm.

It was clear that Commander Blaine didn't share Dinah's enthusiasm at my joining them, but he quickly picked up that Dinah wasn't going to go without me and said something about it being good that there would be another set of arms to carry driftwood. No one brought up the folly of looking for anything in all that fog.

The three of us started along the boardwalk that led through the dunes on the edge of the grounds. The area on either side was

111

strictly off-limits, as it was in the process of being replanted with fragile native plants. Not that we could see it anyway. Nor could we see much ahead or behind us, but the sound of the waves was clear.

At the end of the walkway, we passed through a small gateway that had an Asilomar sign. There was a little bit of sandy sidewalk, and then I recognized the blacktop of the street. When I tried looking both ways, I realized it was useless. I couldn't possibly have seen a car, nor its driver, me, until it was too late. For the first time I really understood why the roads had been shut down and how isolated we were.

Even though there was supposed to be no traffic, habit made me hurry across the street. On the other side, low fencing protected the replanted area. A walkway was formed between the fenced areas and led to the open beach. The sand felt silky soft underfoot and immediately got into my shoes.

I thought the whole looking-for-driftwood thing was a line Commander had used to try to spend some time alone with Dinah, but as soon as we got onto the beach, he handed us each a reusable grocery bag and told us to start looking.

He went on a little ahead and stopped to

pick up something, then dropped it quickly. I saw a dark hunk hit the sand.

"Be careful, somebody had a campfire here and it's still smoldering." He bent down again, then straightened, holding something. "Well, that's not very considerate." We'd caught up with him by then, and the sand was damp and easier to walk on. Ahead there seemed to be some kind of channel in the sand with brackish water moving toward the waves. Commander held two long wire forks identical to the one Mason had used for the marshmallows. "These aren't throw-away items. I need them back for the next s'mores break."

He searched around the area a little more and used one of the forks to pull out the partially burned remains of a s'mores bag. "Looks like somebody decided to do their own campfire. Pretty careless, not even throwing away their trash."

He ran the bag through the sand and then touched it to make sure it was cool. Then he dropped it, along with the fork, in the canvas bag he'd brought to collect the driftwood. We were careful to walk around the remains of the campfire. Dinah went ahead toward something dark on the sand. I saw her take a step, and then she tripped and screamed.

Commander and I rushed toward her. Dinah was sprawled on the ground, and when I got close, I saw an arm clothed in a black wool jacket with pink crocheted flowers around the sleeve sticking out from below her. Commander Blaine pulled Dinah to her feet, and the three of us gasped.

CHAPTER 9

"Turn her over, turn her over," Dinah squealed. When Dinah had gotten up, the rest of Izabelle Landers had become visible as she lay facedown in the sand.

We got Izabelle on her back, and her face looked blue and distorted. Dinah felt her wrist and thought she detected a faint pulse.

"Call 911," she said quickly. The adrenaline rush had given Dinah's voice a high-pitched, panicky sound. I reached for my cell phone, then realized I'd left it in my tote in the administration building. Commander didn't have his phone, either.

"I'll go back and call," he said, gesturing toward the Asilomar grounds, still invisible in the fog. He walked quickly through the sand, the bag for collecting driftwood swinging on his arm.

Dinah and I knelt down in the sand on either side of Izabelle.

She looked terrible. Now that I was closer,

I could see the red blotches on her face. Dinah and I tried to comfort her and tell her that we were getting help. Nothing in her face gave any indication she heard us.

I checked the area around her. A sand-encrusted s'more lay on the ground near her hand.

Commander Blaine came back to tell us the paramedics were on the way, then went to stand by the street to flag down the ambulance. Luckily we had the Asilomar gate as a landmark. It seemed like it took the paramedics forever to arrive. The fog made it impossible for them to drive fast.

Two men in dark blue uniforms hustled across the beach, carrying a stretcher and a large case. They got Izabelle on the stretcher, and one started doing CPR and put some kind of bag on her face. The other asked me what had happened, and I gave him the little information I had. I also mentioned the sandy s'more. He scooped it up and put it in a plastic bag. The paramedic working on Izabelle continued the CPR as Commander helped get the stretcher across the sand. I thought I saw Izabelle move her head as I followed them to the street.

"You better come with us," one of the paramedics said as they loaded the stretcher into the ambulance. A police cruiser had pulled over to the curb, and two officers got out. They walked onto the beach, shaking their heads at the low visibility.

Dinah had followed us. She stood with Commander and told me not to worry, they would take care of things in my absence. All of us were operating on nerves by then. I climbed into the back of the ambulance. When I looked back, Commander and Dinah were talking to the police.

"I'm not an expert, but she looks like she had some kind of attack," I said to the paramedic. He was too busy working on Izabelle to answer.

The ride to the emergency room was painstakingly slow until we got out of the fogged-in area. The man monitoring her vitals was very quiet, and I had a bad feeling.

Izabelle was taken right into the emergency room when we arrived. I was directed to a waiting room. The only good part was that it was empty. I think ER waiting rooms probably all look the same. Uncomfortable but indestructible plastic chairs, a gray linoleum floor, a TV tuned to CNN with the sound tuned so low you get only every fourth word and a vibe of worry.

I wished I had brought some crocheting. I wished I'd brought my purse. Most of all, I wished I wasn't there in the first place. A woman with dark circles under her eyes called me to the reception desk, and I gave her the information I had. Before we finished, a somber-looking doctor walked out. I figured his bad news before he said it. He said he was sorry but they'd lost her.

"It appears she had a severe allergic reaction. It's called anaphylactic shock." He explained that it caused her throat to constrict so she couldn't breathe and her blood pressure to drop. He asked me a lot of questions about Izabelle that I couldn't answer. I didn't even know how old she was, let alone if she was allergic to anything. "Sometimes people suddenly develop a severe allergy and it catches them off guard. A severe reaction can happen in minutes and requires immediate care," the doctor said. "Maybe that's what happened in this case. There was some peanut butter in the food item the paramedics brought in. That might have triggered it." He asked me more questions regarding her family, and again I had no answers. While he was talking, a police officer came in and joined us.

"Sergeant French, Pacific Grove PD," he said, introducing himself to me. The doctor obviously knew him and nodded in greeting. The police officer turned back to me and spoke in a kind tone. "You look a little green around the gills. Are you all right?"

"Not really," I said, feeling my stomach churn and threaten to empty its contents. I suppose someone good at being in charge wouldn't have said that. I should have sounded unflappable, like someone dying while under my authority was something I could completely handle.

The craggy-faced police officer had good people skills. He tried to put me at ease and suggested I sit down. "I just need to get some information from you. When someone dies on the beach, we investigate," he said, keeping a friendly voice.

Of course, Sergeant French knew about the fog and how it had brought everything to a standstill on the tip of the peninsula. I told him about the creative weekend and Commander Blaine and the s'mores. He kept taking notes. When I mentioned finding the burned wood, he looked up. "Fires aren't allowed on the beach," he warned.

It seemed kind of beside the point now.

It was dark when the police cruiser pulled up to the administration building. The only bright spot was that the fog was finally beginning to dissolve. The ride back from the hospital had been at almost normal speed. Dinah was waiting for me, and when

I walked in, she jumped up.

"Tell me everything," she said. She swallowed her words when she saw Sergeant French following me. I crossed to the registration table. Commander Blaine had collected the extra s'mores bags and the container of forks was gone. The folders for the campers were under the table, along with a folder Mrs. Shedd had included for me. I had thumbed through it once before and noticed information sheets for all the presenters and campers. I had wondered why they included emergency contact information. Now I understood.

I pulled out Izabelle's information sheet and showed it to Sergeant French. Her contact was Zak Landers and included a phone number. He wrote down the information and, to my relief, said he'd make the call. Then he left, and I collapsed into one of the easy chairs in the conversation area.

"First of all, Commander took care of dinner and Mason arranged some kind of walking meditation. I told everyone that Izabelle got sick and you went to the hospital with her. They were all understanding." Dinah glanced out the window as Sergeant French got into his cruiser. "She isn't all right, is she?"

I shook my head slowly and then recounted what had happened.

"Did he say how she died?" Dinah asked nervously. I knew she was really asking did they think it was murder. I was embarrassed by the relief in my voice as I explained the doctor said he couldn't say for sure, but he thought she'd had some kind of allergic reaction.

"He said she might have gone into anaphylactic shock and asked me a bunch of questions. I had to tell him I didn't know. I hardly knew her." The word *knew* stuck in my throat. "I can tell you this because you're my best friend and you won't think I'm some kind of cold-hearted monster, but I was really hoping to get through the weekend without anybody dying. There's no way this isn't going to be a black mark against my leadership abilities."

"Yes, but at least it wasn't murder."

"Right," I said, getting up and going back to the registration table. The rhinestone clipboard and my tote bag were still in the corner. "But I still have to call Mrs. Shedd." Reaching her turned out not to be an easy matter.

"I heard about the fog emergency," she said when I finally got her on the phone. "CNN is everywhere, even on the ship. Do they know when this fog problem is going to end?" I told her it had thinned considerably.

"Good," she said. "Well, if that's all —" She was ready to wind down the call.

"No, there's something else."

"I hope it isn't a dead body," she said, obviously joking. When I said nothing, I heard her swallow. "Oh no, there is a dead body, isn't there?" I told her about Izabelle, and she gasped. "How terrible! The poor woman alone on the beach —" Mrs. Shedd clicked her tongue in dismay. "I tried to tell Commander Blaine not to do the s'mores, but he was absolutely insistent about doing them. Then I tried to get him to go the traditional route, but no, he had to make them his gourmet way and stick in peanut butter."

As the news sank in, Mrs. Shedd realized it presented a problem for the weekend program. "That leaves you with a big spot to fill, doesn't it?" Her tone changed, and it was clear she wanted to end the call. "I'm sure you'll think of something. You're good at improvising. Just make the best of it." I heard her call to someone that she'd be there in a minute and to save a space in the mambo class. "By now you've had some experience dealing with deaths. I'm sure you'll do a better job than I would." She started to sign off, but I stopped her long enough to explain that most of the campers hadn't arrived yet because of the fog.

"You said it was clear now. So, they'll probably all show up tomorrow. Tell them we'll do something to make up for the lost day. I have every confidence in you, Molly."

"Thanks, but —" I started to say. It was already too late. She'd hung up and probably headed off to her dance class.

I considered calling Barry, but I wasn't up for it. I knew what he'd say as soon as he heard someone had died: "Stay out of it." But I couldn't. As the holder of the rhinestone clipboard, I was in the middle of it whether I wanted to be or not. Though at least it wasn't murder.

I needed time to think, and I wasn't up for dealing with Adele just then. I saw her march past the window on the driveway side of the building. Any moment she would come through the door and give me the third degree about Izabelle. I just couldn't tell the story one more time.

"I can't face Adele right now," I said, making a beeline for the other door. Dinah followed me out onto the deck. I was still getting used to being able to see beyond the end of my arm. I could actually see the fire circle, where a campfire was giving off a warm glow. I was going to suggest going there since it appeared the benches were empty, but as we crossed the path through the meadow, I saw two people sitting toward the back. The floodlights along the wall illuminated their faces. It was the guy who had made the scene with Izabelle in the kitchen — Spenser somebody — and his niece. I didn't want to talk to them, either.

"Adele won't find us at the beach," I said, pointing toward the entrance to the boardwalk.

"So what was up with the cop?" Dinah asked as we started along the raised walkway. She stopped herself. "Sorry. You said you didn't want to talk."

"To Adele," I said. "I always want to talk to you." The sand was light even in the dark, and the contrast made the silhouettes of the bushes and plants stand out.

"He came to the hospital to write a report because Izabelle died on the beach. They don't have much crime up here, and the police are very community-oriented."

"Which means what?" Dinah zipped her hoodie a little higher.

"I don't know. I guess you could say he was friendly when he asked questions. He wanted to know what Izabelle was doing on the beach."

"What did you tell him?" Dinah stepped from the end of the boardwalk onto the sandy sidewalk.

"I told him about the s'mores and how everyone had gone their own way with theirs. He filled in the rest, saying she must have decided to take hers to the beach."

We reached the street and a white Toyota went by. I watched the red taillights and finally saw the curve of the street. It was like discovering the area for the first time. Seeing the sky and stars was a relief after feeling like I was stuck in a pillow. Once we crossed the street, we started down the opening to the beach. When I looked ahead, even in the dark I could see the waves breaking against the shore. We walked a little farther and the beach seemed empty and peaceful. "I guess they must have finished any investigation. There's no yellow tape," I said as we reached the remains of the fire. I kicked one of the hunks of partially burned wood. "It looks like the fire must have gone out. Otherwise, the wood would have just burned to ash."

"Or maybe someone put it out," Dinah said.

"I don't think Izabelle was worried about the fire. I don't think she had time to be. The doctor said her attack could have come on within minutes after she ate the s'more with the peanut butter."

"How awful. She comes to the beach to enjoy the goodies and then, blam! she's sick," Dinah said.

"It's kind of odd that she'd be eating the s'more. She seemed so careful about her diet."

"Maybe she was one of those people who watch themselves so carefully, and then binge," Dinah said.

"We'll never know." I repeated my relief that her death seemed to be from natural causes. It was bad enough that I'd come across murders in Tarzana, but a murder in another place — it would look like I was some kind of murder magnet. I flopped on the cold, soft sand.

"Right," Dinah said, sitting down next to me. "She just made a deadly choice in snacks."

"I wish I'd paid more attention to everything when we found her," I said, getting up. *The Average Joe's Guide to Criminal Investigation* repeated over and over how important it was to examine a crime scene right away. Then I stopped myself. "But it wasn't a crime scene, right?"

"Right," Dinah said, standing beside me. "I'm sure you've avoided Adele by now. It's getting cold and damp here. I could use a little time in front of a fireplace. Commander Blaine set up board games and hot chocolate in the common living room of our building."

"Aha, so you're changing your opinion of him."

"I still say he's too fussy for my taste, but our campfire dinner the other night was fun, and he certainly came through during the whiteout. And those s'mores . . ." Her voice trailed off as she looked down the beach. "Okay, maybe that was not the best example under the circumstances, but he certainly came up with a lot of variations on the original idea."

"You can argue all you want, but I think you're softening."

"He's not my type," Dinah countered. "I see myself with the brooding poet type. You know: intense, wears turtlenecks. Yeah, and isn't into relationships, and is probably a jerk, too," she added with a groan.

"I don't think Commander is a jerk," I replied. "He might be a little stiff and a little too enthusiastic, but definitely not a jerk."

"Maybe not, but what do we really know about him? Just that he has a postal center in Tarzana and he's very into parties. Doesn't it seem a little odd to you that someone who's so into entertaining is alone?"

I glanced in the direction we'd come from. "Even if he might have a dark past, that cocoa is starting to sound good. You're right, it is cold and damp. We might as well go back." We got up and started to walk toward the street. As we approached the fenced-off area, I made a visual sweep of the planted area. Something got my attention. "What's that?" I asked, pointing at a strange glow.

We moved closer for a better view, but it still appeared to be just a ghostly light.

"Maybe somebody threw one of those light sticks back there," Dinah offered, walking on.

I stood my ground and peered into the darkness. Curiosity had gotten the better of me. I had to know what it was. Dinah saw that I had stopped at the fence and came back. I tried leaning over it to see if I could reach the glowing spot, but it was too far away. "I'm going in," I said, stepping over the low chain. But going in was as far as I got. There seemed to be no way to reach the glow without tromping on some plants. Dinah picked up on my plight and offered to hold my legs so I could lean over the plants without falling in them.

She braced herself, digging her feet in the sand, and held onto my calves as I leaned and reached into the tangle of growth. I tried to avoid thinking what night creatures might be crawling around, just waiting for some tasty fingers to come their way. Instinctively I balled up my hand. I wished I had my son's old Pinchy-Winchy claw toy to use, or at least gloves. I willed my hand open, and as I pushed through the wiry brush, I felt something soft and grabbed it. It came free easily and obviously wasn't attached to the sand.

Dinah pulled me up straight and we both looked at what I was holding. We couldn't make out the color in the darkness, but the shape was clear.

I was holding a small pouch purse, and the glow was coming from something shaped like a flower attached to the front.

That was about all we could make out in the dark.

"Why do I think this has something to do with Izabelle?" I asked as we trudged up the beach toward the street.

CHAPTER 10

"Wow, glow-in-the-dark yarn," Dinah said as I turned off the light in my room. We were examining the pouch purse, which we now knew was lime green and the six-petaled flower was a satiny pink and the whole thing was crocheted. In the darkness the purse disappeared, but the pink flower gave off an eerie light. We had slipped back into Asilomar without crossing paths with anyone from our group. We wanted to keep the bag under wraps until we could check it out, and had avoided the cocoa party by slipping up the back stairs in Lodge.

I flipped the light back on. The purse was on my bed between us. "Okay, now that we've cleared up the strange light thing, you ought to see what's inside," Dinah said.

I knew Dinah was right, but I still hesitated. There was something unsettling about looking into someone's purse. By the design, it was hard to think it was anybody's but

Izabelle's — after all, she was supposed to be the queen of crochet embellishment, and who else would think of using glow-in-the-dark yarn to make flowers? But what was it doing in an off-limits area?

I swallowed and opened the purse, reaching inside. Along with sand sticking to the fibers, I felt something cold and metal that had snagged near the top. It turned out to be a key with an Asilomar tag.

"There's an obvious way to be sure the purse belonged to Izabelle," Dinah said. Of course she was right, and we went out into the hall. We made sure it was empty, then slipped toward the door to Izabelle's room. I had the key in my hand but I hesitated again. In all honesty I didn't want the key to fit. I wanted the purse to belong to some random person who had nothing to do with our group. If it was Izabelle's, it brought up a lot of questions, like how someone in the middle of an allergy attack would decide to lob her purse into the bushes.

Dinah nudged me and spoke in a low voice, urging me to stick the key in the lock. I took a deep breath and tried to put it in. It didn't go. I felt a wave of relief and even laughed a little.

"So, I guess we were wrong," I said, turning to go. Dinah took the key from my hand

131

and turned it around. That way it fit perfectly, and with half a turn the door was unlocked and slipped open.

Neither of us made a move. If opening the purse felt strange, it was nothing compared to looking into her room. I was about to pull the door closed when something moved in the darkness and made a rustling sound. Both Dinah and I jumped as a shadow passed in front of the window. There was someone in the room. Instinctively I lunged forward, then slid on something as the shadow slipped out the window.

A moment later the room was flooded with light as Dinah flipped the switch. I skated across the floor on a flutter of papers, rushing toward the open window. But when I looked out, the small balcony was empty.

"What was that about?" Dinah said, her voice high-pitched with tension. My heart was still pounding as I took a deep breath.

"Somebody was in here." I began to scoop up the papers, looking at them as I did. They had copy centered in the middle of the page. When Dinah saw one, she said they were galley pages.

"They must be from Izabelle's book. The one she was making the big to-do about. Her fusion craft." Dinah put on her creative writing teacher hat and explained the pages were typeset like the book. "It's the last step before the book comes out." Dinah pointed to a notation penciled in the margin. "She must have been proofreading them."

As we piled them on the bed, Dinah held up a page in front of me. "Look at the title: *The Needle and the Hook.*"

"You think her big fusion craft was mixing knitting and crochet?" I asked.

"It looks that way." Dinah riffled through the pages on the bed. "It also looks like most of the book is missing."

We both looked toward the window. "Do you think the shadow was a woman, like maybe Adele? What if she found out the subject of Izabelle's new craft and went bonkers?" I pictured Adele ranting about the fusion craft soiling the purity of crochet.

"I know she had a problem with crochet versus knitting, but do you think she'd go so far as to break into a room? And what would be the point of stealing the galleys? I'm sure the publisher has another copy. Finally, I think we know Adele well enough that if it had been her, we would have recognized her shape," Dinah said.

By now our heartbeats had returned to normal, and all that was left was the rush from the adrenaline. I glanced around the room with a different perspective.

"I guess it'll be my responsibility to pack up her things."

Dinah gave me a sympathetic nod. "Yes, one more responsibility that goes along with the rhinestone clipboard."

The room was laid out about the same as mine, except there was only one twin bed against the wall. Aside from the papers it seemed orderly. Izabelle's personal items were in several unzipped pouches by the sink. A stack of plastic bins sat against the wall. Each of them had a label for a session of her workshop. When I lifted the lid of the top one, I saw pillowcases with thread crochet trim and a lot of flowers in different sizes and yarns, along with a copy of her book. I walked over to the closet and opened the door. A faint scent of her floral cologne clung to her neatly hung clothes and the suitcase stowed below. When I turned back to the room, Dinah was sitting on the bed with a laptop computer open next to her.

"What are you doing?" I asked.

"Checking my e-mail. You know how upset I've been about not bringing my laptop. This is even better. She has one of those cards that makes it so her computer can go online anywhere." Dinah looked up and caught my expression of disapproval. "It's all right. I'm just going to see what I have.

And I want to check a quote for the memoir workshop. So technically I'm using it for the weekend. I'm sure Izabelle wouldn't mind." The reflection from the screen illuminated Dinah's face after she'd pressed the power button.

"Hmm. It looks like Izabelle was in the middle of something and just let it go into hibernate mode." Dinah turned the computer so I could see the screen. The body of an e-mail was in the center of the screen. It had no salutation and said *Don't do anything before you talk to me. Call me or at least answer your phone.* It was signed *Tom, ITA Sponsor.* I sat down on the bed next to Dinah and put the computer on my lap, but I almost dropped it when my cell phone started to vibrate in my tote next to me. I hurried to get it before it started to ring. Dinah and I had kept our conversation to a whisper. Somehow, I didn't want to make any noise.

I answered the phone with a whispered hello.

"Hey, babe," Barry said. "Just calling to see how it's going. I figured by now you'd be in your room . . . alone. Right, you are alone?"

There was dead air. I couldn't lie when asked a direct question, but I also didn't want to answer. Saying nothing seemed the safest bet. Unless you're talking to a top-flight homicide detective who knows how to squeeze information out of the most reluctant suspects. In my case it was easy. He knew me well enough to recognize that the dead air meant something was up, probably something he wouldn't be happy about. "Okay, Molly, let's just save us both a lot of time and cut to the chase. Where are you, and what are you doing?"

"I was going to call you. There's been a little incident." I paused; what I was going to say next was going to get the reaction. "One of the presenters died."

"What?" Barry said. I could practically hear his blood pressure go up.

"The doctor and the police think it was from some kind of allergic reaction." I heard his breath come out in a gush.

"Then it wasn't homicide. Good."

I told him the doctor thought Izabelle had suddenly developed a life-threatening allergy.

"That sounds reasonable." He began his standard speech. "The police will investigate. Stay out of it. Leave it to the professionals la la la la." He didn't actually say la la la la. That was the part where I wasn't listening anymore. Eventually he figured out something else was up, and he knew me well enough to ask me directly. Like I said, when someone asks me a specific question, I always tell the truth. Barry asked where I was. I thought he took the information that I was in Izabelle's room rather well. But since he didn't ask about the purse, I didn't tell. I let him think I was being overzealous about my responsibility to handle things.

"I understand you think it's your task to pack up her things. But you have all weekend, and you might want to wait until you talk to her next of kin."

Barry seemed pleased when I said I would definitely take what he said into consideration. Then he signed off after telling me how much he missed me.

"He just wants to protect you," Dinah said when I flipped my phone shut. It was pointless to try and keep our conversation private. Besides, Dinah knew all my business anyway.

"The trouble is," I said, putting my phone away, "he makes it so I can't discuss things with him. I can just imagine what he'd say if I told him someone was in the room when we got here and went out the window. And he'd get crazy if I told him we thought that what we'd just read on Izabelle's computer made it sound like she was planning to do something that would cause trouble."

"We do?" Dinah said.

"Sure, look at it. It sounds like some person is telling her not to do something rashly." Dinah read it again and nodded in agreement.

"I wonder what ITA is?" she said.

I looked at it again, too. "I bet the *A* stands for anonymous. Like Alcoholics Anonymous. They always give people sponsors."

"And the *I* probably stands for independent or international," Dinah said. "All we have to do is figure out the *T*."

For a few minutes Dinah and I thought of words beginning with T that might go with Anonymous and Independent or International. We got teetotalers, tap dancers, taskmasters, tastemakers, tattletales, techies and taxi drivers before we gave up.

"Let's check Izabelle's favorite Web sites. Maybe that will give us a clue," Dinah said, clicking on a button on the computer.

A list came up. A number of the Web sites had to do with crochet, but one popped out at me. I told Dinah to click on it. When the opening page loaded and I read it over, I nodded toward the screen.

"You realize what this means," I said as we looked at the home page of peanutallergies.com. "She knew she was allergic to

peanuts. It wasn't a sudden allergic reaction."

"Then why would she eat a s'more laced
with peanut butter?" Dinah said. I flipped
through some more screens that described
first aid maneuvers. I pointed at the screen.
We both looked at the slender cylinder
with the designation EpiPen. Underneath
was a diagram of how to use it. Apparently
you stabbed it in your thigh if you had a reaction to something and it would keep you
going until you could get further help. The
lime green pouch bag was still hanging on
my wrist. I reeled it in and turned it upside
down. A cell phone fell out along with a
match of what we were looking at on the
screen.

"Hmm, one more thing that proves she
was aware of her allergy and had taken
precautions," Dinah said, examining the
EpiPen.

I checked the cell phone; the battery was
completely dead. "Then how did she die
from an allergy attack?"

CHAPTER 11

The whole group was already at breakfast when I came into the dining hall. Outside, the sky was an overcast white with haze in the air, but when I stopped at the registration desk, the clerk assured me it was completely normal and not the beginning of another fog emergency. The redheaded clerk had finally gone home, and this morning two women were manning the desk. They gave me a pile of phone messages. They were all from people who were on their way and wanted to make sure I knew they were coming. Now that the operations of Asilomar were back to normal, there were pots of coffee on the table and the smell of pancakes and maple syrup in the air.

Only Commander Blaine seemed disappointed that breakfast apparently was going along without his help. I heard him comment to Dinah, who was sitting across the table, that if it had been up to him, he'd have set up the breakfast buffet style, with lots of choices for pancake toppings besides the mundane, overly sweet syrup that was the only option.

The knitting couple, Jym and Jeen Wolf, were at the same table, wearing matching tee shirts with the saying *Born to Knit.* They greeted me with enthusiastic smiles and asked about the status of the retreaters. I held up the handful of messages in answer. Miss Lavender Pants and her brother and sister-in-law were next to the Wolfs. Miss Lavender Pants seemed happy that the real workshops were going to begin, and hoped there would be no more incidents like Adele's big scene.

Mason waved me over to the next table and pulled out a chair in anticipation. Apparently, he'd brought a wardrobe of loose-fitting pants and kimono jackets. Today's outfit was navy blue with an olive green tee shirt underneath. Only his smile was the same.

"Hey, Sunshine," he said in a reassuring tone. "If you need any help, just give me a nudge." He and Dinah were the only ones who knew Izabelle was dead. After what I'd found in Izabelle's room, I'd gone to talk to Mason. I had tried to get Dinah to come with me — maybe more as a chaperone than anything else — but she was more interested in going to bed. After what I'd been through, I was too wired to sleep anyway.

I had felt a little odd knocking at Mason's door both because it was late and because the rooms didn't have any space for socializing. But I wanted to run our experiences in Izabelle's room past him. Since he was a criminal attorney, I wanted to hear his take on things.

When Mason answered the door, it was obvious he'd been sleeping. I don't know why I was surprised. There wasn't much else to do in the small, televison-free rooms. His eyes were glazed and his hair was all tousled. The unfocused look on his face changed to a slightly surprised smile when he saw it was me.

"What's up, Sunshine?" I was relieved he didn't make some smarmy remark. I knew he might be thinking it, but at least he didn't say anything. He was clearly waiting to see what move I was going to make. He'd made it clear he was ready, willing and more than able to step into the boyfriend slot, but had left it up to me to give the okay.

"I need some advice," I said. Was there just a little disappointment in his eyes as his smile went down a notch?

"C'mon in." He stepped aside and shut

the door behind me. I swallowed when I saw his room was smaller than mine and had only one single bed. "Sorry there's no chair," he said, pulling the covers up over the small bed. We both sat down.

I usually felt very comfortable with Mason. There was something about the way he handled things, like coming by helicopter when I got detained on Catalina. And he was always such a good sport, like coming on this weekend and teaching tai chi. And I liked the way he'd said that there was always fun where I was. He hadn't even minded the fog.

Only this time what I felt had nothing to do with comfort. I tried not to look at his pajamas or what he wore as pajamas — a tee shirt and soft knit pants. I realized I'd never seen his bare feet before. Or realized how big his feet were. I tore my eyes away and glanced around the room, trying to ignore the faint smell of his cologne.

I didn't know where to look when I talked to him. Definitely not the same as talking to Mason in a suit. I told him about finding Izabelle and what they thought was the cause of death. I moved on to Dinah's and my walk to the beach. When I got to the part about going in Izabelle's room and someone being in there, and then mentioned what we had found, he sat forward a little.

This was what I loved about Mason. He didn't discount what I said or tell me to leave it alone or that I had murder on the brain.

"So, I gather you aren't so sure it was an accident?"

"Right," I said. "But I really don't want it to be homicide. I mean, what a perfect crime, but I don't want it to be a crime. I wanted this weekend to be crime-free. Mrs. Shedd can't blame me for the fog, but it still looks bad that the one weekend she puts me in charge of is the one when there's a fog emergency. She can't count what happened to Izabelle as my fault, either, but someone getting sick and dying doesn't look as bad as someone getting killed."

"I think I have an answer," Mason said. "Here's a problem for a murder scenario. S'mores aren't like cyanide. You can't mix them with something. You know the one about you can get a horse to water, but you can't make it drink? Well, somebody could have handed the s'more to Izabelle, but they couldn't have made her eat it. She must have picked up the wrong bag, or maybe it was mismarked. Feel better?"

"Yes," I said, sighing in relief.

"As for the person in the room, I don't have enough information to give you an answer. But it's probably something stupid like someone who couldn't wait for her book to come out and wanted to see it. So, there you are, no murder this weekend."

I turned toward him, ready to give him a thank-you hug, but I stopped short. Along with his other attributes, Mason had a high cuddle quotient. And it would have been all too easy to let the hug morph into curling up next to him.

"Got to go," I said, my voice cracking, as I jumped off the bed and made it to the doorway in two steps. I heard Mason chuckling behind me, and I bet he'd had the same smile then as he was wearing here now at breakfast.

Mason reached for the coffee pot and poured me a cup as I glanced around the table. Sheila was sitting next to Adele. I think their sharing a room was really getting to Sheila. Her shoulders were hunched and she was crocheting in her lap. It was therapeutic crochet. I doubted she even knew what she was making or cared if her stitches were all over the place. This was about the meditative quality. Besides, she knew she could rip it out later.

When Adele turned to hang her jacket on

the back of her chair, I saw something that made me jump. "Where did you get that?" I said, pointing as she held a pouch purse with the strap hanging down.

Adele reacted with a funny look, and I realized I might have sounded a little frantic. She set it in the middle of the table with a gesture that implied it was there for me to admire. Hers was red and the flowers were white, but the style was identical to the bag I'd found in the plants. "What do you think? I made it, Pink." Dinah looked over from the other table, and when she saw the purse, her eyes widened. "If you want, I can help you make one," Adele said. "The directions are in Izabelle's book. She used some glow-in-the-dark stuff for the flowers, but I just went for the sport-weight yarn I'd used for the bag." At the mention of Izabelle's name, Jym asked how she was doing.

I took a deep breath. I wasn't looking forward to what I had to do. Everyone turned toward me, waiting for an answer, which confirmed that no one knew yet. I was still composing my thoughts when Bennett and Nora came in and went to the neighboring table, and momentarily the attention turned to them. Even if nobody exactly recognized him, he had a kind of magnetism that drew your eyes to him. His manner was gentlemanly as he pulled out a chair for his wife and gestured for her to sit. I was glad she'd decided to give the dining hall food a try after all. Bennett made a little nod of greeting to the group, and then everyone turned back to me.

"Well, Pink," Adele said finally, "is Izabelle going to make it back from the hospital in time to do her workshop?"

"Not exactly." Did I really say that? How lame. Once I actually said she was dead, everyone would realize what a bad comment it was. Better just to be direct. I was about to say it when Sergeant French came into the dining room and glanced around until he saw our group. As he walked toward our table, he put on a somber expression. I might as well leave the job of telling the group to him. He certainly had far more experience. And, maybe, it was the coward's way out.

"Ms. Pink." He acknowledged me with a nod when he stopped next to me; then he greeted the rest of our group. He turned back to me with a question in his eyes: "They don't know, do they?" I guess it was pretty obvious. All the smiling and cheerful conversations didn't go with having just heard someone had died.

Sergeant French checked out the group

some more. I suppose he was sizing them up, trying to figure if anybody was going to faint or anything. His head stopped moving when his gaze reached Bennett. It was obvious, from the perplexed squint of his eyes, that he was trying to place Bennett, as if maybe he had seen him on the Ten Most Wanted list.

Nora apparently was used to people staring at her husband that way and volunteered that he was on *Raf Gibraltar.*

Sergeant French studied Bennett's face and then brightened. "That's right. He plays the older brother. What's his name?"

"Buzz Gibraltar," Nora said. "If you watch the show, you probably realize the story always turns on his assessment of the situation. Nobody understands, but he's really the star."

Nora always seemed to be playing the manager, talking up her client. Did she have any life of her own? Did she want any life of her own? Or was she content to be an extension of Bennett?

By now everybody was staring at the craggy-faced policeman in the dark uniform — and not in a good way. I had to do something. How would it look that I hadn't told them?

"Look, everybody, I need to tell you about

Izabelle," I said quickly. "You all know she got sick on the beach last night. There isn't any soft way to put it. She isn't coming back. She died right after she got to the hospital."

The group gave a collective gasp, and a few people made comments that got lost in the din.

Bennett's voice was heard over the noise. "What happened? The last time I saw her, she looked fine."

"And when was that, Mr. Franklyn?" Sergeant French asked, taking out his notebook.

"I don't remember the exact time, but everyone was checking out the s'mores bags Commander Blaine set out. I think she was picking out one."

"And then?" Sergeant French said. Bennett just shrugged and said he'd walked away after that. "Got to keep trim for my show, so I passed on the snacks." Nora gave Bennett a little shake of her head, as if she was upset that he'd said anything.

Before Sergeant French could ask any more questions, Jeen asked for details about what had happened. She pursed her lips and gave me a disparaging look. "I don't think saying she died is enough. We want to know how she died."

I started to explain that Dinah, Commander, and I had found her on the beach and that we'd called the paramedics, but Jym interrupted me.

"I think what my wife was asking was what happened to her. Was it foul play?"

Sergeant French took over the floor and put up his hand in a reassuring gesture. "From what the ER doctor said, it looks like Ms. Landers had a severe allergic reaction to something in the s'mores, so there's no reason for you people to worry about being in danger."

Commander Blaine popped out of his chair. "There was nothing wrong with the s'mores," he protested.

Sergeant French kept an even tone. "I'm not saying there was. We're investigating her death as being from natural causes. Did any of you happen to go to the beach with Ms. Landers?"

There was a hum of conversation and a lot of head shakes.

Miss Lavender Pants raised her hand and jumped up. "If I were you, I wouldn't rush and be so sure it was natural causes." Her tightly curled brown hair bobbled as she swiveled and pointed directly at Adele. "She threatened the vic." When Miss Lavender Pants got weird looks for her word choice, she put her hand on her hip. "All right, I watch *CSI NYC,* and they always call them vics." She rolled her eyes and continued, "Like I said, she threatened Izabelle, and the next thing we hear is the woman is dead. It sounds a little too coincidental to me. If I were you, I wouldn't be so quick to be sure it isn't murder."

Now all heads turned toward Adele, whose eyes bugged out as she stood up. "Are you crazy? I didn't kill Izabelle. I didn't even threaten her. What I said was something like it wasn't over, and maybe I said something about her not getting away with it. But that didn't mean I intended to kill her. I meant I wasn't going to give in just because she denied stealing my work," Adele said. Her demeanor changed slightly. Obviously she didn't like being accused of killing someone, but she liked having everyone's attention. She began to address the group. "You can understand why I'd be angry. She used my work to figure out the stitch I created, and then added on to it and had the nerve to wear it."

It was obvious Adele wasn't going to let up, so Sheila and I got on either side of her and acted as a human hook to get her away from the table. "Why are you dragging me out? She's the one who started it." Adele

151

pointed an accusing finger at Miss Lavender Pants, who gasped.

"You heard her. Now she's threatening me."

I noticed Sergeant French was following us out. "Ms. Abrams, I'd like to talk to you."

I felt Adele grab my arm with such force I knew she was leaving marks.

"Pink, stay with me. He's going to haul me off to some interrogation room and shine bright lights in my eyes until I give in and confess to something I didn't do."

I tried to tell Adele she was being overly dramatic, but she was too busy being overly dramatic to listen. Typical Adele. One minute she'd be lobbing zingers at me, but as soon as there was some kind of problem, I was suddenly her best friend and savior. Even if the rhinestone clipboard hadn't put me in the position of being responsible for her, I wouldn't have abandoned her.

Sergeant French led Adele to a bench and then told Sheila and me that he wanted to speak to her alone, but Adele set up such a ruckus he finally agreed to let us stay.

"Am I a person of interest?" Adele demanded. There was just the tiniest curve to her mouth, and I wanted to roll my eyes. Only Adele would think being a person of interest made her special.

Sergeant French didn't know Adele, so he took her seriously and said he was just trying to find out what happened to Izabelle.

"Well, I certainly don't know. I was so upset after the workshop — there she was wearing that choker made with the stitch I came up with. Do you have any idea how upsetting that was? Here I had been putting her on a pedestal as this crochet goddess, and then she turns out to be a stitch thief."

Adele went on and on after that, giving Sergeant French probably far more information than he wanted about the ins and outs of crochet. When she got to explaining how she needed the choker back because she couldn't remember how many yarn overs she'd done before pulling the yarn through all the loops, his eyes glazed over.

"I really need to get that piece of my work back. Is it with her things?"

I wanted to throw up my hands. Adele was outdoing herself. Was she actually asking Sergeant French to go through Izabelle's things?

"I can prove it's my work," Adele said. "I spilled a little drop of pink pearl nail polish on the inside. So all you have to do is check it and you'll know it's really mine." Adele turned to me. "You know, Miss Rhinestone Clipboard, you've got another problem. The retreaters are arriving this morning, and at least some of them are expecting to have workshops with Izabelle this afternoon."

I had been so concerned with Izabelle dying, I hadn't thought about her workshops until that moment. But as usual with Adele, everything she had said was really a setup.

"Of course, I could take her place. No problem with teaching people to crochet. Sheila can assist me," she said, nodding toward her roommate. "And as for the workshop she called A Subtle Touch of Crochet" — she jiggled her head so that the big, floppy flower on her cloche wobbled — "I know how to make flowers and I'm an expert at trim. As for the last one, her world premiere fusion craft, sorry, no can do."

Sergeant French listened to the interchange while staring intently at Adele. First, she'd said that Izabelle had stolen her work, and now she was only too glad to take her place. Was she trying to move up from person of interest to suspect? You never knew with Adele.

Sergeant French asked her where she was during the s'more time. "Did you perhaps go to the beach and meet Ms. Landers to discuss that stitch you were talking about?"

"Of course not," Adele said with a harrumph. "Who'd want to go to the beach in all that fog? I took one of the bags with the classic s'mores and went to the fire pit. I don't know why Commander Blaine had to go all fancy with —"

"I think that's all," Sergeant French said abruptly. Apparently, dealing with Adele had pushed his community-relations skills to the limit. He told Adele and Sheila that they could go, but I was to stay.

"I contacted Zak Landers," Sergeant French said. "Turns out he's her ex-husband. He seemed surprised she'd listed him. You should probably call him about her things."

I glanced in Adele's direction. "Are you considering her a person of interest?"

He didn't answer but instead asked me if I knew the whereabouts of my people during the snack break.

"Why do you want to know?"

He appeared disgruntled and ran his hand over his slicked-back strawberry blond hair. "You're not supposed to answer a question with a question." He looked down at his notebook and seemed to consider his words. "I don't think she was on the beach alone. It's the campfire."

"I get it. Who would go to the trouble of building a fire to toast a few marshmallows? Right?"

"Yes," he said finally. "I asked her ex-husband if she would be likely to make a fire on the beach. He kind of choked."

"You know she knew she was allergic to peanuts," I said.

"Her ex told me," Sergeant French said.

"Did he tell you she carried an EpiPen?"

Sergeant French began to eye me warily.

"As a matter of fact, he did. How did you know? Last night at the hospital, all you knew was her name."

I took a deep breath and told him about finding the pouch bag in the plants and using the key to open Izabelle's door.

"I was just trying to confirm that the bag was hers," I said. "And you should know that someone was in the room when I opened the door." I mentioned seeing a shadow go out the window and that I was sure the person had taken most of the pages of Izabelle's manuscript with them.

Sergeant French was starting to give me a funny look. It got more pronounced when I mentioned how Dinah had just happened to turn the computer on and we'd seen the peanut allergy Web site.

"Maybe I better have a look at the room," he said. He pulled out his cell phone and made a call to Zak Landers to get permission to check out the room.

I took Sergeant French back to Lodge. I retrieved the key and pouch purse from my room and took him down the hall. Once Izabelle's door was open, we walked in and I pointed to the window, which was now closed, and again explained how I'd seen something dark go out the window. Then I pointed to the floor where the remnants of the manuscript had been. The spot was empty now, and a neat stack of papers was sitting on the bedside table.

"Are these the papers?" Sergeant French said, picking up the top sheet. It was the title page, and I explained that Dinah and I thought it was her book about the fusion craft. Of course, he didn't know what I was talking about.

"Fusion craft? Enlighten me," he said. As soon as I started talking about knitting and crochet, I sensed he was losing interest. "Okay, I get it. She was mixing two things. You said most of the pages were missing. He picked up the manuscript and thumbed through it. "Well, it looks like they're all here now." He paused a moment and then, in his best community-relations voice, sug-gested that maybe we'd been mistaken about a person being in the room. "A crow might have come in the open window. They can sure make a mess. Maybe the pages you

157

thought were missing just got knocked under the bed." He glanced around the room. "Housekeeping probably found them when they did the room." He gestured toward the open door, signifying it was time to go.

"I can buy you trying the key, and when you saw something flapping around inside, going in, but looking at her computer is kind of a stretch. You should talk to her ex and find out how he wants to handle her things."

I know I said I didn't want it to be murder, but I couldn't ignore a nagging question. Before I walked out into the hall, I posed it to Sergeant French.

"Izabelle Landers was extremely careful about what she ate. I thought she was on a diet, but now I realize it was because of her allergy. Why would she have taken the s'mores that contained peanut butter, and how did the bag with her EpiPen end up in the plants? I'm just saying it seems kind of suspicious. And I think you're definitely right. I think there was somebody on the beach with her."

Sergeant French appeared impatient. "Oh no, you aren't going amateur sleuth on me, are you?" He rolled his eyes. "I appreciate your input, but we professionals have it under control. Are you trying to say you think somebody murdered her with a s'more?" He took a moment to collect himself and go back to his community-relations voice. "There's an easy explanation. Maybe the s'more bag was mismarked, and she could have dropped the purse with the EpiPen without realizing it." He draped the crocheted bag over his little finger to demonstrate how lightweight it was.

"But she'd have had to make the s'more, and she'd have realized there was peanut butter right away. Have you seen how those things ooze? And peanut butter has a definite smell. She'd never have made the whole thing and then eaten it without realizing what she was eating."

Sergeant French threw up his hands. "Okay, so maybe she did know what she was eating. I had an aunt who was allergic to cranberries. She knew it, but every Thanksgiving she'd eat them anyway. She always said this year it was going to be different, that she wasn't allergic anymore. Plus, I've heard that people crave what they're allergic to. I'm sorry, Ms. Pink, there is just no way I'm going to buy that somebody killed her with a s'more. And here's one other little problem with your scenario. Let's just say someone did make the s'more for her. How would they have gotten her to eat it? You admit she'd have to have known about the peanut butter." He shook his head and looked skyward. "Am I really having this conversation?"

CHAPTER 12

"Maybe it's not the worst thing that Sergeant French doesn't think it's murder," Dinah said. "Remember how you wanted this to be a no-dead-body weekend?" She caught herself. "Okay, maybe there is a dead body — but I think what you really meant was a no-murder weekend. Right?" She realized she'd spoken a little too loudly and threw me an apologetic smile.

"Yes, that's what I meant, but having a no-murder weekend doesn't mean a pretend-it's-not-a-murder weekend. Even Sergeant French thinks there was someone else on the beach with Izabelle. I'm just going to do a little quiet investigating," I said. We were stationed at the registration table in the administration building. There had been a steady stream of campers checking in, though the number was less than we had originally expected. The fog delay had caused some people to cancel. I wondered if more people would have canceled if they'd heard about Izabelle's death.

Somehow I was going to have to turn things around on this weekend. I thought of my late husband, Charlie, and wondered what he would do. He was an expert at putting a positive spin on things. But even he would have had trouble putting a spin on the fog emergency and Izabelle's death.

The thought of Charlie brought a wave of sadness. It had been over two years since he died, and I had picked up the pieces of my life and started anew. I was proud of myself for getting the job at Shedd & Royal and making new friends, but a part of me wished it had never been necessary. You moved on, but you didn't forget. Not a day went by that something didn't remind me of our previous life.

I suppose that was why I still resisted Barry's desire to take our relationship to another level.

I heard the musical flourish that was my cell phone's ring tone. It took a moment to locate my tote bag in the corner and then I answered it. It was Barry checking in.

"Hey, babe, remember the boxes? Well, there are more of them in your hall now. Do you want me to check with your sons?"

I said no a little too fast. Maybe that was

another reason Barry's and my relationship hadn't progressed. My older son, Peter, just didn't like Barry, and Samuel viewed him as an intruder. I softened it by saying I'd checked with them already. Peter knew nothing about them, and Samuel hadn't answered his voice mail.

It was frustrating to Barry that he couldn't get along with my boys the way I got along with his son, so he changed the subject. "How's it going there?"

I mentioned the retreaters arriving and the workshops starting in the afternoon.

"That isn't what I meant." As usual, he saw right through what I said or, more important, didn't say. "Okay, Molly, let me guess. Even though this Sergeant French is satisfied your crochet person died from an accidental allergic reaction, you don't buy it." Barry didn't approve of my amateur sleuthing and found it very frustrating that no matter how much he told me to stay out of things, I got involved anyway. And even more upsetting to his worldview, I had actually solved a number of cases.

"Well, you wouldn't either, if you knew all the facts."

Barry tried to resist, but he couldn't, and finally asked me for the facts I was talking about. At the end, I heard him blow out his breath.

"You do realize if you get this French to think it's murder, the number one suspect is Adele. It certainly wasn't very smart of her to go on and on about how Izabelle had done her wrong."

I'd already thought about that and come to the obvious conclusion that there was no point in trying to convince Sergeant French that it was homicide. I would just have to figure the whole thing out myself. I didn't tell Barry the last part, but he figured it out.

"Molly, you have a bad track record for getting into trouble. I'd jump in the Tahoe and be up there in six hours, but when you canceled on me, I let somebody else have the weekend off," he said.

I looked over at the registration table. Suddenly Dinah was swamped with a bunch of people. I told Barry I had to go, and got off the phone quickly.

What did he mean I had a bad track record for getting in trouble? Maybe I had gotten into a few embarrassing situations in my past investigations, but this time I was sure nothing like that was going to happen.

"What do you mean Izabelle Landers won't be doing her workshops?" a woman in a khaki safari jacket was demanding of

Dinah when I reached the table. I had wondered how to handle the situation with the new arrivals. Dinah, Adele, Sheila, and I had gone through the schedules in the folders and crossed out Izabelle's name and written in Adele and Sheila. I thought I would tastefully tell each person that Izabelle wouldn't be with us as they registered, but this woman had opened her program folder too quickly.

I thought about using one of the terms doctors use and say we'd lost Izabelle, but it sounded like we'd misplaced her or she was wandering somewhere without a compass. I decided just to be direct. "I'm sorry to have to tell you, but Izabelle Landers died last night."

"Oh," the woman in the safari jacket said, looking stunned. I assured her we had a replacement for all Izabelle's sessions except the one featuring the fusion craft.

"I'm afraid Izabelle was the only one who could do it," I said.

Another woman with light brown hair that draped over her shoulders and the most beautiful turquoise earrings huddled in close and pulled a man with her. "I get it. That's the surprise Mrs. Shedd talked about. This is one of those mystery weekends, isn't it?" the woman said with an excited note in her voice. She turned to her husband. "Davis, you're going to love it. We all get to play detective."

A woman in a red sweater stepped closer. "What kind of weekend? I came here to crochet."

"Ladies," I said, then considered Davis. "Sorry, I mean people, this isn't some kind of whodunit game. Izabelle Landers really died. But I can assure you the people we have in her place will do a wonderful job and we're going to have a wonderful week-end."

Of course, then they wanted to know how Izabelle died. I decided the best thing to do was to give them what Sergeant French had said about the allergic reaction, with no editorial comments from me.

More people came, and I repeated the story over and over. I thought it was going well until I noticed that Miss Lavender Pants — now technically Miss Lavender Sweatshirt — was hanging off to the side and talking to people as they left. Judging by their expressions, she was giving them her take on things. The woman with the turquoise earrings shot me a knowing look. Great! She probably thought the game was on.

When the table finally cleared, Dinah

shook her head. "I've been thinking. I don't care what that sergeant said, that wasn't a crow in the room. It was too big to be a bird, and I didn't hear any wings flapping."

CHAPTER 13

"Pink, I need to talk to you. This is urgent," Adele said, stopping at the registration table. The lunch bell was ringing, and Dinah and I were just getting ready to leave; we had put up a sign saying to see me in the dining hall. Adele was outdoing herself. In the short time since I'd agreed to let her run the crochet workshops, she had let it go completely to her head. She didn't seem to care about the rhinestone clipboard anymore. She was too busy trying to order me around. Now that she was a presenter, her inner diva had kicked in. I had to keep telling myself not to let her get under my skin and to remember that she was crochet family.

"I need Izabelle's supplies for the first workshop." Adele was glancing around at the people congregated in the administration building with a newfound air of importance. She'd even changed her clothes. Her outfit could best be described as purple haze. The long sweater, the pants, and even her suede boots were shades of the color. She'd topped off the outfit with a crocheted royal purple beanie. Then, just to be sure she had enough color, she'd added ropes of large crocheted beads in yellow, orange and fuchsia.

I knew exactly where the supplies were. I'd seen the boxes piled in Izabelle's room, each marked for a different session. But after my talk with Sergeant French I felt uneasy about going in the room, and even more uneasy about taking anything out of it.

When I hesitated, Adele grew agitated. "What's the holdup? You can't expect me to conduct the classes if I have nothing to work with." Adele let out a sigh of displeasure, and Dinah looked like she was ready to punch Adele.

"Hey," Dinah said, "who died and made you queen?" Then Dinah's eyes opened wide in horror as she realized the truth in what she'd said. "Oops, bad choice of words."

In the meantime I'd come up with a solution. I did as Sergeant French had told me and called Izabelle's ex. The sheet with his number was in the file box under the table.

I almost wanted to call Barry and tell him what I'd done, just to show him I wasn't going to get in trouble this time.

Once I reached Zak Landers, I expressed my condolences and explained the situation; it turned out he was fine with us going in her room. I also found out he was her third husband and she didn't like people to know she was allergic to peanuts because it made her seem less than perfect.

"Use whatever you want," he said. "And if you wouldn't mind packing the stuff up at the end of the weekend, I'll arrange to pick it up." He sighed. "I don't know why she put me down as her emergency contact. She has a sister, you know. I don't even know her name. In the years we were together, they never had any contact." He seemed to be half talking to himself as he mumbled something about how he was trying to get in touch with the sister. Then he hung up.

"I might as well get the stuff before lunch," I said, putting away my cell phone and grabbing my purse.

"I'm coming with you," Dinah said. "As long as he gave us carte blanche, I'm checking my e-mails."

"Hey, wait for me." Adele rushed to keep up with us. "Say, Pink, I've been meaning to ask you. When you were at the hospital with Izabelle, did you happen to notice what they did with the white choker?"

I turned back to Adele as we walked up the low hill to Lodge. "After you made that ridiculous remark to Sergeant French, I thought back to when we found Izabelle on the beach and remembered she wasn't wearing the choker."

When we got to Izabelle's room, all three of us tried to go through the door at once, but Dinah, being the smallest, pushed in ahead.

"As long as Izabelle's ex said to use anything," Dinah said, going right for the laptop. I headed for the boxes I'd noticed before. I turned to show them to Adele, but she was busy sorting through the bag of incidentals Izabelle had set by the sink.

"Here's the container she used for the beginning crochet session. She must have brought it back here after the workshop and before she went to the beach." I moved to look through it, but Adele beat me to it and I watched as she pulled out skeins of different kinds of yarn with descriptions attached to them. And a bunch of swatches that showed different stitches. Izabelle had made a stack of handouts, too, with instructions for single, double, half-double, and triple crochet. When Adele got to the hooks and samples of some bigger items, Dinah got my attention.

"She got another e-mail from that sponsor person." I went and stood behind Dinah, reading over her shoulder. It said *Don't do something you'll regret. Let's talk about it.* As before it was signed *Tom, ITA sponsor.*

"Do you suppose we should send him an e-mail and tell him what happened to her?" Dinah said, and I asked her to go back to the other e-mail we'd seen. In a moment she had it on the screen. I read it and reread it. It had warned her not to do anything without talking to him.

"I wonder if she did whatever he was warning her not to," I said, staring at the message.

"We could e-mail him, tell him what happened, and ask him," Dinah suggested.

Adele had moved on to going through the things on the night table.

"What are you doing?" I asked. Adele looked up at me with her storm cloud expression.

"I thought as long as I was here, I'd see if I could find the choker." She stepped back, and her elbow hit an open zippered case on top of the dresser. It hit the floor and the contents fell out. Adele moved on to look through the things on the nightstand while

I retrieved everything and put it back. I noticed a small, clear plastic case holding a pair of green contacts. I showed them to Dinah.

"Oh, so her eyes weren't really green," Adele said as I took the case back and put it with the other stuff. "The woman was a fake. I can't believe I thought she was so great."

Dinah pulled a copy of *A Subtle Touch of Crochet* out of the top box and thumbed through it. She stopped at the photo of Izabelle and examined it.

Adele looked at the picture from a distance. "Look at those cheekbones. I bet they're fake. Maybe her chin as well. For sure the nose — and her lips, oh please." She tossed her head in disgust. I thought it might just be Adele's anger speaking, but when I looked at the photo, I had to agree.

"It's as if she totally made herself over. I wonder what she looked like before all the work," I said. I glanced at the photo again, this time checking out the surroundings. It appeared to have been taken in Izabelle's craft room.

"That's how I want my crochet room to look," I said, pointing.

Dinah looked and laughed. "I bet they just fixed it up for the photo. She probably had grocery bags of yarn all over the place, like the rest of us. And blankets that just need the fringe, along with shawls waiting for the ends to be woven in. The doll and those stuffed bears are just in there for show."

Adele had found the manuscript pages and made a loud squeal when she read the title.

"The Needle and the Hook," she said in disbelief. "That's what her fusion craft is. I can't believe what a traitor she was on top of everything else. And not even that original. Other people have mixed knitting and crochet. But then I know she wasn't really original. She stole my work. She probably stole other people's, too." With that Adele began rummaging anew.

"That's it, ladies," I said closing the book and putting it back in the box. "Time to go."

The dining hall was buzzing when we got there. I had stowed Adele's box by the registration materials in the administration building. Dinah and Adele went to different tables and found seats. I had asked the presenters to spread themselves around and more or less host their table. I was too tense to sit and circulated around, making sure everything was going okay.

Adele started talking crochet before she

even hit the seat and was polling the people at her table to find out if they were crochet novices or experienced. She was using her hat and beads as examples of crochet embellishment.

Jym and Jeen Wolf, the knitting couple, were holding court at another table. The jeans and tucked-in tee shirts with clever sayings seemed to be their uniform. Jym appeared very animated and friendly. I envied their perfect posture. They passed around a mint green baby sweater as the iced tea circulated the other way. They both nodded a greeting as I passed. Jeen snagged me and whispered that Sergeant French had stopped her on the way to lunch to ask her a few questions about where she was during the s'more time and what her relationship with Izabelle was. "He's convinced somebody was on the beach with her. Can't you do something to get whoever it was to come forward, so he leaves the rest of us alone?" I told her I'd see what I could do.

Mason greeted me as I reached his table. I wondered if his tablemates had any idea of his day job. The kimono-style jacket and loose cotton pants hardly looked like lawyer wear. I heard a snippet of the conversation, which seemed to be about yoga versus tai chi. "In yoga," Mason explained, "you hold a pose, while in tai chi, which incidentally is a martial art, you flow through poses almost like a slow-motion dance. Breathing is important in both of them." It was obvious that Mason was serious about the tai chi. He really did make an effort to balance his life.

Dinah seemed even more energized as she talked to the group at her table. Her spiky salt-and-pepper hair seemed to exemplify her enthusiasm. She had been so excited about this weekend and working with people who wanted to be there instead of her usual freshmen who had to be present. I doubted she even noticed me go by.

Bennett had everyone at his table laughing. As I got close enough to hear what was going on, he was finishing an anecdote about his show. His group seemed to be hanging on every word. Not a big surprise, really; he was an actor, and being able to tell a good story was a given.

Sheila was at the last table. I felt for her when I saw the way her eyebrows were knit together. Being the host was not her kind of activity. But then this weekend had turned out to be a lot different than she'd expected. It was supposed to be a change from her busy life. But rooming with Adele and now helping her with the workshops were all pressure. Hesitantly, she showed off the scarf in shades of blues and lavender she was wearing. I knew right away it was one she'd made. The dreamy look similar to an Impressionist painting was as good as a trademark. It was no wonder she sold so many. Each one was different and exquisite. Miss Lavender Pants looked over from Bennett's table and almost drooled over the scarf.

I leaned against the partition that separated the entrance area from the dining room after I passed Commander Blaine's table. He was demonstrating how to make a swan out of one of the cloth napkins while talking about his workshop and how much fun it was going to be. He had everyone at the table abandoning their food and following along. I watched as he bustled around the table, coaching the napkin folders.

I was distracted by a ruckus at Adele's table and went over to investigate. "I thought Izabelle Landers was supposed to be here," a woman said to me as I approached.

I sighed and tried to explain in a concerned, hushed voice, but I'd said the same thing so many times it was impossible not to make it come out like a recording. The woman's eyes widened with distress.

"What about her world premiere workshop? I love her *Subtle Touch of Crochet* and I was so looking forward to her new fusion craft. What with the fog delaying everything, this weekend just isn't like the other years."

"Trust me, you're not missing a thing," Adele interjected. I gave her a sharp look and took over.

"What Adele means is that the workshops she and Sheila are going to put on will be so exceptional you won't feel like you missed anything." The woman accepted the comment and Adele stared at me with her mouth open.

"Pink, thanks for the vote of confidence. You really mean it, right?"

I muttered a positive answer as I glanced up and looked out the window. I noticed the housekeeping crew pushing their cart down the walkway. I might be only an amateur sleuth, but I wasn't giving up investigating. What was it Sergeant French had said when he was trying to convince me that the shadow in Izabelle's room had been a crow? After the alleged bird had knocked the manuscript pages under the bed, he thought the cleaning crew had found them when they were doing the room and put them in an orderly stack on the night table.

Well, now was my chance to check it out. I left the dining hall and caught up with the crew down the walkway.

"Excuse me, but which of you did the rooms in Lodge?" I said. The group eyed me warily before two women put up their hands in acknowledgment. I suppose they were expecting me to complain or accuse them of something.

I did my best to short-circuit that fear by thanking them for the nice job on my room. The tension left their faces and they smiled.

"I wanted to ask you about another room. It had a stack of plastic containers with a lot of yarn."

One of the women nodded. "The one with the already made bed. Yes."

I didn't want to tell her it was more accurately not slept in, because the resident was dead, so I just nodded as an answer.

"Did you find a lot of papers under the bed and put them on the night table?"

One of the women nodded. "Papers? You mean like a stack about this big?" She held her thumb and forefinger out in a space that would hold maybe one hundred sheets, in the ballpark of what I was asking about.

I attempted to keep the surprise out of my face. Maybe I was going to owe Sergeant French a mental apology. "You found them under the bed?"

And maybe not.

She shook her head. "I didn't find them anywhere. I get it. This is a setup. You're trying to get me to incriminate myself. I didn't let that man in the room even though he said he just wanted to drop something off. I took the pile of papers from him. I'd already picked some off the floor and put them on the night table. I just added the ones he gave me to them."

"Some guy brought the papers?"

"Okay, I know it's against the rules. We're not supposed to let anyone in without having them show us their key. And I didn't let him in," the housekeeper said. The rest of her group had started to move on, and she looked like she was planning to join them.

I had to come up with something to get more details. Think fast, I ordered myself, mentally running through the table of contents of the *Average Joe* book. What it said was that sometimes the basic truth worked best.

"Wait," I said as she turned to join the rest of the crew. "The room I'm talking about. Well, that woman is dead. She died on the beach yesterday."

The girl's face fell and she seemed in more of a hurry to leave, so I started to talk faster. "Everybody thinks it was an accident, that she was allergic to the peanut butter in the gourmet s'mores."

"Peanut butter in s'mores? I've never heard of that. There is a lot of s'more business up here. Every group seems to make them in the fire circle, but they just go the usual way. So, she got sick from the campfire treats and —" She shrugged.

"I think she might have had help eating them and I'm investigating. So finding out who the man with the papers is is important."

The girl's mouth quivered. "You mean like in that old TV show where that woman who lived in Vermont or somewhere always was smarter than the cops?"

"Sort of like that." As I watched the quiver turn into a giggle, I got annoyed. "I'll have you know I have successfully investigated a number of murders."

"Okay, sure," she said in a patronizing tone. "I got to go. I don't know who the guy was. I don't keep track of guests' names.

I took her arm and eased her up the path toward the dining hall. "If you could just have a look inside and tell me if you see him."

"No way," she said, pulling away from me. It occurred to me that sometimes you had to pay for information, so I offered to give her the tip that Izabelle might have left. The girl snatched the ten-dollar bill.

"I'm not going in, but I'll look through the window." She leaned toward the windowed wall and I pointed toward our group and asked if she saw the man. She just kept shaking her head, and I suddenly had the feeling that was all she was going to do even if she saw him. There was nothing in it for her to give him up.

I was about to let her go when the door to the dining hall opened and some people walked out. The movement drew her eyes to the group. *The Average Joe's Guide to Criminal Investigation* had a whole section on observing people's responses. Some were involuntary, like your pupils got bigger when you liked something, whether you wanted to admit it or not. And some were under your control, but still automatic, like the way the housekeeper straightened suddenly as she looked at one of the exiters.

"That's him, isn't it?" I said softly.

What was Spenser Futterman doing with Izabelle's manuscript?

CHAPTER 14

The first sessions of the workshops were scheduled to start right after lunch. No time to talk to Spenser Futterman and no chance to tell Dinah that he was the crow. Dinah walked out surrounded by people from her table who were taking her workshop. She appeared happy and excited, and I didn't want to ruin it for her by interrupting. I was discovering it's lonely at the top.

The workshops were all meeting simultaneously except for Mason's. But then his wasn't really a workshop and more of an activity, and we'd scheduled several time slots so the whole group could attend the tai chi sessions if they wanted to.

Mason caught up with me as I walked up the pathway past Lodge. I was clutching the rhinestone clipboard, ready to make my rounds. Mason had changed out of the tai chi clothes into well-fitting jeans and a blue oxford cloth shirt. The color of the shirt brought out the color in his face, and as usual a tousle of hair had fallen free and dangled over his forehead.

"Hey, Sunshine, where are you headed?"

I held up the rhinestone clipboard in response. "I'm going to stop in all the workshops and make sure everything's going okay."

I looked at his clothes. "What about you?"

His mouth eased into a grin. "No tai chi until late in the afternoon, so I thought I'd head over to Carmel for a while." He glanced around the empty walkway. "You look tense around the eyes. How about joining me? Take an hour or so off. I noticed you didn't eat breakfast, or lunch either."

"Mason," I said, rolling my eyes, "I can't leave. After everything that's happened, from the fog to Izabelle, well, I have to keep an eye on things." I held up the clipboard. "The buck stops with me."

He nodded and let me know he understood. "I thought that's what you'd say, but I figured I'd ask anyway. What's on the schedule for tonight?"

I asked if he hadn't gotten a schedule, and he admitted to having paid attention only to the times set for tai chi. I had a convenient copy and pulled it out, showing him that after dinner, Commander Blaine was setting up board games in the lobby area of a building called Scripps. "There's going to be informal crocheting and knitting as well."

"You ought to be off duty by nine. How about you and I slip out then? The Seventeen Mile Drive is just over there," he said, referring to the private scenic roadway that wound through the Del Monte Forest and hugged the ocean as it ran past some famous golf courses and resorts. "There are some great restaurants."

"Mason, I can't go on a dinner date. I'm working," I protested.

"It's not a date, Molly, just two out-of-town Tarzanians discussing the weekend. Nobody will miss you for an hour or two." He put his hand on my arm. "Everybody gets a break. Besides, if you don't eat soon, you're going to pass out."

He had a point about needing to eat something and I certainly needed a break, though it was kind of funny to need a break from a supposedly fun weekend. Besides, now that I had accepted that Izabelle's death was murder, we could talk about the case. Mason had helped me before by using his resources to find out information. So, I said yes. His smile broadened and he said he'd make a reservation.

"Nine o'clock, remember," he said as he

walked away and I left to make my rounds of the workshops.

I was curious to see Bennett in action, so his workshop was my first stop. It had been set up in a meeting room in one of the small newer buildings, and I stopped in the doorway. He was straddling a chair in the front of the room and wore a baseball cap backward. His group seemed to be mesmerized by whatever he was saying. Miss Lavender Pants and her crew were hanging on his every word, and I stepped closer to hear better. He said something about playing some acting games to loosen everyone up, and then he'd be passing each person their lines in a one-act play.

"We'll work on them today and tomorrow, and then tomorrow night you'll present the play for everyone at the last night party." Miss Lavender Pants seemed to like the idea, but some of the others appeared nervous and complained about not having enough time before they had to perform.

Bennett put his hand up. "It would be nice to have more time, but you'll all do fine. I know most of you are doing this for amusement, but our activities will help you all in your regular life. They'll boost your confidence and you'll have fun."

He seemed to have things under control,

so I moved on to look in on the others. As I was going down the walkway, I saw a figure headed toward me. I swallowed hard when I recognized the short man with the brick-shaped head. I wasn't going to let Spenser Futterman get away without talking to him. I put on my best smile as he got closer, though I had no idea what I was going to say. I couldn't very well just start out saying, "Hey, what was that about you messing with Izabelle's manuscript and by the way, did you kill her?"

He actually appeared friendly when he saw me and stopped as our paths crossed. He made small talk about the weather improving and operations at Asilomar being back to normal. He asked about our group, but before I could bring up Izabelle, he did. Was it true she died?

I nodded with a solemn face. "Did you know her?" Of course I knew the answer, but I hoped it would get him talking about her.

His eyes narrowed warily. "I wouldn't say I knew her. More like I saw her around. We both have mailboxes at the same postal center. The one the guy with your group owns. Captain somebody."

"Commander," I corrected. "His name is Commander Blaine." Spenser nodded and then shrugged off the information. He seemed much more interested in finding out about our creative weekend and what part Izabelle played in it. When he heard she was a workshop leader, he wanted to know what we were going to do without her. This wasn't how it was supposed to go. He was supposed to give me information, not ask for it.

"We have it covered," I said, trying to get the upper hand of the conversation. "If you knew her, then you probably know about the book she has coming out featuring her new fusion craft." I tried to read his face as he answered.

"She has a book coming out? I didn't know," he said, seeming surprised. "Like I said, I only knew her in passing." Then he looked at his watch and muttered something about having to be somewhere, and wished me a good day before taking off down the path.

Okay, he was lying, but he seemed to be good at it, which meant I probably wasn't going to be able to get any more information out of him.

I'd used up my casual conversation card. It was time for my secret weapon.

"You want me to do what?" Dinah said. I'd timed my arrival to coincide with the memoir writers' break. Most of them had gone down to the gift shop to hit the coffee cart. I knew Dinah's head was all into the workshop now, but I was hoping to get her help.

"I don't think I can get any more information out of Spenser Futterman." I had already relayed my conversation with him to her and mentioned I was sure he knew more than he was saying. "He told me how he knew Izabelle, so I can't very well bring it up again. But you," I said with a hopeful look, "could use your charm and find out everything."

"You think I'm that charming?" Dinah said with a throaty laugh.

"Commander certainly seems to think so," I said.

"So, what do I do, flirt with Futterman?" She slumped. "Maybe that's why it's been so hard for me to meet anyone. I've been spending too much time whipping freshmen into shape. I've lost my soft side." She sighed. "I'm out of practice in that department. Plus, I don't want to look pathetic. Or desperate."

"That's only if it's real flirting. This would be phony flirting, and you'll look just fine. It's not like you really want him — just information."

"Good point," Dinah said, watching as her writers came back up the path. Her whole demeanor perked up. "Did I tell you what a treat it is to work with people who are excited to be here? I don't have to fight anybody about wearing a baseball hat inside or deal with any attitudes. My writers worship me," she said with a happy smile. She headed back in the room with her group close behind. "Okay, people, let's get back to mining those memories."

The yarn workshops were up next. Not only did I want to check on them, I also wanted to remind the participants of Mrs. Shedd's promise of blankets to a local shelter, and whatever they could do would be appreciated.

I stopped in at the knitting group first. Jeen and Jym were going around, helping members cast on. They were exacting in their movements. Only a few people seemed to be experienced knitters, and they were already working on something. I watched the casting-on process with interest and once again appreciated crochet. Making the row of chain stitches was really the same thing. Both casting on and the row of chains provided something to begin with, but the foundation chain in crochet was so much easier to do.

Jeen looked up, and when she saw me in the doorway, waved me in and met me at the front of the room.

"Everything going okay?" I asked, and she nodded. The center of the table had a neatly arranged selection of worsted-weight acrylic yarn and sets of needles. There were also samples of scarves with copies of patterns next to them.

"I was expecting people with a little more experience. Most of them have none. But we'll get them going in no time."

I reminded her about Mrs. Shedd's promise of the blankets, and an expression of concern passed over her face. "I'm afraid there won't be blankets. We'll be lucky to get one. As soon as we show all the newbies how to cast on, we'll teach knit and purl. I thought I'd have them make practice swatches, which hopefully we can put together into a blanket. The good part is the group is all for it."

She invited me to stay and join them, but I passed. I started to leave, but she looked like there was something she wanted to say.

"Is there anything else?" I prodded.

"Well, yes. This is kind of awkward." She appeared momentarily perturbed. "As I said to you before, I sincerely wish whoever was on the beach with Izabelle would just come

191

forward and settle things." She composed herself and began again. "When we talked to Sergeant French, we said we didn't know Izabelle before this weekend. It just seemed like a way to end his questions." She bent her head in a pleading gesture. "So, I'd appreciate it if you would leave it that way."

At first I didn't know what she was talking about. Then I remembered the way Jeen had greeted Izabelle and commented on her weight loss, and realized they obviously did know each other from before.

I said yes, without bothering to explain that even if I did say something, Sergeant French would probably file it under "annoying amateur sleuth."

It wasn't quite as peaceful in the crochet room. Adele stood in the front, showing off samples of things from Izabelle's box. When I walked in, she was holding up a lap blanket made of soft gray squares with different stitches. They were joined with white yarn that also was used for a border.

Sheila was moving among the people, who were hunched over their work. Boy, did I recognize that posture. For something that was so relaxing, meditative and restoring, when you first started out, crochet was just the opposite.

If anyone knew how to deal with too-tight

stitches, it was Sheila. As accomplished a crocheter as she'd become, she still slipped up sometimes and let her emotions rule her crocheting. All the Tarzana Hookers knew to automatically hand her a smaller size hook when she ended up with a row of tightly knotted stitches she couldn't get her hook into and to remind her to take her time and make the stitches loose enough so she could go back to the bigger hook. She was so busy helping the others, she'd forgotten about her own tension. She pushed her hair behind her ear to keep it from blocking her view as she helped a man in a striped sweater. When I caught sight of her expression, she seemed animated and happy, but most of all, calm.

Adele tried to ignore my presence, but finally acknowledged it, and with a diva-ish sigh asked if I was just going to stand there or come in.

It was lucky for Adele that Sergeant French wasn't watching her. She seemed to be enjoying being in charge all too much. She might as well have been wearing a banner that said *I have a motive.* But, I reminded myself, he just thought someone had been on the beach with Izabelle — he didn't think the someone had killed her.

As soon as I brought up the blankets,

Adele flashed a self-satisfied smile. "Pink, I'm way ahead of you. I already have them working on blocks." She suggested I join them, and while I could certainly have used some crochet time, I thought it would compromise my authority to have Adele acting like she was in charge of me.

I went back outside and took a deep breath of the pine scented air. So far, so good. There was just Commander Blaine's group to check. He had brought all kinds of equipment with him, and the room bristled with enthusiasm. He had set up several stations and was moving between them to check on his students. One group was doing origami with napkins, and another was making flowers out of radishes, cucumbers and carrots. I heard him talking about how everything they would be doing in the workshop sessions was leading up to what they would do for the final evening's party.

His group members were all so occupied they didn't even look up when I stuck my head in the door.

Commander Blaine didn't seem quite as happy the next time I saw him.

CHAPTER 15

"What's she doing with him?" Commander Blaine said with a grunt of disgust. He wasn't really talking to me, more to himself, as he followed me down the stairs of Lodge. His comment was directed at Dinah, who was sitting in one of the easy chairs by the fireplace, talking to Spenser Futterman. My take was a little different. Good for Dinah! She was already working on her mission, and from here it looked like she was doing a good job with the phony flirting. She was doing a lot of blinking, and her amethyst drop earrings did a jiggly dance as if she was oh-so-amused at whatever he was saying.

The workshops had broken up for the day and everyone was wandering around, still caught in the afterglow of the creative afternoon, and had changed into loose-fitting clothes. Next up was tai chi on the beach.

Commander Blaine caught up with me on the landing, and grumbled again about Dinah talking to Spenser. This time he seemed to be talking to me.

"Do you know him from Tarzana?" I asked innocently. I already knew Spenser was one of Commander's customers. "I keep seeing him around, but he doesn't seem to be with our group."

"Yes, I know him," Commander said, not taking his eyes off the couple below us. He was silent after that, and it appeared that was all he was going to say. But I wanted to know more. I had a feeling what I was about to say was going to start trouble, but it would get him to talk.

"I was just wondering about him, you know, kind of doing girlfriend duty to check up on Dinah's guy."

"Her guy?" Commander sputtered. "When did that happen?" He took my arm and led me back up the stairs to the empty hallway. "He's not right for her. If you're really her friend, you'll tell her he's all wrong for her."

And then tell her you're perfect for her, right? Actually, the more I'd seen of Commander, the more we were on the same page about that. If Dinah could get past a few details, I knew she'd appreciate his good traits.

"How, exactly, do you know him?"

"You know I have a mail center in Tarzana, right? He has a mailbox at my place, and he does his copying there. Even with the copying ability of everyone's printer, when they need a lot done, they still come to me." He seemed to want to dismiss Spenser and get back to talking about himself. "Maybe if you understand —" He seemed thoughtful for a moment before he spoke. "I really like your friend. She's the first person who's sparked any interest in me since . . ." His voice trailed off and he looked down. When he put his head back up, his eyes were watery. "My wife died three years ago. We'd been married for a very long time, and I fell into kind of a black hole without her. When I finally started to get myself together again, I found I was terribly lonely. And you know how they say if you think about somebody else's loneliness, it helps with your own? I got to know some of the people who have mailboxes at my place. Most of them work out of their houses and are pretty isolated. When you have a home office, there's no socializing in the coffee room. Sometimes I thought I was the only person they talked to all day. So, I started to organize get-togethers, and since they were all strangers, I made sure there were activities that would get them talking. And it went from there." He was facing me. "I want you to understand that I'm not some playboy type who's after every woman. Dinah is special to me."

I had to admit that what he said touched me, though when he got to the playboy part, I had a hard time not laughing. If there was any label I wouldn't stick on him, that was it. I knew from my own experience of losing Charlie how hard it is to start over again. Commander certainly had come up with a unique and positive way of handling his own problem. And probably helped a lot of his customers, too.

"Did Spenser come to your parties?" I asked, not giving up on getting information.

"No, he was never interested — or very friendly, for that matter. When I first saw him up here, he just nodded a greeting, not even a friendly hello. I think he has some kind of accounting business, but there's something else he does. I never got a look at what he was copying, but he seemed very excited about it."

"What about Izabelle Landers?" I asked, suddenly remembering all the handouts she'd brought.

"What about her?" Commander sounded wary.

"Did she come into your shop?"

"Sure. She had a mailbox there, too. She came in to make the copies for her workshops."

"So you knew she was coming up here," I said.

"I saw her name on the schedule."

"What about Spenser Futterman? Did Izabelle know him?"

Commander was getting impatient. It was obvious all he wanted to do was bury Spenser and talk himself up, and I wasn't cooperating by asking all my questions.

"I don't know, maybe. I think I saw them talking once. He was showing her something." I asked if he had heard what they said, and his face grew stern.

"I respect my customers' privacy and I don't snoop." He had gone back to the stairs and was looking over the banister. I could tell by his expression that Dinah and Spenser were still in conversation. "Put in a good word with your friend for me, will you?" With that he went down the stairs and through the communal living room without stopping.

When I finally got outside, I was surprised to see sunshine and blue sky. How nice, just in time for tai chi. Dinah had been deeply entrenched in her conversation with Spenser. I'm sure she saw me when I went past, though she certainly didn't show it. If she was getting some good information, I certainly didn't want to disturb her. I wondered if she had noticed Commander go by.

Everything seemed to sparkle and look more cheerful with the addition of the sun. A trickle of people were walking on the boardwalk toward the beach. I joined them, thinking about Izabelle. A day ago at almost the same time she had been going this same way. I pictured her with her pouch purse dangling at her side. What was her mood when she headed toward the beach? Most important, who was she meeting? I walked out through the gate and crossed the street. The entrance to the beach was shaped by the fenced-off planted areas on either side. It was in one of those that we'd found the pouch purse. As I walked down the sandy entrance, I tried to figure out how Izabelle could have accidentally dropped her bag on the other side of the fence, as Sergeant French thought. Could she have been so impatient that she decided to cut through the plants? Maybe she was carrying shopping bags with the s'more ingredients and some wood for the fire, and with her arms full took the shortcut and the bag fell off her arm and she didn't even notice. Still, the biggest question was how she came to eat the peanut butter–laced s'more.

It was giving me a headache to think about it, and I put all thoughts on hold as I walked across the sand toward where Mason was setting up.

This was the first time I was really seeing the beach. Before, it had been either foggy or night. Now I could see the huge waves rolling to the shore and admire their color. The water was actually sea foam green. As I stepped through the sand, I was taken with how white and silky it was. Adele had said the sand on this beach was unusual because it was formed by the waves wearing away granodiorite rocks along the shoreline. As I looked out over the open water, I pictured a map and saw myself standing on the edge of the peninsula between Carmel Bay and Monterey Bay. As Commander had said, it was the edge of the continent. Just a little way down, the Point Pinos lighthouse, with its beacon and foghorn, had been protecting sailors from crashing onto this outcropping of land since the 1850s. The breeze was fresh and constant — invigorating without being cold.

I had briefly wondered about taking part in the tai chi. Would it compromise my authority if people saw me stumbling in the sand? I'd never done tai chi, and the pull of the chance to try it won. Besides, I wanted to support Mason.

Mason had chosen a spot where the sand was firm and damp. Beyond, a little rivulet came from somewhere inland and made a channel to the water. Adele arrived and positioned herself right in the front. She made sure to tell the people around her that she was an experienced tai chier and showed off her outfit of bright orange loose pants and a matching kimono-style jacket open over a white tee shirt. As she turned, I caught a glimpse of her pouch purse. Something about it struck me, but before it could compute, Commander arrived and asked where Dinah was. My shrug of ignorance didn't please him, and he took a spot off to the side. Miss Lavender Pants had dragged her crew with her and they took positions next to Adele. Sheila came over by me.

"It's good you're trying this. I hear it's very relaxing," Sheila said. "Molly, I know about tension, and you've got it in spades." Bennett arrived and bumped fists with Mason in greeting. He still had on the backward baseball cap, though he'd changed into soft gray sweatpants. And he wasn't alone. I was surprised to see Nora walking next to him. There was some discussion between Bennett and Nora as they took spots next to Adele. I was just about to go up and tell Nora how glad I was that she was joining us, when she marched over to Mason. The next thing I knew, Mason told the group to move down to the beach to drier sand. How foolish of me to think she could take part in anything without ruffling some feathers.

More retreaters trudged across the sand and joined the group. When it appeared all who were going to come had gotten there, Mason began. He explained there were different schools of thought on how to teach tai chi, but he liked the way he'd learned the best. He had simply watched his teacher and mimicked his moves. Eventually he'd picked them up.

"Tai chi is supposed to be meditative, and I think that it's best to keep it that way." Mason liked using music, too, and had brought a boom box with him. He turned it on, and what I could describe only as Eastern ethereal music poured forth.

And then he began. At first I was concerned that my arms weren't flowing up and down the way Mason's were, but then the music and the rhythm of the waves kicked in and I went with the flow. I lost track of the others on the beach as Mason's moves and mine became one, or so I hoped. Actually, I knew I was a step behind and not nearly as fluid, but when he finished, the tai chi had done its trick. I felt renewed.

There was a little spattering of applause, barely audible above the waves, and Mason took a humble bow. As I looked over the group to check their reactions, something about Adele made me stop. The wind fluttered her orange jacket open, and I saw the pouch purse and realized she'd worn it all during the tai chi session. She didn't have it on her shoulder, but instead wore it with the strap across her chest. That seemed the way it was meant to be positioned. Wearing it like that, you could do just about anything and have it stay put, including walking onto the beach even if you cut through the plants. I was suddenly sure there was no way the pouch purse fell off of Izabelle by accident.

"How'd I do?" Mason asked as he caught up with me on the way back.

"It was magnificent," I said with a satisfied sigh.

"I'm glad you liked it. Some people get frustrated because they don't get it right away, but a lot of the benefit is just doing it, whether it's perfect or not."

"See you later," Mason said with a wink when we got back on the Asilomar grounds.

Most of the group was heading toward the dining hall, and Mason was going back toward Lodge to change and get ready for our meeting. There was no way I was going to call it a date.

I didn't catch up with Dinah until I saw her in the dining hall. It was still a little surprising to see how crowded it was now that Asilomar was back in business. Our group had gravitated toward the same area of the dining hall, though now we took up more tables. I heard snippets of conversations as our campers found seats. Everyone sounded charged up about their workshop. I had wondered if it seemed cold to go on with the weekend as if nothing had happened, but Izabelle had died before most of them got there. And only the crocheters were really impacted.

"So what did you find out?" I said, grabbing Dinah as she came from the food line with a plate of what looked like pot roast with carrots and oven-roasted potatoes. She set her plate down and we went into a corner out of earshot.

"He's very charming," Dinah said with a laugh. "I barely had to bat my eyelashes at all before he got into the conversation. I kept trying to get him to talk about himself, but he kept saying he wanted to know about me and the group."

"What did he want to know?" I asked.

"I guess he must have overheard Adele fussing. He wanted to know if it was true someone had stolen her work. He asked about our group's program and what kind of workshops we were having. Oh, and that woman he said was his niece? I guess he forgot who he said she was, because this time he said she was his cousin. My guess is she's his girlfriend, but he's trying to keep his options open."

"Really? What about the manuscript? Did you find anything out? Or bring up Izabelle?"

"No, but I'm not giving up. We're meeting later for a walk on the beach." When she saw my concerned look, she stopped me. "I'm doing it for you. Just to get information." She glanced down at her black jeans and tee shirt. She had a long, cream colored scarf wound around her neck and the amethyst earrings. "Do you think I should change?"

"No," I said firmly, and suddenly regretted asking her to do the information thing. "And be careful. Maybe you shouldn't go walking on the beach alone with him."

Dinah swallowed hard. "It figures. I meet somebody I like, and he might be dangerous and has a girlfriend. I have to do something about being attracted to jerks. I guess you're right about the walk. I'll change it to a game of Ping-Pong in the administration building."

"There's something else," I said, thinking of what Commander Blaine had said. I just got his name out when Dinah waved me off.

"First of all, there's nothing between Commander Blaine and me besides a little conversation. Don't worry, I'm turning over a new leaf. No more jerks or possible murderers. All I'm interested in with Spenser is getting him to talk. Okay?"

I felt a little better. The last thing I wanted to do was end up fixing up my best friend with trouble. We headed back to the table, and when I made no move to get food, she questioned it. I mentioned my dinner with Mason.

"It's a meeting," I said before she could give me one of her looks. Dinah knew all about my relationships with Barry and Mason. For now, Barry and I were a couple and Mason was relegated to friend. But it hadn't always been that way. Barry's and my relationship had been anything but smooth, and still had its bumps due to our different styles. I liked some notice. He believed in just showing up, and used the unpredictability of his job as an excuse. He had backed off a little, but he still occasionally brought up the idea of us getting married. No matter what he said to the contrary, I thought it was because he had failed at it before and wanted another chance. I wasn't looking to get married again — at least not now. In the past, we'd broken up once over his attempt to run my life, and again when it came out he had omitted some major portions of his past. There was also the issue with my sons. He and Peter basically avoided eye contact, and my younger son, Samuel, was polite but still treated him like an intruder.

On the plus side, Barry could fix anything that got broken. He was hot in all ways, and I admit I had a certain fascination about the world he inhabited. And I cared about him. Okay, maybe it was more like love. And ditto for his son, Jeffrey.

For a time, Mason with his desire for a casual relationship seemed more appealing and without all the bumps in the road, until I'd found out Mason's definition of "casual" and mine weren't the same.

I poured myself a glass of iced tea from the pitcher on the lazy Susan in the middle of the table and took a slice of lemon. I couldn't vouch for the food, but the Asilo-mar staff did a great job with iced tea. Some of Dinah's writers had found her and took seats at the table. A man with a goatee held up a journal and said that the class had been so inspiring; he hadn't stopped writing since he'd left the workshop.

Adele was at the next table, surrounded by crocheters. They seemed to have forgot-ten completely that Izabelle was supposed to have been in charge. One woman actu-ally approached Adele with a copy of *A Subtle Touch of Crochet* and handed Adele a pen to sign it. This was Adele's chance at the power position she'd always coveted with the Tarzana Hookers. She was over the top as usual, but other than that she seemed to be doing a good job.

I had stopped back at the crochet work-shop later in the afternoon. By then Adele had shifted from how to crochet to embel-lishments and had opened another of the boxes from Izabelle's room. This one had supplies, samples, and handouts for a group project. I was surprised to see what Izabelle had planned.

Adele held up two pouch bags, one of which was identical to the one we'd found on the beach. Adele explained she'd had some other projects in mind for the group to do, but since there was yarn and directions for the bags, they would make them as a crochet-along. Adele showed off her red bag with white flowers. The only difference was she hadn't used the same kind of yarn for the flowers that Izabelle's directions listed. As everyone got up and began to pick their yarn, Adele said the good thing was that the project was doable in the time they had.

I stood watching as they began making their foundation chains. I longed to go in and join them — just for a while, to set aside being the boss and lose myself in crochet. Besides, the bag was just what I needed. It was just the size to keep my essentials in.

Adele had seen me standing in the doorway. "C'mon in, Pink. You know you want to join us." I waited for a zinger to follow, but this time none came. She was actually sincere, but I still couldn't join them. The tai chi was one thing, but there was no way I could sit in on the crochet-along. I was supposed to be in charge of the retreat. It was the downside of being the holder of the rhinestone clipboard.

I noticed the group had brought their projects to the dining room and were more interested in adding rows to the purses than in checking out the food. They were all looking to Adele as their leader. I nudged Dinah, and she watched Adele as well.

"It's like she's holding court over there. Lucky for her Sergeant French seems content that Izabelle died from an accidental allergic reaction. Because if you were looking for somebody who certainly gained from Izabelle's death and had threatened her . . ." Dinah said, letting me fill in the rest of the thought.

"You don't think she could have —" I watched as Adele signed the woman's book. "Nah," I said, answering my own question. "The whole thing with the s'more took planning. Adele flies by the seat of her pants. If she'd done it, she'd have strangled Izabelle with the choker, probably by mistake as she was trying to pull it off of her neck."

There was much less action going on at the knitters' table. Jym was passing the salad dressing to the person next to him, and Jeen was shaking her head at a woman across the table who'd taken out her needles and work-in-progress. I don't know what Jeen said, but the woman quickly put away her work. It was all too orderly for my taste. Adele would have been happy to know that I thought the crochet chaos at her table was far more appealing than what was going on with the knitters.

I was surprised to see that Bennett hadn't come in. I think his group missed him, too. I saw them look up expectantly every time someone came in. Finally, they started to talk among themselves.

The rest of dinner went by without incident. I reminded everyone about the evening's activities and then hung around until all the retreaters had finished. Dinah stopped off at the administration building for her Ping-Pong match with Spenser, and I went on to the communal living room of the Scripps building. Commander was already setting up board games along with a bowl filled with scraps of paper with entries for charades. People started coming in. There was lots of talking and upbeat expressions, as if they were ready to have a good time. Even if I hadn't been able to prevent Izabelle's death or solve the mystery yet, at least the retreat seemed to be going ahead successfully. That should count for something.

Some of the arrivals gravitated toward the games area. Jeen and Jym arrived and brought some of the knitters to the chairs arranged by the fireplace. Adele and Sheila had the crochet group with them when they walked in and they made their own little area. A couple more showed up and joined their group. I hung around for an hour or so. I was glad to see both groups of yarn people spent their time working on blocks for the blankets, though living up to Mrs. Shedd's commitment still seemed like a long shot.

I hurried back to my room to change out of the sweats I'd put on for tai chi. Mason had said the resort where we were having dinner was casual, but still I didn't think the jeans, turtleneck, and corduroy blazer I'd been wearing were appropriate and went for the outfit I'd brought for the last night party. I'd have to wear it twice, I thought, pulling out the black jeans that promised to lift my butt and make my stomach look washboard thin. I added the white shirt and black pullover sweater and left the shirttails hanging out. Tossing on a burnt orange scarf I'd crocheted on a big hook in cotton yarn, I headed out to meet Mason.

CHAPTER 16

No matter how much I had told myself that I deserved a break, that the retreaters were all adults, and that the activities for the day were all basically over, I still felt guilty about leaving. I was glad it was dark and the walkway was empty as I headed for the parking lot near the Asilomar entrance. Still, I walked off the edge of the path, staying in the shadow. Mason was leaning against his rental Explorer as I approached. I was sure I heard him chuckle.

"C'mon, the coast is clear," he said in a conspiratorial whisper as he slipped around to the passenger side and opened the door.

"So you saw me," I said in a disappointed tone. Here I thought I'd done such a good job of hiding. He was quick to reassure me that even though I was visible on the way to the car, probably nobody was paying any attention, and even if they were, would they really care?

"What if something happens while I'm gone?" I opened the car door and started to get out. "I better not leave. Already there's been a fog emergency and a death. Haven't you ever heard that things travel in threes?"

Mason put his hand on my arm. "It's only for an hour or so. Besides, you missed dinner. Have you eaten anything since the first night?"

My stomach rumbled in answer and I pulled the SUV's door shut.

I must admit that as we drove out of the Asilomar gates, I felt my shoulders unhunch. Sheila was right about me having tension in spades. As we got a block or so away, I started to feel a giddy sense of naughtiness. Dinah had promised to keep an eye on things and I had my cell phone.

Mason knew his way around the area and pulled up to an entrance gate. Once we'd paid the fee, we entered the Seventeen Mile Drive, which was in the privately owned town of Pebble Beach; hence the gate and entrance fee. At night there wasn't much to see besides spots with clear views of the dark ocean and lights in the mansions set back from the road.

I knew more than saw that we were passing through the Del Monte Forest, and somewhere out in the darkness the Lone

Cypress sat on the edge of a rock, catching the constant breeze.

"Well, here we are," Mason said, steering the car in a driveway. Before he'd completely stopped the car, a man in a white uniform stepped out to open the door and take care of the car.

We walked under a large overhang and into a low building.

"Nothing against Asilomar," Mason said. "I like the rustic quality and camplike atmosphere, but a little luxury is nice, too."

No pool or Ping-Pong tables here. The lobby we walked through was all thick carpet and lots and lots of comfortable chairs and sofas. The clothes were all high-end casual. No sweatshirts or baseball caps. Mason had explained that the resort had a world-famous golf course attached to it and any kind of spa facility you could imagine. "And the rooms all have telephones and televisions," he said with his trademark chuckle.

Mason took my arm and led me to the back of the lobby. A wide doorway opened onto a restaurant. The lights were low and the walls all glass. Floodlights on the roof illuminated the area outside, and I saw the edge of the golf course. I knew the beach was on the other side.

I was enjoying the surroundings, but the sense of guilt about leaving was still hanging on my shoulders like a shawl. At least if I talked about Izabelle's death, it would make the occasion seem work-related rather than fun.

As soon as the host seated us, I started talking about Izabelle. Mason looked up from his menu and rolled his eyes. "You don't have to justify being here. I'm sure Mrs. Shedd wouldn't mind. She took off on a cruise. It's okay to be off duty," he said. "See, me too." He pointed to the line on the menu that said no cell phone conversations were allowed in the dining room, and took out his phone and shut it off.

"I'm not supposed to be having any fun," I said in a serious tone. "I'm not sure I like being the boss. I miss fun."

Mason picked up his menu. "It's okay. I won't tell anyone if you enjoy yourself."

"But I've only got the weekend to figure out who killed Izabelle," I said.

"I thought you didn't want it to be murder. Remember how I said it would be impossible to get somebody to eat a s'more against their will and it was just what you wanted to hear."

I sighed. "Okay, I didn't want it to be murder, but I can't ignore the facts just because a murder makes me look bad."

"Even the local cop is only interested in finding out if someone was on the beach with her. He's investigating it as an accident," Mason said.

I leaned forward. "Did he question you?"

Mason nodded. "He hung around all day, grabbing people. I'm surprised you didn't see him. But then I guess he was done with you."

"So, what did he ask you?"

"Probably the same as everyone else. What did I know about Izabelle Landers and did I meet her on the beach. He seemed to be going the direct question route. I suppose he was looking for reactions. You know, not being able to look somebody in the eye if you're lying. I had nothing to tell him, but I did get a little info out of him." Mason seemed pleased with himself. "Want to know what he said?" It was just a tease. Mason knew I wanted to know.

"French is only looking for someone who was on the beach with her, and if the retreat ends and everybody keeps denying they were the one, he'll probably close the investigation since he's convinced it wasn't foul play."

The waiter came by, and I waited while Mason ordered a stuffed mushroom appetizer and a bottle of wine.

"French thinks either she was so crazed for chocolate, she ate the s'more without realizing it had peanut butter on it, or she had a mad craving for peanut butter and gave in to it. Apparently her ex-husband said she had a thing for chocolate. French seems to think she met somebody on the beach about something else. And that person left the beach before Izabelle got sick. He thinks the pouch bag just fell off her arm on the way to the beach and she didn't realize until too late that she didn't have it."

Mason leaned back in his chair. "Sunshine, I hate to say it, but it sounds reasonable. She seemed so controlled about everything, not even reacting when Adele accused her of stealing her work. Sometimes those supercontrolled types come unhinged." The waiter brought the wine and had Mason taste it. Once he'd given his okay, the waiter poured us each a glass and left.

"Molly, why not just accept it was an accident? It lets you off the hook. An accident doesn't have near the stigma a murder does."

"I can't help it." I paused and sighed. "It happened on my watch, and I feel responsible."

Mason's eyes lit with a warm smile. "That's what I love about you. Someone with scruples even when they're not in your best interest."

The waiter took our dinner order, and when he left, Mason looked at me intently. "So, Sherlock, who are your suspects? Maybe your compadre Adele?"

"My compadre?" I said with a laugh. "I wouldn't exactly call her that." I agreed that Adele had the most obvious motive, but while she was lots of things, I was sure she wasn't a murderer.

I brought up Spenser Futterman and the reappearing pages. "There's certainly something fishy with him and the woman who he claims is his niece or his cousin."

"Did you tell Sergeant French that the maid ID'd him?"

"No, and I'm not going to. After his amateur sleuthing comment, I'm sure he wouldn't pay any attention." I mentioned the connections that Izabelle had with some of the others. Jeen admitted knowing her from before, and Jym had seemed to know her as well. I mentioned Commander Blaine's postal center and the social events he planned for his customers. "Maybe there was more to their relationship than he said. Maybe he tried to be friendly and she blew him off. Maybe he took it badly," I offered.

"What about the ex-husband?" Mason suggested.

"Interesting," I said, brightening. "I was going to say that when I talked to him, he was in Tarzana. But who knows if he really was? I could have been calling him on his cell phone and he could have been anywhere. Even up here."

"He certainly would have known about her peanut allergy," Mason added.

The trouble was, there were a lot of possibilities, but nothing pointing to any one person. I reached for my wineglass, and as I did, something appeared in my peripheral vision that made me almost drop it. I suddenly bent forward in the chair, doing my best to hide. Mason reacted, and I pointed toward a table by the windows. The host pulled out the chairs for Nora and Bennett.

"They can't see me here," I said under my breath. "How would it look after the number I did on her, trying to convince her how great the food is at Asilomar?" I could feel my shoulders hunching as I spoke. "That woman has done nothing but complain all weekend. She'll make an issue about me leaving Asilomar to eat, and tell the others. I'll never hear the end of it. Look, she even made a problem with your tai chi. What was that about?"

Mason waved his hand in front of my face to get my attention. "Molly, take a breath," he said in a reassuring tone. "They're not paying any attention to you. They're so wrapped up in themselves, they won't notice you. The thing at the beach was nothing. She said something about the damp sand bothering Bennett, so I moved us."

I stole a look and realized he was probably right about them not noticing me. Nora had a pleased smile, no doubt because the waiter appeared to be fawning over them. At last they were getting the treatment she thought they deserved.

"She's been so angry all weekend. Why did she even agree to come?"

Mason reminded me that I'd said something that made it obvious it hadn't been her choice and that Bennett had agreed without consulting her.

"Okay, then why would he do it?"

"I don't know, but I bet there's something in it for him," Mason said.

It sounded possible, and I started to nod in agreement when my cell phone began to ring. I'd recently adjusted it so it went right to ring and turned the volume up as high as it would go. I was afraid that otherwise I'd miss calls during the weekend. My ring of choice was a royal flourish that kept playing while I searched in my bag for it. It slipped out of my hand and landed on the floor before I finally retrieved it.

I hastily flipped it open to stop the noise.

"Hello," I said in a low voice, praying that it wasn't Dinah with a catastrophe. It was worse. It was Barry.

"Don't hang up," he said right after his initial hello. Several times before when he'd called, I just said I couldn't talk and clicked off.

"This isn't a good time," I said, but Barry got my attention by saying it was something about my house. I sensed people coming from the side, and when I turned, the waiter and host were approaching.

"I'm sorry, but no cell phones in the dining room," the host said in a low voice. I gave him an apologetic smile and flipped the phone shut. But before I could put it away, it began to ring again, and I noticed that I now had the attention of most of the diners.

"I'll have to ask you to step out into the lounge," the host said firmly, taking my arm in a helpful but determined manner.

I answered the phone to stop the ringing and accidentally hit the speaker phone button as I did. Barry's voice blared out, demanding to know what was going on and not to hang up. I caught sight of Nora's expression as I rushed toward the exit. She didn't look happy to see me.

I slumped into one of the easy chairs in the lobby. "What is it?" I said, looking over my shoulder toward the dining room. Only a few people were still looking in my direction.

"What's going on?" Barry said. "What were all those voices?"

Mason came out a moment later and said our dinner had just arrived.

"Who's that?" Barry's voice squawked as I tried to shut off the speaker phone feature.

Mason was chuckling as he headed back to the table after I told him I'd be there momentarily.

Detective Barry by now had figured out who the voice belonged to, and when someone from the bar came by and asked me if I'd like a drink, he made an educated guess that I wasn't at Asilomar.

He sounded hurt, and I rushed to tell him about being too tense to eat, that being in charge was turning out to be more than I thought, particularly with Izabelle's death, which I now believed was murder. "Mason was just trying to help release some of my tension."

"I just bet he was," Barry said in a low voice. "I can help you release some tension, too. Leave the investigating to the Pacific Grove PD."

"How'd you know?" I finally asked him.

"I know you, Molly, and if you think it's murder, you're getting in the middle of it. Babe, it's not your responsibility." His voice softened. "I bet your shoulders are all hunched up. If I was there, I'd get the knots out." I knew that Barry was clenching his jaw and probably pacing. "I don't mean to add to your concerns, but when I stopped by your house, the dogs barely ate and didn't care about going outside to play. It was almost as if they'd already been fed and someone had played a lot of fetch with them." I pleaded ignorance and got off the phone quickly. Who knew Barry and my sons would all do their job?

When I finally came back to the table, Mason looked far too amused. "I never have fun like this with my other friends."

I noted with relief that he didn't say his other girlfriends. Even though technically I'm a girl and a friend, I'm not what the words used together connote. I knew Mason well enough to know his choice of words was no accident.

CHAPTER 17

It looked like all of Asilomar was asleep when we drove back through the entrance.

When we'd finally left the restaurant, after Mason talked me into having the super deluxe flaming bananas over ice cream, Nora and Bennett were having after-dinner drinks at their table. I think she must have been trying to delay going back as long as possible. No doubt this was the kind of place Nora thought they were coming to. All I could do was hope that neither Nora nor Bennett would mention where they'd seen me.

Mason thought I was overreacting, but I had been promoting the rustic accommodations and the hearty camp food, saying it was all part of the workshop atmosphere. How would it look if the retreaters knew I'd run off for flaming bananas over ice cream?

Mason walked me to my room and stopped. He reminded me that he was going to his aunt's birthday brunch in Santa Cruz the next day.

"You're welcome to join me," he said in a soft voice. He didn't argue when I said I couldn't leave. His point wasn't whether I went or didn't go, but that he'd invited me. It was his way of telling me his definition of casual had changed. That had been the stumbling block when it looked like Mason and I were on the road to becoming a couple. When he'd made it clear that his idea of a casual relationship meant keeping his girlfriends separate from his family, I'd seen red. First, it sounded like he had a parade of women going through his life, and second, not being included in his family made any relationship seem kind of cheesy.

"Think about it," he said before brushing my cheek with a soft kiss. Mason was persistent, but he didn't push. Oh dear, just when I thought I had found a place in my life for both men, Mason had to go and confuse things.

No sooner had I closed my door than I heard a knock.

I knew it was Dinah before I opened the door. She must have been just sitting in her room, listening for footsteps.

"How was everything while I was gone?" I

asked even before she stepped into the room.

"Fine. The charades were a big hit. Commander's group made hot spiced cider and popcorn. He had one of those things you stick in the fire to make the popcorn."

"What happened with your Ping-Pong game with Spenser? What did you find out?"

Dinah laughed. "Mostly that he is a much better Ping-Pong player than I am. Whenever I tried to ask him anything, he said he couldn't play and talk. When we finally finished, he went back to trying to ask me questions. He was curious about the knitting couple for a moment or so, and then he lost interest. I brought up Izabelle again, and this time he admitted that maybe he did know her a little. Something about he'd seen her at the place where he has his mailbox."

"Seen her, hah! He's done more than that, according to Commander Blaine. He mentioned them talking. Commander isn't sure what he does for a living," I said.

Dinah looked disappointed. "I thought I was supposed to be getting the information." When I told her I'd ended up talking to Commander because he was upset when he saw her with Spenser, she rolled her eyes. "Don't you think he's a little possessive, considering there's really nothing between us?"

When I mentioned the whole thing about his late wife, Dinah started to soften, then seemed to reconsider. "I'm not saying the story about his wife is fake, but the whole thing about me being the first woman he's been interested in — it's flattering and all, but also sounds like a line." Then she reconsidered again. "And maybe it isn't a line. Maybe I'm a little uncomfortable with how open he is about being interested. But enough about that," she said. "I have something to show you." I hadn't noticed the composition book in Dinah's hand until she held it up.

"I was trying to get my workshop things in order and I came across this notebook from the session we had during the fogout. Remember I had everyone write about orange soda? After Izabelle presented her piece, she must have left the notebook on the table. I read it over, and I bet her ex-husband is never going to find her sister." Dinah opened the book and handed it to me.

I vaguely remembered the piece. I'd been more concerned with the fog and keeping Miss Lavender Pants and her crew without a reason to make trouble. This time I paid attention as I read how Izabelle had taken the last glass of orange soda, which she didn't really want, just to spite her sister.

"Izabelle was certainly mean-spirited," I said. "Judging by the fact that her ex doesn't even know the sister's name, I'm guessing they've had no relationship for a while. They probably had no relationship when they got older." I glanced at the notebook again. "What should we do with this?" Dinah decided to keep it for the time being. She wanted to know about my evening out, and I thought her eyes would fall out when I told her about seeing Nora and Bennett at the resort.

"It figures she'd be happy at a posh resort, since that's where she thinks they really belong. How did CeeCee ever get him to stand in for her this weekend?" Dinah asked.

"I'm still trying to figure that out. I heard him make a comment about getting some kind of payoff for doing it. We'll have to ask CeeCee when she comes up here."

There was a lull in our conversation after that, and it took Dinah all of about two seconds to figure out there'd been more to my time with Mason than I had mentioned. Of course she got me to tell her about his invitation and what it meant.

"Nothing is going to change," I said.

"Mason had his chance before, and now it's too late."

"Are you so sure?" Dinah asked as she headed to the door. I *was* sure, wasn't I? When she'd gone, I tried to call Barry to smooth things over, but I got his voice mail. I hated to admit it, but I was relieved. There was no way I could explain the dinner with Mason that wouldn't upset him. I was too keyed-up to sleep. I had gotten the pattern for the pouch purse and some yarn. I did the foundation row for one side and then began to do rows until my eyes got heavy. When I finally went to bed, instead of counting sheep, I counted suspects.

The next morning I caught sight of the sky as I looked out my window. It was white, and I got worried about another fogout, but as soon as I realized I could see the administration building at the bottom of the hill, I relaxed.

No time to loll under the covers. I threw them back and dashed across the cold floor to the bathroom. I showered quickly and pulled on sweats and was out the door. Dinah stepped into the hall, similarly dressed, at the same time. Mason was already on his way down the stairs.

He had pulled a heavy gray hooded sweatshirt over his tai chi outfit and carried his boom box. He waited at the bottom of the stairs for us, and we headed for the beach together.

Even with the chill and early time, a nice-sized group showed up. No Nora and Bennett this time, but Jeen and Jym Wolf, the knitting couple, came.

Mason began by telling the new people to follow along and not to worry if they didn't get it exactly. Jym interrupted and asked if there was a handout detailing the particular moves.

"I looked into it. They have wonderful names like Wave Hands Like Clouds and Grasp the Bird's Tail," Jym said, speaking to the gathered group. He turned back to Mason and said the proper way to teach was with verbal instructions. I knew Mason was annoyed by the comments, but he hid it well and thanked Jym for his input, then turned the music on and began.

The Wolfs stayed, but they had matching exasperated expressions that only got more pronounced, as they couldn't keep up with Mason's movements. Jeen stopped altogether and tapped her husband's arm, making it clear she was going. With a last look of disapproval, the two headed off down the sand. Sheila arrived, nodding in apology to Mason. I saw her check out the group, and when she realized there was no Adele, her shoulders relaxed. Sheila joined right in and already seemed to be picking it up.

I loved Dinah's take on the tai chi. She was into the music, and even with its ethereal feel she was moving in time to it and throwing in a dash of attitude.

Everyone scattered after Mason's final move of making a door out of his hands, opening them and stepping forward, which marked the end of the routine. Dinah and I headed back, leaving Mason surrounded by enthusiastic retreaters. I was glad he was getting some positive attention for his efforts after Jym's remarks.

"I want to check my workshop room for my pen," Dinah said when we were back in the Asilomar grounds. As we headed up the path, we passed Commander Blaine's meeting room. The lights were on, and when we stopped by the open door, I saw that he was busy setting up cooking supplies. His silver hair was perfectly smoothed back, and like his other pants, today's khakis had sharp creases. He waved at us, but the warm smile was all for Dinah. I wondered if she realized the smile she gave back. No matter how much she objected, the quality of her smile said he had a chance.

When we reached the knitters' room, Jeen was arranging some yarn on the long table. I stopped in to find out about her abrupt tai chi departure.

Before I could speak, she began. "I'm speaking for my husband and myself when I say this. If you're going to teach something, you have to map it out. You have to provide a handout with details of what you're going to teach. Then do a demonstration while explaining what you're doing verbally. You can't just stand there and do it and tell people to follow along. Imagine if I did that with knitting."

She showed me the handouts explaining casting on, and more with instructions how to knit and purl. "Here, let me show you," she said, handing me a pair of green metallic needles and a ball of moss green yarn. She pointed to the handout with directions and then began to demonstrate how to do her favorite method of getting the yarn on the needle.

"I want to thank you and Jym for doing so well this weekend. What with the fog emergency and then Izabelle's death, well, things haven't exactly been going as originally scheduled."

After casting on only a few stitches, Jeen laid down the yarn and needle she'd been demonstrating with. "It hasn't been the weekend we expected by any means, but Jym and I are good at going with the flow." I almost choked at her comment. Going with the flow? Was she nuts? I hid my reaction by appearing to admire her *Needle Mania* tee shirt. I sputtered out a compliment, and she beamed a stiff smile and thanked me. As before, the tee shirt was tucked into the jeans that hung loosely on her angular frame.

"It's so sad about Izabelle. How, exactly, did you know her?"

Jeen regarded me with an inscrutable expression and seemed to take her time gathering what she was going to say. It made me wonder — was she taking time because she had something to hide, or because she was such a precise person she wanted to get the facts exact?

"We worked together a while back at The Yarn Source." Jeen picked up the needle and yarn and once again began demonstrating casting on. She barely looked at her work as she talked. I was familiar with the Tarzana yarn store. It had been the original home of the Tarzana Hookers until it closed down. That was when Mrs. Shedd invited the crochet group to meet at the bookstore.

Dinah and I hadn't joined until after the move.

"I didn't realize you were that close. Then her death must have really been a shock." Adele and I had our differences, but if something had happened to her, I would have been a lot more emotional than the woman in front of me. And, I reluctantly admitted to myself, I would have missed her.

"It was quite a while ago, and we weren't close. Izabelle never got close to anybody. I was already an accomplished knitter when I started at the store. On the other hand, Izabelle was a newbie at crochet, not that it stopped her from coming up with a plan. She had decided crochet was her golden ticket. I don't know how she did it, but by the time she left The Yarn Source, she'd come up with *A Subtle Touch of Crochet.*"

"And what did you do when you left the yarn store?" I asked. She'd finished demonstrating the single needle version of casting on and urged me to try. Actually, I was curious. After several muffed attempts, I finally got it and kept going until I had ten stitches on the needle.

A hint of annoyance moved over Jeen's face, and she dropped her voice. "I taught a knitting class at Beasley Community College's Extension Program."

Okay, on one hand we had a woman just starting out who had managed to parlay her skill into a successful book, and an accomplished one who ended up teaching an extension class. Seeing how Jeen was so into rules and the proper way of doing things, I had to believe that didn't sit well with her. I came right out and asked her how she felt about Izabelle's success.

"I was happy for her," Jeen said in a careful tone. "But she was never happy with herself. She seemed obsessed with changing her appearance. I gather she still was — those green eyes were brown when I knew her, and she weighed more." Jeen picked up her needles and began doing a first row on what she'd cast on. She nodded, encouraging me to do the same, as she pushed a sheet of paper toward me that had diagrams and instructions on how to knit. I hesitated, but she nodded again and I picked up the other needle. The pair felt awkward in my hands after using a hook. Well, at least Jeen did what she expected of others. She gave me verbal instructions, the written ones, and then she demonstrated by slowly moving her needles. After a stitch or two, I got it and went on down the rest of the row.

"I really felt sorry for Izabelle. I think she

kept going through husbands. And if she had any family, she never talked about them. She was all about making something of herself." Jeen smiled. "I'm lucky to have a wonderful partner like Jym." I took the mention of his name as an opening and asked if knitting was his full-time business, too.

"Oh, no," Jeen said with a laugh, as if I'd just said the most ridiculous thing. "He's a structural engineer." She went on about how he'd taken up knitting so they'd have something they could do together. When she got to the part where he'd whittled special sets of knitting needles, I started to zone out, and when she took a breath, I changed the subject back to Izabelle.

"Besides the eye color and weight, what kinds of changes did Izabelle make in herself?"

"I don't know what she did before I met her, but while we worked at the yarn store, she kept changing the style and color of her hair, and she went to a voice coach. It seemed like she was trying to reinvent herself." I had reached the end of the row, and Jeen demonstrated by turning her work and beginning another row. She said she wanted to make sure I had the knit stitch down before she moved on to purl.

"The trouble was that no matter what she did to the outside, the inside was the same old Izabelle. I ran into her after dinner the first night. I tried to be friendly and ask about her new fusion craft, but she was barely cordial and in a hurry."

"Why be in a hurry here?" I said, gesturing toward the tree-filled grounds. "There was nothing going on that night."

"I think she was meeting someone," Jeen said. "Or she might have just been trying to get rid of me. Izabelle was not a gracious person." Jeen sighed. "Oh dear, and I wasn't going to speak unkindly of the dead."

"Did you know about her peanut allergy?" I pressed.

Jeen seemed to be getting tired of answering questions, particularly about someone she didn't care for. She looked at her watch, readjusted some of the things on the table.

"Izabelle always made a big fuss about what she ate. I never thought about it, but it was probably a cover-up of her allergy."

"Why did you tell Sergeant French you and Jym didn't know Izabelle from before?" The question had been on my mind ever since Jeen had told me what she'd said to the police officer and asked me not to contradict her.

Jeen's calm demeanor suddenly got agitated, and her movements were jerky as she wound the yarn around her needle. "It's nothing, really. I just thought that since I'm sure neither Jym nor I was on the beach with Izabelle, why say we knew her at all? Why should we open ourselves up for a bunch of questions for no reason?" She glanced at me. "What's with all your questions?"

I thought quickly and said I planned to say a few words in remembrance at the last night party, and since I didn't know Izabelle, I was trying to get a feeling of who she was from people who did. I was going to use that as a springboard to asking more questions, but there was suddenly another presence in the room. Someone whose outfit of shimmery white pants with a long white cowl-neck top finished off with a white turban could have been called fog.

Adele stood at the table, staring at my hands. "I can't believe it, Pink. You've gone over to the other side."

CHAPTER 18

"You'll be glad I got you out of there, Pink," Adele said as we stopped outside the class-room. I didn't look back, but I was sure Jeen's face probably still had the look of horror. Adele's actions must have broken every rule of Jeen's code of proper behavior. My fellow Hooker had snatched the needles out of my hand and thrown them down on the table with such force, they bounced. Then she grabbed my hand and pulled me out of the room as if she was rescuing me from being kidnapped.

Dinah came out of her classroom, holding the pen she'd been concerned about. "What's going on?"

Adele answered before I could open my mouth and launched into a tirade about Jeen's efforts to turn me into a knitter.

"She almost had Pink, too. First it was just casting on, then why not try a few rows, and the next thing you know, you're making a baby blanket." Adele adjusted her white turban that had gotten knocked off-kilter during my rescue.

"You really should thank —" Adele said, but I put up my hand to stop her as I gave her my rendition of CeeCee Collins's cease-and-desist look. Nobody could carry it off with the same power as our crochet group leader, but whatever I managed was sufficient to make Adele close her mouth without saying anything more.

"Not that I have to explain, but nobody was getting me to do anything. I went along with learning how to knit to keep Jeen talking about Izabelle. It turns out they have a history."

"Oh," Adele said as her frenzied expression relaxed. "Why did you want her to talk about Izabelle?"

Dinah and I looked at each other, and Dinah gave me a why-not-go-for-it half shrug of one shoulder, so I told Adele I didn't believe Izabelle had eaten the s'more on her own.

"You think somebody killed her?" Adele appeared stricken. "But you're not telling anyone, right?" She grabbed my arm. "Look, Nancy Poirot Fletcher Drew, nobody else thinks it was murder, and you've got to leave it that way." She made some loud dramatic sighs. "Pink, if the cops start looking for a murderer, you know their first stop is going to be me." It wasn't enough for Adele to just say it, she had to point to herself with both hands as well.

"You know I didn't do it, right? I was just so upset when I saw she was wearing my work and calling it her own, I lost it for a minute. That's all." Adele tried to get me to promise to stop investigating, but I said nothing. I wasn't going to lie to her, but telling her I planned to continue would only lead to more hysterics.

I had hoped to change into a more in-charge sort of outfit before breakfast, but when I saw people were already gathering outside the dining hall, waiting for it to open, the sweats were going to have to do it for now. By the time the three of us reached the building, the bell had rung, marking the start of breakfast, and people were already filing in.

The warm air inside carried the pungent aroma of coffee and bacon mixed with the slightly sweet smell of pancakes. As I watched people from our group head to the area we'd come to call our own, I noticed their animated faces and the friendly sound of their conversations. If there hadn't been the fog emergency and Izabelle's murder —

no matter what anyone said, I was calling it that — this would have been an easy weekend. Asilomar took care of the lodging and food and provided a rustic backdrop. Commander Blaine was on top of activities. And the presenters were doing a good job tending to their groups. After registration, all I would have had to worry about was picking up sunglasses people left in the meeting rooms and replacing lost name tags.

As soon as we cleared the door, Dinah was surrounded by some of her memoir writers. It was great to see how enthusiastic they were, and I knew Dinah was loving it. Adele started to gather up her people and marched them to one of the tables. She got a glimpse of Sheila coming in and snapped a sharp wave at her — clearly a command to join them.

Jeen and Jym took seats and moments later were surrounded by their people. Commander Blaine drew his group to him like he was a magnet and they were iron filings.

Mason was probably already on his way to Santa Cruz for his aunt's eightieth birthday brunch. I felt a twinge when I thought of his invitation to join him. Just when it seemed I had worked everything out, he'd confused things.

I went to the food line and passed on the plate-sized pancakes. It was definitely hearty food, but too heavy for my taste. I just took some fruit and a bowl of oatmeal which I flavored with a pat of butter, a light sprinkle of brown sugar, and a few raisins. Not that I expected to get to eat it. Why should this meal be any different from the others?

When I reentered the dining area, Sheila got my attention and pointed to the empty seat next to her. I noticed it wasn't at Adele's table.

As I took the offered chair, I saw that Sheila's whole body seemed rigid.

"The tai chi was great," she said as she put a napkin across her lap. "It was really relaxing." She glanced toward Adele's table. "But I think I already need another session." Sheila looked at the pancakes in front of her and gave the plate a little push away. "It's nothing against the food," she said apologetically.

I laid my hand on her arm in a reassuring manner. "I know. You need a retreat from the retreat."

We both turned our attention to the reigning crochet goddess, who was parading around her subjects, letting them admire the white flowers she'd attached to the white cowl top.

Sheila nodded in agreement and took something out of her pocket. Her hands started moving in her lap, and when I glanced over, I saw she had a magenta metal hook and a ball of cream-colored cotton yarn. She'd already made a slipknot, and as the hook moved through the yarn, a longer and longer length of chain stitches dangled from the hook. She took a few deep breaths and began moving the hook back over the stitches. Her fingers started to move fast, and as the new stitches pulled tight, she mouthed "loose," drawing it out into a long exhale. The mantra succeeded, and her single crochets became loopy. The tightness literally left her shoulders as she worked down the row. When she reached the end, she turned it and did another, then slipped the whole thing back in the patch pocket of her jacket.

She knew I'd been watching her and turned toward me, her eyes now with a little sparkle. "I decided to call it tranquilizer crochet. When I feel my shoulders hunching, I just do a few rows. Since I'm not making anything, there's no pressure to count stitches or worry if they're uneven. It seems to be working pretty well."

Sheila had tried so many methods of dealing with her runaway nerves, I was glad this one seemed to work. And it had no side effects like medicinal tranquilizers.

Some latecomers arrived in the dining hall, and I noticed a dark blue uniform among them. Sergeant French separated himself from the clump of guests and surveyed the room. As soon as he saw me, he nodded in acknowledgment and walked over.

"Ms. Pink, sorry to interrupt your breakfast," he said, stopping next to my chair. He mentioned trying to reach my cell phone and getting voice mail. While he explained he wanted to go over a few things for his report, I checked my phone. I'd forgotten to plug it into the charger, and it was dead. How many other calls had I missed?

There's something about a cop's uniform that makes it a magnet for attention. It seemed like most of the room was staring in my direction. I heard Sheila suck in her breath.

"I just wanted to go over the sequence of events when you found Ms. Lander," Sergeant French said, taking out his pad and pen. I hadn't noticed before how big his head was compared to the rest of him. I repeated how Dinah, Commander, and I had gone to the beach to look for driftwood in the fog. We'd found the remnants of the fire first, and then Izabelle. The fog had made it hard to see, and we'd almost tripped over her.

"And then what happened?" he asked, scribbling something down.

"We thought she was still alive, but none of us had a phone with us. Commander Blaine said he'd go back to Asilomar and call 911. My friend and I stayed with Izabelle until the paramedics came."

"So Commander Blaine never came back to the beach?" Sergeant French asked.

"He came with the paramedics. After he called, he waited for the ambulance at the back entrance to Asilomar, so he could help them find us." I watched as he wrote something else down.

"Did anybody mention to you that they were on the beach with Ms. Landers?" He said it like an afterthought, but I thought it was an effort to catch me off guard in case I'd been withholding any information.

I shook my head in response and tried to see what he'd written down, but he did a good job of covering up his scribbles. "Are you going over your report because you changed your mind and think there was foul play involved?" I asked in a low voice.

Ever the community-minded police officer, he was careful about his tone and word choice. There was nothing condescending in the way he told me what they had determined from the information they had. "No, Ms. Pink, no foul play. The medical examiner has ruled it accidental. We think that small purse was so lightweight, Ms. Landers didn't notice she'd dropped it. She was carrying the shopping bag with the s'more ingredients and maybe even some wood she'd found for the fire. Commander Blaine confirmed that each bag had enough to make two s'mores. He also said the bags were marked, but admitted there could have been a mistake. We think there was a certain frenzy on her part to eat the sweets, and she might not have noticed the peanut butter. It is, after all, the same color as graham crackers, and according to Commander Blaine the blocks of chocolate stuck to it and probably covered it up. We checked, and the standard ingredients for s'mores are graham cracker squares, blocks of milk chocolate, and roasted marshmallows. There was a whole s'more on the beach, and we assume she ate the other one. At some point she must have detected the peanut butter and realized she didn't have the bag with the EpiPen. It only takes a short time for anaphylactic shock to set in, and she was on the beach alone in all that fog. It appears that it was just the perfect storm of an accident."

"Or the perfect crime," I said before I could stop myself.

"Ms. Pink," he said, straining to keep his friendly expression from fading, "I hate to pull rank on you, but I'm a professional, and other professionals like the medical examiner and the ER doctor all agree that Izabelle Landers died because of an allergic reaction from something ingested by her own hand." He started to go, then turned back. "Think about it, Ms. Pink, what kind of person would try to kill somebody with a s'more? And how would you get someone to eat it against their will?"

Okay, maybe I didn't have the answer to either of those questions, but I could have provided Sergeant French with a list of suspects if he wasn't so sure the case was closed. I wouldn't have included Adele — even with all her shortcomings I didn't believe she would kill anybody. Commander Blaine knew all about the contents of the s'mores, and he had admitted to being slighted by Izabelle. I really didn't want to believe it was him because even though Dinah was still fighting it, I thought there were definite possibilities for them. Spenser Futterman belonged on the list, too. No matter what Sergeant French had said about the shadow Dinah and I had seen being a crow, I was just about a hundred percent sure it was Spenser. After all, the maid had identified him as the one who left the manuscript pages.

Would there have been any point to telling Sergeant French what the maid said? Probably not. And what about Jeen? She seemed to take Izabelle's success so well, but maybe it was all an act. Then there was Jym. Could there have been something between him and Izabelle? Maybe Jeen was trying to cover up something when she made a point that she was sure that neither she nor her husband had been on the beach with Izabelle. It was certainly odd that they had lied to Sergeant French and said they didn't know Izabelle before the weekend.

The conversation in the dining hall had dropped off during Sergeant French's visit, and as he left, I noticed the volume came back up. I helped myself to a cup of coffee from the vacuum pot on the lazy Susan, but it was lukewarm and not the kind of industrial-strength caffeine hit I needed. A red-eye from the coffee wagon sounded a lot better. Dinah had left her charges, and stopped between me and Sheila.

"What was that about?" she asked, nodding her head toward Sergeant French as he went out the dining hall door. I mentioned him asking about the sequence of events for his report and that he was still trying to find out if someone was on the beach with Izabelle. I noticed Sheila's eyes getting rounder as she listened.

"He must be questioning everyone," she said.

"And requestioning, too," I added. "It's obvious nobody has admitted to being on the beach with her, and he's trying to get tricky now and see if someone admitted it to someone else."

I noticed Jym and Jeen had gotten up from their table. They had rounded up their knitters and were heading for the exit. At the next table Commander Blaine collected some tools he'd used to demonstrate carving an eggplant to look like a penguin. Something struck me about the way he put the tools in the canvas tote bag hanging on the back of his chair. It was the same canvas tote he'd used to collect the driftwood. I stared so long Dinah turned to see what I was looking at. And then suddenly I got it.

"French was right. She wasn't alone," I said. It all came back to me now, and I reminded Dinah how we'd found the remnants of the fire first. "Commander was all upset because someone had left two of his wire forks on the beach. He used one of them to pull the partially burned s'mores bag out of the hot ashes." I watched as Commander clutched the bag and got up. "And then he put them in that canvas bag." We were all staring at Commander now. "I guess finding Izabelle made me forget about the forks. Do you remember him picking them up?" I stopped to think about the implications.

"Yes, now that you mention it, I do recall him fussing about the two forks and I remember the bag," Dinah said, growing more excited.

"The question is, was he really concerned about collecting his tools and cleaning up litter, or was he trying to get rid of evidence?"

"Great! It figures the guy who likes me turns out to be a murderer." Dinah groaned.

"Maybe I should call Sergeant French and tell him," I said, but both Dinah and Sheila shook their heads. "Right, he already thinks I have murder on the brain. Besides, the marshmallow forks have probably been thoroughly cleaned and mixed in with all the others. So, what's the point?"

Dinah looked back toward her people. They were still in their seats, obviously waiting for something. "I have to go," she said with a guilty furrow of her brow. "I promised to take them on an outdoor writing exercise. It's just a little something extra I thought I'd do. They are so enthusiastic. Did I tell you how much I'm loving this workshop?"

I laughed. "You might have mentioned it a few times. Go, go, I don't want to stand in the way of anything that's going well." I took a sip of the now cold coffee and made a face. A red-eye was definitely a priority. The dining room was clearing out. Adele and her crocheters separated. They headed outside and she cruised by our table. Sheila's shoulders sprang into a hunch as Adele stopped next to her.

"I guess you didn't see me when I waved for you to join us at the other table," Adele said. There was no sarcastic edge in her voice. I don't think it occurred to her that Sheila ignored her deliberately. Why wouldn't Sheila want to sit with the reigning crochet queen?

"Whatever," Adele said quickly. "Just be sure to get the containers of yarn for the crochet session." And then, in a whirl of too much white, Adele caught up with her crochet groupies and rushed ahead to get in the front. She waved for them to follow her. It occurred to me that if she'd worn that outfit during the fogout, she would have disappeared.

"You think all this has gone to her head?" I said with a sigh. "C'mon, I'll help you get the yarn."

After a brief stop to put my phone in the charger, I led Sheila to Izabelle's room. "Maybe I should just wait here," Sheila said, hanging back. I knew she felt apprehensive about going into the dead woman's room. Who could blame her? There was something eerie about seeing Izabelle's toothbrush still sitting in a glass on the sink. Or thinking of the clothes in the closet she packed for the weekend and now would never wear.

I promised Sheila it was all right and she finally came in, but it was obvious she didn't want to stay.

There were two containers marked "Supplies," and Sheila grabbed one and headed toward the door. As I went to take the other, I saw the laptop sitting on the night table. With everything going on, I had forgotten all about the e-mail Dinah and I had sent to the ITA sponsor. Wondering if he'd sent an answer, I powered it up. I went through the motions of getting to Izabelle's e-mails, and along with some junk e-mails there was a reply from Tom.

When I opened it, a full page of text appeared. He explained that he had never actually met Izabelle. He was her sponsor and everything between them was supposed to be confidential, and even though she had died, he was still going to honor that. There was only one small piece of information he offered. Maybe small to him, but very large to me. He said that ITA stood for Identical Twins Anonymous. As the information registered, I got it. We knew that Izabelle had a sister, and now I realized it was a twin sister. And suddenly the green contacts, the plastic surgery, and the voice coach made sense.

It had been all about creating her own identity. I always thought that it would be neat to have a twin, that it would be like having another you to be friends with. But apparently not all twins felt that way. I did a quick search on the organization. It had been started to help identical twins with an identity crisis. I went back and reread the original e-mail Tom had sent. It was obvious Izabelle had told him she was going to do something, and he was trying to stop her. Considering the organization, it seemed like a safe assumption it had something to do with her twin. Did that mean the twin was here?

I couldn't wait to tell Dinah all that I'd

found out. And Sheila couldn't wait to get out of the room.

"I'll help you get these to your classroom, but I'm stopping for a red-eye first," I said when we'd gotten outside.

As we headed around the administration building to the side with the deck, I noticed that Spenser and his mysterious female companion were sitting on a corner bench with their backs to us. They were talking about something. I didn't want to tell Dinah, but her undercover work had been a little weak. I'd hoped she would get information, but it sounded like all she'd done was give it.

"Why don't you go on ahead to your meeting room?" I said to Sheila, never taking my eyes off the pair. This was my chance to find out what was really going on with those two.

Sheila saw me staring and asked what was up. Then she nodded her head in sudden understanding. "You think they have something to do with Izabelle's death, right?" I motioned for her to keep her voice down, and she started talking in an excited whisper. "You're going to eavesdrop, aren't you?" She took another look at Spenser's back. "I'm staying. Two sets of ears are better than one."

257

The deck was raised off the ground, and the spot where they were seated was bordered by bushes taller than me. Sheila and I checked the area around us, and the footpaths were empty in all directions. Sheila stuck to me like glue as we walked closer to the deck, still carrying the boxes of crochet supplies. When we were even with the bushes, I abruptly made a side move off the footpath and behind a leafy bush. Sheila paused for a beat and did the same move, which sent her crashing into me behind the bush. We put our burdens down and slipped farther behind the brush.

At first I could only make out their voices, but not what they were saying. I took Sheila's hand and we moved farther along the wall until we were directly beneath Spenser and his lady friend.

"Keep on good terms with Dinah Lyons," the woman said. "She's a good source if I need any more information. We took care of almost everything regarding Izabelle Landers. I can't believe nobody figured out what was going on."

"What else is there?" Spenser asked.

"I need to take care of the one who's running the crochet workshop now. All I need is a clear shot, and I can check her off my list."

CHAPTER 19

My head was spinning by now. In a small space of time I'd found out that the sister Izabelle didn't get along with was her identical twin, that Commander Blaine may or may not have been tampering with evidence and that Spenser Futterman's companion wanted to shoot Adele.

Sheila and I had slipped unnoticed from behind the bushes. Once I got my coffee drink, we'd found a bench and I was trying to regroup. I let the red-eye circulate through my brain. I was thrilled that Dinah was doing such a great job with the writers, but I missed having her to talk to. Sheila was definitely trying to be helpful, but she was already a wreck from driving with Adele, then sharing a room with her and then becoming her crochet assistant.

"The obvious priority here is Adele," I said. "I have to warn her."

"Good luck getting her to listen to you."

Sheila had taken out her tranquilizer crochet supplies and was adding a row. Her breath immediately smoothed out.

I sighed and asked if I could do some; I certainly needed something to calm my thoughts. Instead of giving me her crocheting, Sheila produced a ball of sunny yellow worsted and another hook and said I could do my own. A few minutes of crocheting did wonders for me, and I was ready to save Adele as we headed for her workshop.

"Adele, I have to talk to you," I said as I came into the meeting room with Sheila close behind. Adele was standing at the front end of the table with seven women and one man arranged around the other end.

"Not now," she said. "Pink, just put down the box. I have a workshop to run. She gestured toward the crocheters. "People, while I set up, you can work on the blocks for the shelter blanket." She nodded at Sheila. "Leave yours on the table and go help them."

Adele was in full attitude with her hand on her hip, glaring at me until I set the box on the table. She waved for me to leave and immediately began taking out Izabelle's sample pouch bags, tee shirts with a row of trim along the bottom, and flowers that could be attached to anything from purses to jean pockets, along with several copies of *A Subtle Touch of Crochet.* Apparently ignoring Adele's order, two of the women left their seats and began looking through what Adele was setting out. A woman with long, prematurely gray hair joined them, picked up one of the copies of Izabelle's book, and began thumbing through it. Meanwhile, Adele was managing to totally ignore me.

The woman with the book held it open and showed it to the others. "Look at the doll clothes," she said, and the three women started discussing making clothes for some dolls they had.

"People, please keep your seats," Adele said, annoyed that no one seemed to be listening to her.

"Adele, it's important," I said, taking her arm, but she pulled it away.

"Pink, what's with you? Can't you see I'm busy?"

Now the women had moved from discussing the doll clothes to the doll model in the picture. "Look at that nose," one of them said. "That's definitely not a regulation doll nose. I'm sure it's one of those dolls I was telling you about."

I caught a glimpse of the picture over one of their shoulders and recognized it as the doll in the background of the photo of Izabelle on the back of the book. "It's an odd-looking doll," I said, jumping into their conversation. "So you think it's some special kind?"

"Pink, you're interrupting. Leave," Adele said, sounding exasperated. But it was too late; the women had already picked up on my question.

"We collect dolls, which I guess makes us kind of experts," the woman in a red sweater said, "and this doll looks like what I call a 'little me' doll. There are various methods, some better than others, but the idea is the same — basically a doll is crafted from a photograph to look like a child. I've seen some where they just go for face shape and hair color, but this one looks like they went all out."

Adele was out of patience. She took the book from the woman's hand and strongly suggested all of them take their seats. She glared at me and pointed toward the door. I happened to look at the doorway behind Adele. Spenser's friend abruptly stepped into view. I saw her hands go up. There was no time to consider alternatives, I just had to act. On pure impulse I dived toward Adele, tackling her, and yelled for everyone to hit the floor.

"Pink, you've really lost it this time!" Adele screamed as we landed on the floor together.

CHAPTER 20

I rolled off Adele and sat up. Ten pairs of eyes were all on me, mostly with a look of concern attached. Only Adele's eyes had the additional flare that implied she'd like to do me bodily harm.

Of course, when I looked toward the door, no one was there. "Sorry everyone," I said, getting up. I needed to think fast and give an explanation for my actions. "Just a little emergency drill." I held up the rhinestone clipboard which had gone down with me. "It's one of the duties that go along with having this." Thankfully, nobody questioned what kind of emergency it was a drill for, and they all began to get up.

No problem getting Adele to talk to me now. She didn't resist when I led her to the corner of the room. The rest of the group went back to their seats, and Sheila took a few deep breaths and resumed helping them.

I quickly told Adele what I'd overheard and mentioned seeing the woman at the doorway. When Adele rolled her eyes in disbelief, I called Sheila over to back up my story.

"Now you're pulling Sheila into your investigations?" Adele said, giving us both a hopeless look. "You overheard who?" As I began the second telling of the story, even though I'd been there and heard what Spenser's companion had said, it sounded ridiculous. Why would anybody want to shoot Adele unless it was the fashion police? As I tried to explain who everyone was and what I thought they might have done, it got too convoluted and I gave up. "Never mind," I said walking away. "You're on your own."

There's nothing like a little yelling with a few screams thrown in to attract a crowd. As I exited, I walked into a bunch of people who were straining to look in the doorway. Dinah pushed her way through the onlookers with her aquamarine scarf flying in the breeze. The woman with the turquoise earrings rushed past her and stopped next to me.

"Was that part of the mystery weekend?" She glanced around. "Is there another body somewhere we're supposed to find?"

How many ways could I tell that woman there was no mystery game? I repeated that the weekend activities didn't include a mystery game. She was one of Dinah's writers, and my friend urged her to rejoin the others.

I waved to the onlookers and said everything was fine and they should go back to their workshops. Dinah glanced toward her people clustered on the path and stepped closer to me.

"We were on our way to the deck by the social hall for another outdoor writing exercise. What happened?" She turned away and called out to her writers to go on ahead and to pick out a tree and describe it. "Okay, tell me everything, and don't leave out any details."

I started with what I'd found out about Izabelle.

"So, Izabelle was a twin," Dinah said, her eyes sparkling with interest. "A twin who didn't like being a twin. No doubt that was why she made herself over. That would end her being a mirror image of someone. Izabelle probably isn't her real name, either."

I moved on to what I'd overheard, along with possibly saving Adele's life.

"Hmm, so Mr. Futterman's charm was as fake as mine," she said. "If he thinks he's

266

going to keep me around to pump more information from —" She stopped. "All I talked about was Adele stepping into Izabelle's shoes." Dinah stopped and seemed worried. "I hope it isn't something I said that made them want to shoot Adele."

"What did you tell him?" I asked.

"Maybe I did say something about Adele thinking Izabelle had stolen her work."

I shrugged it off. "It doesn't matter. Adele wouldn't listen to me when I tried to warn her."

"What about calling Sergeant French and telling him about the threat?"

"I couldn't even explain it to Adele without realizing how ridiculous it sounds. So, no, I'm not going to call Sergeant French. He already thinks I'm nuts."

Dinah squeezed my hand in support and then went on to catch up with her writers. By then the onlookers had realized there was nothing to see and the path was deserted. The air was silvery with the morning haze and the light was flat. I didn't even have my shadow as company as I walked down the path away from the low building housing the crochet and knitting meeting rooms.

I clutched the rhinestone clipboard to my chest and hung my head. That last little fiasco wasn't helping my image as the person in charge. I thought coming up with the emergency drill excuse was pretty creative, though, and people seemed to buy it. At least the workshops all seemed to be a success. I sighed. But time was running out to figure out who killed Izabelle. There was just lunch, the afternoon sessions, and the last night party. After breakfast the next morning everyone would start to scatter, and Sergeant French would probably give up and say an unknown person may have been on the beach with Izabelle.

I walked up the hill to the Lodge building. Even the smell of pine trees and the air fresh off the ocean didn't cheer me up. Somebody was going to get away with murder if I didn't get going.

The housekeepers had finished their duties and were rolling their cart down the first-floor hall as I came in. The building was quiet as I walked up the stairs and down the hall toward my room. When I got inside, I sat down on the bed and checked my cell phone, which was now fully charged. I'd been in a hurry when I dropped it off and hadn't checked my voice mail, but now I had time. Three calls from Barry, starting late last night and ending early this morning. He'd sounded more and more upset with each message. I punched in his number and held my breath.

"Greenberg," he answered in his all-business voice. As soon as he heard it was me, his voice softened only as long as it took to say my name, then it went right to agitated.

"Where were you?" he demanded. "Or should I say who were you with?"

"I was snug in my bed alone," I said, rolling my eyes. "My phone's battery ran down and I didn't realize it until this morning."

There was silence on his end and I knew he was evaluating what I'd said. One of the drawbacks of being involved with a cop is that he's used to dealing with people who don't always tell the truth. By now I knew what he was waiting for. Would I gush forth with too many details? Like saying I'd had my phone where I couldn't see it and therefore had missed its flashing screen before it shut down, and talking about what time I went to bed and what time I'd gotten up and how quiet the room was, since I was all alone? Too many details spelled cover-up to him.

Two could play that game, so I just said nothing until he finally spoke, apparently accepting my excuse as being true.

"Babe, I just want you to know I had

nothing to do with your new residents."

"Whoa," I said, "what are you talking about?"

"The two cats."

I asked the obvious question. "What two cats?"

The story unfolded that when Barry had stopped by the first time to let the dogs out and make sure everything was okay, there had been two cats sleeping on a lounge chair in the backyard. But when he'd come by late last night, the cats had been inside and there were some cat bowls, cat food, a cat box and even some cat toys on the floor in my crochet room, which, according to Barry, seemed to have become cat central. And as far as he could tell, all my yarn was okay, but then who could tell, since it always seemed to be all over the place?

"Cats? What kind of cats?" I said as visions of a yarn nightmare danced through my mind.

"They look like the regular kind to me. One of them is black and white and the other is kind of gray. I'm guessing they have something to do with the stuff accumulating in your front hall. Did I mention there were some chairs along with the cartons?"

"You mentioned cat bowls and cat food separately. Is there some cat food in the cat bowls and some water? You said a cat box, too, right?"

"Don't worry. Everybody seems to have lots of whatever they need."

"I'll have to deal with everything when I get back." A little weariness crept into my voice and Barry picked up on it immediately.

"Not much fun without me, is it?" he said in a teasing voice.

"No," I said, and meant it.

Barry laughed. "So Mason isn't keeping you amused?" He sounded all too happy when I mentioned Mason was gone for the day to his family event. I didn't say anything about Izabelle's death or my investigation. I should have figured that was the same as giving too many details when you were trying to cover up a lie. It was like a red flag to Barry.

"Okay, Molly, let's put all the cards on the table," Barry said at last. "What's going on with your crochet instructor's death?"

I tried to say nothing, but Barry used his whole arsenal of investigating tricks, from "You'll feel better if you tell me the whole story" to saying that maybe he could help straighten things out.

The funny thing was, it did feel good to tell him the whole story, at first, anyway. He listened patiently as I gave him all the details. Almost all the details. I left out tackling Adele.

"Now what in that makes you so sure someone killed the woman?" he asked in an understanding voice, which surprised me. When I'd gotten involved in investigating other murders, he'd been far more disturbed and irrational. Maybe because those were in his jurisdiction, or maybe because he was trying a new tactic to deal with me — being reasonable.

"Molly, it sounds like Sergeant French and his people have it covered." He still sounded calm. "You were so worried about being in charge this weekend. Wouldn't it be better if you spent your time on the retreat and trust the cop to do his job?"

Not a chance.

CHAPTER 21

I was determined to juggle handling the retreat and checking out my list of suspects. After all the fuss to get her more of Izabelle's supplies for the workshops, Adele had complained there was too much clutter and insisted I take back one carton. I opened the door to Izabelle's room and took it inside. A copy of *A Subtle Touch of Crochet* fell out of the box. When I picked it up, I thumbed through it and stopped when I got to the doll picture. I saw what those women meant — the face didn't look like any doll I'd ever seen. Before I could really study the picture, I heard some fumbling at the door. I had every right to be in there since Zak Landers had given me the okay, but still instinct kicked in and I slipped into the closet, leaving the door open a crack.

It took a few more moments of fumbling and then I heard the door open, followed by nervous whispers.

"We have to hurry. My boss will have a fit if we get caught." I recognized Spenser's female companion as she slipped in. He held up some kind of device and said something about being surprised that it really worked.

"If all else fails, I might have a future as a burglar," he said with a grin. She glared at him in response.

"It's in there," he said, pointing at the closet. I just had time to move behind the clothes before the closet door swung open. Spenser leaned in and began moving things along the clothes rod. I flattened myself against the back wall as he took a hanger containing a jacket.

"Hold it up," she ordered, and he complied. The dark space was filled with flashes of light. Between seeing spots from the brightness, I caught a glimpse of her single-lens reflex camera. If I hadn't been hiding, I would have hit my forehead with my hand. So that was the kind of shooting they had in mind for Adele!

"Got it," she said, and headed for the door as he rehung the jacket.

"It's a lot easier exiting by the door than by the window," Spenser said, following her out.

I waited a few moments and then stepped

out into the room. All was quiet. The jacket was in the middle of the clothes rod, and I took it into the light to see what the fuss was about. The body was cream-colored denim and the sleeves were crocheted in coral yarn. Another strip of coral crochet ran down the front and around the neckline. I checked the inside for a label and found one of the kind I'd seen advertised in craft magazines. It said "An Izabelle Landers Original Design." The style reminded me of a baseball jacket.

After Spenser's comment, I opened the window and stuck my head out. In the daylight his means of escape the other night was obvious. The balcony almost touched the back stairs.

When we met after the morning sessions ended, Dinah got a good laugh about the real meaning of *shoot* and was curious about the jacket.

"I could go undercover again and see what I could find out about it," Dinah offered, but I told her to put it on hold for now. I also told her how glad I was I hadn't decided to call Sergeant French about the *threat* against Adele. Talk about embarrassing! We had stopped by the entrance to the dining hall. Dinah seemed supercharged with energy.

"I know this weekend has been tough for you, but my students are a teacher's dream. How am I ever going to go back to my restless freshmen at Beasley Community College?" She went on some more about not having to waste time arguing about what was or wasn't acceptable to wear in class and being respectful of others. I didn't mean to, but I kind of tuned out as she went back to raving about her group, and I didn't come back into focus until she said she'd been thinking about what I'd said about Izabelle being a twin.

"Remember that first e-mail we saw from Tom? He was reacting to something she had said she was going to do. It probably had something to do with her twin. I was thinking," Dinah said, glancing into the interior of the large dining hall, "what if her twin was here, and whatever she planned to do, she planned to do this weekend?"

I told her I'd been thinking along the same lines, and we began surveying the people coming out of the food line, picking out those from our group and checking them for resemblance to Izabelle. But after a moment I rocked my head in a hopeless gesture. "How can we tell? It's pretty obvious that after all that work Izabelle had done, they're no longer identical."

"Look for height and build," Dinah said, studying Jeen. She fit the bill, but so did a lot of others — Miss Lavender Pants, the woman in the safari jacket, even the one who kept thinking it was a mystery weekend. I was about to give up when I noticed a head of long, prematurely gray hair come into view.

"I have an idea," I said, but when I turned to Dinah, her students were beckoning her to their table. Her whole demeanor brightened as she went to join them. I was on my own.

"Excuse me," I said to the gray-haired woman. She looked up from her plate of macaroni and cheese and smiled. I asked her how she was enjoying the crochet workshop to break the ice, and then worked back to where I wanted to go.

"You mentioned something about the doll model in Izabelle Landers's book." She brightened with recognition almost immediately.

"It was quite something, wasn't it?" she said. "Personally, I find those dolls a little too wax museum for my taste, but to each their own."

"So you think the doll was made to resemble a real person?" I said, and she nodded.

"Just a guess, but since it was in her book, probably the author as a child. Personally, I'll take a Madame Alexander doll any day over one of those."

I thanked her and said I hoped she enjoyed her lunch. While I mentally went over what she had just said, I had a sudden desire to get another look at that doll. I slipped out of the dining hall, greeting people as they came in.

Outside, the sky was white. Even though it was midday, the light looked the same as it had in the early morning. I walked up the main path toward the meeting room that housed the crochet group. Since they were gathering again in the afternoon, Adele would have left everything as is. And the door was unlocked as well.

The table was littered with yarn and hooks. Izabelle's sample flowers and lacy trims were in the center of the table along with several copies of the book. I felt a surge of excitement as I fluttered through the pages, looking for the doll model.

I looked at it through new eyes now. Was this how Izabelle had looked as a child?

"I'm glad to catch up with you," Bennett said, coming through the open door. "The actors need a few props, and I wondered if you could snag them." When he described what they needed, they sounded like the kinds of things Commander Blaine had brought, and I suggested asking him. It was the first time I'd really had a chance to talk to Bennett alone. I apologized for the bumps that had started off the retreat.

"It was too bad about the Landers woman, but hardly your fault, any more than the fog." He smiled and I got a dose of his charisma. Like Dinah, he was enthusiastic about his group. "Even in this short time, it's been fun watching them come out of their shells. I guess there's a ham hiding in all of us," he said. He thanked me, and with a wave said his group was saving him a seat in the dining hall.

I glanced at the book in my hands and hoped my idea would work.

Adele was in full crochet diva mode when I came back to the dining hall. She held up a purple pouch purse she'd just completed and was showing off the chartreuse flowers she was going to add. The women and one man around her all oohed and aahed. Adele didn't seem happy when I interrupted.

"Adele, I have to use your car," I said softly. She instantly made a negative face and shook her head. "It's important," I persisted. She still didn't budge. "Okay, how about this — it might permanently get

Sergeant French off your back."

That got through to Adele. At first she'd seemed to like the attention she got from being a person of interest or, as she called it, an important witness, but after the third time Sergeant French had tried to get her to admit that she'd been on the beach with Izabelle, she had complained to me and wanted to know if I was the one who told him she'd been bragging about what a great campfire maker she was.

"I'll have to see your license," she said finally. "And what kind of driving record do you have? Any accidents?" Even though I assured her I'd had no bad accidents and yes, I would show her my license, she kept on, telling me I needed to be aware of her car's little idiosyncrasies. There was something about how you had to turn the key to lock the door, and not slamming on the brakes or revving the engine. It was too much to absorb, but I was sure I'd do fine. What did she think, that I was some kind of teenage hot-rodder?

"Where are you going?" she demanded. "And how long will you be gone?" I mentioned the Del Monte Mall, and she threw me an exasperated groan. "Shopping, Pink?"

"Not shopping," I protested. "I have to

take care of something that has to do with Izabelle Landers. Are you going to let me use your car or not?"

Adele finally handed me the keys. "But I'm in charge while you're gone, right?"

"Whatever," I said, handing her the rhinestone clipboard.

A few minutes later, she stood watching as I got into her old silver Honda. She had actually made me show her my license. Sometimes she was just too over-the-top. What the fuss was, was beyond me. The car was well worn and not exactly what I'd call orderly. She'd re-covered the front bucket seats with what I hoped was fake black-and-white cow skin. The backseat was littered with skeins of yarn that were tangled together and a bag from a craft store with more supplies. I chuckled at the box of bubble gum packets. Who knew Adele chewed that stuff that came in shreds and was supposed to look like chewing tobacco? She never ceased to surprise me. I laid my tote bag with Izabelle's crochet book on the passenger seat.

I started to roll down the window, but Adele yelled for me to halt and pulled open the door.

"Pink, did you pay any attention to what I said? My car is fragile. If you open the window, it won't shut." She touched the roof of the car protectively. "Maybe I should drive."

I reminded her she had the rhinestone clipboard for now, shut the door and turned on the motor. I know she was watching as I finally drove away.

I felt strange driving out of the Asilomar gate, as if I was suddenly reentering the real hustle-and-bustle world. Well, maybe not exactly hustle-and-bustle, but suddenly there were stoplights and traffic, houses and stores and an abrupt end to the feeling of being off somewhere.

Shortly beyond the business area, the road became curvy as it went over a ridge and through a forest of Monterey pines before I saw the signs for the Del Monte Mall. It had taken a bunch of phone calls to listings in the yellow pages before I found someone at a photo center who said he could do what I wanted.

I found a parking spot on the perimeter of the large mall and checked the directory for the store I wanted. A tall, skinny college-age clerk looked up when I walked in.

When I explained I was the one who'd called, he said, "You understand we don't have the actual software that does age progression, like they use for the milk carton photos. That's strictly for FBI and law enforcement." I nodded and he asked to see the photo.

I opened Izabelle's book and showed him the picture. "You want me to age-progress a doll?" he said, giving me a weird look. Not a big surprise; it was an odd request. I thought of explaining why I wanted the altered photo, but I couldn't come up with an easy explanation that didn't make me seem even weirder.

"I think I can do it with Photo Shop. How about next week?"

"I was thinking of something more along the lines of in an hour or so."

He swallowed hard. "Okay. I'm always up for a challenge." He took the book and said something about scanning the photo, followed by a lot of computer mumbo jumbo. With that settled, I rushed back to Adele's car.

I returned to Asilomar just as lunch was ending. The driveway was clogged with people from our retreat on their way to the afternoon sessions as I parked the car in one of the few spots near the administration building. Adele had made me promise to drop off the keys the moment I got back. She was already in the crochet workshop room. When she saw me, she put down the purple pouch bag she was finishing and got up, insisting on inspecting her car.

She walked all the way around it, checking for damage. I rolled my eyes in disbelief as she opened the back door and rearranged the yarn, bag of craft supplies and box of bubble gum packets in the backseat and complained that everything had gotten jostled around, no doubt because of my harsh driving.

She held out her hand for the keys. "Ah, there's one more thing," I said, giving them to her.

"What now, Pink? My people are waiting." She began walking, and I followed.

I broke the news that I had to go back. You'd think I'd just asked Adele for a seat on a rocket to the moon.

"What, exactly, is all this about?" she asked, putting her hand on her cloud-colored encased hip. She wasn't going to give back the keys without the whole story. She stopped in the middle of the path and waited while I told her about the doll in Izabelle's book and how I thought if I got it age-progressed, I'd know what she looked like as an adult.

"But we know what she looked like, Pink. I think you're losing your detective touch."

I reminded Adele how she'd brought up

that Izabelle's perfect looks weren't natural.

"Right," she said. "My eagle eye did pick out the fake cheekbones and redone nose. And the puffy lips, ha!" I threw in the eye and hair color. Then I dropped the bombshell and told her Izabelle had an identical twin and that she might be among us.

Adele took a moment to process the information and then got it. "And I bet if someone was on the beach with Izabelle, it was her," Adele said, handing back the keys. "Okay, you didn't wreck my car the first time, so you won't this time, right?"

In all our negotiations, I hadn't noticed that there were people around us until Jym called out a greeting. Jeen's acknowledgment came out like a combination groan and sigh as her eyes locked on Adele. I looked past Bennett, who appeared deep in thought, to a dark blue uniform that immediately grabbed my attention.

"There you are," Sergeant French said in a studied friendly voice. He stopped next to Adele. "Ms. Abrams, I just want to talk to you again about the afternoon Ms. Landers died."

Adele grabbed the fabric of my corduroy blazer. "Here, Pink has some information for you. I really have nothing more to add. Like I said all those times before, I didn't talk to Izabelle after the incident in the crochet workshop. I didn't follow her to the beach. I didn't have any of the s'mores. I went to my room alone, where I could concentrate, and tried to re-create the stitch she had stolen from me."

The police officer shifted his weight and sighed. He obviously hadn't given up on Adele being the person with Izabelle on the beach.

"Ms. Abrams, you know you'll feel better if you tell me the real story."

"That *is* the real story," she protested. "Talk to Pink. She's got it all figured out. I've got a workshop to run."

She marched off, and Sergeant French turned his attention to me. "More amateur sleuthing, Ms. Pink?" he said with another sigh.

"I'm going to have something this afternoon that's going to rock your investigation."

"Right," he said without looking at me, probably because he was rolling his eyes. Commander came by, carrying a grocery bag. He stopped to remind me that his group was making a special appetizer for the evening get-together. Sergeant French nodded at him.

"Anything else you want to add to your

statement?" the police officer asked.

Commander merely shook his head as an answer. So, Sergeant French had talked to him, too.

When Commander was out of earshot, I asked the sergeant if Commander had mentioned that he'd picked up marshmallow forks on the beach. I was expecting a big gasp of surprise before he asked me for details, but he gave me his blank cop face.

"I don't have to discuss this with you. We're not working together, remember? At first Mr. Blaine didn't mention it, but it came back to him, and he called me. He said he'd picked them up along with a partially burned bag. He claimed it was his natural tendency to pick up his things others had left. He didn't remember exactly, but was pretty sure he'd thrown the bag away and cleaned up the forks and put them back with the others."

"Well, there goes any forensic evidence," I said. I think Sergeant French was back to rolling his eyes as he prepared to leave.

"You should talk to Spenser Futterman," I said quickly.

"Who?" Sergeant French asked. His cop face was all gone as I described Spenser and his female companion and said that Spenser was the crow.

"The what?" he asked. He was trying to keep a serious look, but his mouth wanted to grin. I reminded him that someone was in Izabelle's room when Dinah and I had first used the key. "There were papers missing and we saw a shadow go out the window. You said it was a crow, remember?" He gave me a condescending nod and I explained how Spenser and his lady friend had come into Izabelle's room and I'd heard Spenser admit that he'd been in there before and had exited through the window. "So you see, he's the crow." It was a little tricky explaining why I was in the closet.

"I guess that's part of your amateur sleuthing," Sergeant French said. He couldn't hide the grin anymore. He took out his notebook and wrote something down. "See, I'm making a note of it. You said they didn't take anything other than pictures, right? I'll have my men check this guy out."

Right. I knew when someone was humoring me.

The call that my photo was ready came as the workshops took their break. I walked through the throng of people quickly, not wanting to be stopped by anyone, and made a direct line to Adele's car.

I struggled with the lock, not remembering what special move I was supposed to use, and finally jiggled it enough that it moved and the button popped up. A few moments later, I zipped back out through the gate, elated at the prospect of seeing the altered photo. In a few minutes I'd know for sure if Izabelle's twin was among us and, more important, who she was. I barely noticed the ride and pulled into the large parking lot of the Del Monte Mall.

Rather than deal with Adele's weird lock, I just left the car open. How long would I be, anyway, and who in their right mind would want to steal her car? The layout of the mall confused me, and I didn't realize until I was walking into it that I had parked at the wrong end. By then it seemed longer to walk back and move the car than to go the extra distance. I felt a surge of excitement as I reached the walkway between the stores and headed toward the photo studio. I was priding myself on my creativity at age-progressing the doll. Amateur sleuth, hah!

When I walked in the store, the kid straightened. "I think you're going to be very happy with this," he said as he showed me the sealed, large manila envelope sitting on top of the book behind the counter.

"Can I see it?" I said, reaching for it, but he handed me the bill instead. When the transaction was complete, he handed me the charge slip, book, and envelope, and walked me to the door. "We close early on Sunday."

Since I had waited this long, I decided to do the unveiling in the car, where I could sit and examine the picture. The only problem was, finding Adele's car turned out to be a chore. I'd been so focused on getting to the photo place, I hadn't paid any attention to where I had left the car. Silver cars don't exactly stand out the way my greenmobile does. A 1993 Mercedes 190E in teal green is hard to miss. When I finally located it, I slid in, shut the door, and tore open the envelope.

When I looked at the print, I didn't know whether to laugh or cry. I certainly understood why the clerk had been so quick to show me the door and discourage my viewing his work in front of him.

How to describe what I was looking at? Basically, he had taken the doll's head and given it some wrinkles and gray hair. Apparently he had understood that noses and ears keep growing, and had extended the doll's nose until she looked like a witch and her ears hung to her chin line. Discouraged, I threw it on the seat and turned the engine on.

The parking lot opened right onto the highway and I stepped on the gas, very anxious to get back now. I had spent too much time away from my duties, and for nothing. Up ahead the stoplight went to yellow, and I stepped on the brake. The pedal went down, but the car didn't slow. As the car flew through the intersection, I looked ahead at the road and realized I was in big trouble.

CHAPTER 22

"Oh my God, oh my God — this can't be happening," I said out loud, as if it would make any difference. I took my foot off the accelerator again, and again the car didn't slow at all. I tried the brake, but the car just made an angry noise and kept roaring down the road. What was wrong with Adele's Honda?

A picture flashed through my mind — a retreating figure in a hooded sweatshirt as I approached the car. I hadn't paid enough attention to know if it was a man or a woman. Had that mysterious person done something to the car? I felt the pit of my stomach squeeze and started saying "Oh my God" again over and over out loud. I needed time to figure out what to do. Time I didn't have at the moment. I was closing in on a yellow Ford Focus in front of me. I was going to hit it if I didn't do something fast. I tend to be a cautious driver, not changing lanes unless there's lots and lots of room. I glanced to my left, hoping for a big open space. No such luck: a black Cadillac was barreling along, catching up to me. Hoping for the best, I pulled in front of the fast-moving dark car.

I made it, but just barely. I heard the driver honking behind me and could only imagine what he was doing with his middle finger. The Ford became a yellow blur as I zoomed past it. I felt giddy at my momentary success.

The road sloped upward, but that barely slowed the car. Both sides of the road were bordered by giant Monterey pines, though I saw them as more of a green blur as I put all my attention on the road ahead. Someone must have heard me talking about getting the picture of the doll altered and figured out what it meant. So, I had been on the right track. A lot of good that was going to do me. I got it. Whoever had overheard me didn't want me to make it back.

And unless I could figure out what to do, whoever was going to get his or her wish. The realization of what that meant hit me like a thud. Was this going to be the end for me?

Barry would blame himself. He'd think if

only he hadn't listened to me and had come anyway, nothing would have happened. Would he be the one to break the news to my sons? I felt my eyes fill with tears. I knew Peter would be okay, but I worried about my younger son, Samuel. And what about Mason? He'd blame himself, too.

I thought about my late husband. Would Charlie be waiting for me? I felt a momentary comfort. I knew he would. He'd hold out his hand and help me through the tunnel all the people who'd been dead and come back talked about. Charlie would help me to the light. But that wouldn't help those I'd left behind.

Dinah would be heartbroken. Sheila would be sad. And Adele — the jury was still out. She'd probably inherit my job at the bookstore. My death would be chalked up as an accident. Sergeant French would give up and accept that Izabelle was alone on the beach. And her killer and mine would get away with it.

I didn't want to die. Not now, not yet.

I put more effort into working my foot against the accelerator, trying to get it unstuck, not that it helped. My cell phone was in my purse on the floor, out of reach. Who would I call, anyway? I looked toward either side of the road, hoping there would be an open field to steer into, but I saw only trees.

Another stoplight was coming up. It was green, and I hoped it would stay that way. It was still green as I got closer. I let out my breath, thinking I would make it through. But it went to yellow. Thankfully, the car in front of me didn't consider stopping, and sped through the intersection. The light was red when I got to it. I choked on my breath as the silver Honda zoomed through the intersection. In the rearview mirror I caught sight of the cross traffic surging into the spot I had barely vacated. I caught sight of something else, too. A cop car pulled onto the road from behind a tree and, lights flashing, came up behind me.

My breath poured out in a gush. Someone was coming to help. Or not. I heard a disembodied voice over a loudspeaker order me to pull over. He didn't want to help. He wanted to give me a ticket.

I opened the window — who cared now if it stuck? — and tried waving my hand out of it, hoping they'd realize I was in trouble. I don't think they got the message. The cruiser stayed on my tail, and the voice over the loudspeaker kept ordering me to pull over. I saw more flashing lights in my rearview mirror. Three cruisers were after me now. It was like those car chases I'd seen on TV.

I was so occupied with what was going on behind me, I momentarily lost track of what was in front of me. When I refocused, I saw that I was closing in on a blue Neon. Worse, there was a white minivan in the lane next to it, matching its speed. It seemed like I had no way out. It got worse as I saw the Neon's brake lights go on. I pulled hard on the wheel and drove onto the shoulder just in time. As soon as I got ahead of the two cars, I steered back onto the road. The cop cars did the same.

The road was empty ahead. Had the cops cleared it? I hoped so. All I had to do was steer now — and figure out how to stop. In my peripheral vision I saw one of the police cars had pulled alongside and was driving next to me. A voice barked through the loudspeaker, commanding me to pull over. I yelled back, with all the voice that I could find, that the accelerator was stuck.

I roared past stores and businesses in Pacific Grove. The turnoff to Asilomar went by in a flash, and then the street turned and ran along the beach. There were dunes on one side and a rocky beach on the other. I thought of those piles of sand I'd seen on the sides of highways to stop runaway trucks and tried to aim the car toward a sand hill, but all my years of trying to avoid hitting things kicked in and I couldn't do it. I just grazed the sand and was back on the road. I looked toward the beach side and was relieved to see the rocky area give way to plants and sand. Much as I hated to damage the fragile plants, as soon as I saw an area that looked level, I pulled the wheel hard to the left. The car went off the road, and I bumped through the low fence and over the plants, finally hitting the soft sand. The wheels got stuck and the engine stalled out as the car finally stopped. For a moment I just sat there stunned. Then I opened the door and got out. As soon as I stood, my legs gave out.

CHAPTER 23

A strong pair of hands caught me before I hit the sand. I instinctively tried to fight my way free of being held. The first backward swing of my elbow made contact.

"Ouch, tough girl, I was just trying to help," a familiar voice said as my rescuer let me go. I looked back just as I hit the sand. Mason was rubbing his arm. "You've got quite an elbow swing."

He looked down at me with concern. "Are you okay?"

I did a quick survey of myself. Somehow I had avoided any kind of injury — not even a bump on the arm. Mentally I felt a little shaky, but an inner voice ordered me to snap out of it and I obeyed. "I think so," I said as Mason held out his arm and helped me up. It was still sinking in that I was safe. I apologized for the elbow strike and threw my arms around him, grateful to have the chance to do it.

The relief at being out of the car had made me forget my police entourage until a voice over the loudspeaker ordered me and my accomplice to put our hands on the roof of the car. The three police cars had stopped on the street. All three had their doors open as shields. This had happened before, and I knew enough to simply follow their command instead of trying to explain what had happened.

"This is why I came here this weekend," Mason said as we both stepped out of the hug and complied with the order. "I never know what's going to happen with you around."

"How did you just happen to be here?" I asked as we stood side by side with our arms on top of Adele's sand-locked car.

Mason said he'd gotten back from his aunt's party. "You know how it is with family. I needed a tai chi break and headed to the beach. Here I was, expecting peace, and suddenly a car comes rolling on the sand. Obviously, it got my attention."

I glanced toward the area across the street, and for the first time it registered that I was only a short distance from the gateway to the Asilomar boardwalk. After a moment the police officers came onto the beach and approached the car.

"Ms. Pink?" Sergeant French said, separating from the others. "Are you okay?" As soon as I told him I was, his tone changed. "What was all that about? Did you really think you'd get away? You would just have gotten a ticket if you'd pulled over. I'm afraid you're in a lot more trouble now."

"I wasn't trying to run away from your officers," I said. "The accelerator in the car stuck. I couldn't stop. You really should check it out. Remember I told you about getting some information that was going to rock your case? I think someone didn't want me to make it back."

Sergeant French let us take our hands down and we all stepped away from the car. He stared at Mason's tai chi outfit. "How does he fit into the picture?"

"He doesn't," I said. I was a little out of it from the shock of everything and started to babble that Mason was a high-level attorney from L.A. and a tai chi expert who needed to recover from a family party and had come to the beach to do some tai chi. Mason threw me a concerned look and said he'd take over.

"When I saw Molly get out of the car, it was a natural instinct to come over and help her."

Sergeant French called over one of his

officers and told him to check out the accelerator. Then he turned his attention back to me. "Okay, now why would someone not want you to make it back, and from where?"

He had his friendly face on, but I knew he was probably thinking "Humor the crazy amateur sleuth." Mason nodded. "Molly, I'm curious, too. What's going on?"

We were interrupted by the officer Sergeant French had sent to look over Adele's car.

"Hey, Sarge, you aren't going to believe this." The uniform gave me an odd look. Sergeant French followed him. The car door was open and the officer pointed to something. Then they both knelt down. I was trying to see what they were doing and overhear their conversation. Mason reached out and touched my arm. "I'm just glad you're all right."

"You and me both," I said, remembering how I'd thought it was the end. I was sure Charlie wouldn't mind waiting a little longer.

A few moments later, Sergeant French and the other officer came back to us, both of them wearing odd expressions, and took us to the car.

"Show her what you found," the sergeant said. The officer used a stick to fold back the floor mat, which I now saw had covered part of the accelerator. A mélange of yarn with something pink and sticky mixed in was stuck on the mat. I knelt down and leaned in to get a closer look. The smell gave it away.

"Bubble gum?" I said with surprise.

"Yes, somehow the bubble gum and that yarn mess got caught under there. The mat must have moved when you were driving and held the pedal down. The gum and yarn obviously came from the backseat. There are balls of yarn all over the place and an open bag of bubble gum.

"But don't you see? That didn't just happen. Someone did it to the floor mat," I protested.

Mason was all business now. "What my client is trying to say is that she has good reason to think that someone deliberately placed that glob so the floor mat would stick to the pedal."

"Thanks for your input, counselor, but I'd really like to hear why Ms. Pink is so sure someone wants to harm her."

Was there any way I could explain what I'd been trying to do so it didn't sound ridiculous? I took a deep breath and decided to give it my best shot. I said I thought Sergeant French was right that Izabelle had been meeting somebody on the beach. I explained the e-mails from the Identical Twins Anonymous sponsor. "It seems the whole point of the group is for identical twins who are having problems with being identical twins. Izabelle changed her appearance so she wouldn't be identical anymore. She never even mentioned her sister was her twin in the memoir piece she wrote in one of the workshops. The e-mail made it sound like there was something she was going to do this weekend that involved her twin," I said.

"So, you're saying you think her twin was on the beach with her?" Sergeant French said. To my surprise, he was actually paying attention to what I was saying.

I nodded. "Her twin would know about her peanut allergy and probably that she had an EpiPen with her. And since Izabelle didn't like her twin, there's a good chance the feeling was mutual. Who better to feed her sister the peanut butter-laced s'more?" Sergeant French put up his hand.

"Sorry, Ms. Pink, I still don't buy it that the woman was killed with a s'more. But them meeting on the beach, one way or the other, seems reasonable."

I shrugged off his critique of my murder plan and continued. "Because of the e-mail from the Twins Anonymous guy, I began to think her twin might be here. But how to figure out who was her twin?" I asked if I could retrieve the crochet book and the manila envelope, and he gave his okay. I opened to the page with the doll model and repeated what the gray-haired woman had told me about the doll probably being made from a photo of a real little girl.

"I thought there was a good chance the doll was made from a photograph of Izabelle when she was around five years old." I mentioned remembering the photo of the missing child I'd seen on the milk carton and how it had gotten me thinking. I swallowed, then told him about my plan to get the photo in the book age-progressed. I went over my phone search to find the photo studio. To my surprise, Sergeant French's face lit up with interest.

"What an interesting idea," he said. He noticed the manila envelope in my hand, and before I could react, he'd taken it and was pulling out the photo. He might have been actually taking me seriously until then, but when he saw the picture, he seemed as if he didn't know how to react. Finally he tried to speak, but choked on a laugh.

"Okay, maybe the execution didn't work out quite right," I said, wincing at the print that clearly just looked like a freaky doll head. Mason had his hand over his mouth, no doubt to hide his grin.

"But the idea could work," Sergeant French said, taking the book from my arm. He studied the photograph of the doll. "The features and head shape do seem as though they were based on a real child. With the right software it could be very interesting. I have access to the real deal," he said. "I'll have to try to pull some strings, seeing it's Sunday afternoon, but I know somebody who owes me a favor."

"You mean you're really going to try to do age progression on the doll?"

His face took on a wary expression. "But if my picture turns out like yours, then it never happened, got it?" I nodded in agreement and he glanced toward the car. "I'm not saying someone did that to the mat. People don't use bubble gum and yarn to sabotage a car. They use bombs and cut brake lines." Sergeant French measured his words. "But I'll acknowledge someone could have. I'm going to err on the side of caution and assume someone did try to sabotage the car, and suggest that you stay low until I get back. The twin could have heard what you were doing and realized the altered photo could identify her." He turned to Mason. Do you think you can keep her hidden? Let them think she's over a cliff somewhere and they're home free."

"I think that can be arranged," Mason said. "There's a chapel just inside the grounds. No one would see us in there. They're all still tied up with the workshops."

"Then you really believe me about the s'mores and the twin and — ?" I said in surprise.

Sergeant French put up his hand, interrupting me. "Don't get too carried away. I'm limiting what I believe to the fact somebody might have put the gum and yarn together and stuck them to the floor mat, but that's it."

A cop carrying a roll of yellow tape came toward the car as Mason and I walked quickly toward the boardwalk. A few people on the beach had stopped when I'd first landed there, but by now they'd realized there was nothing going on and had drifted off. The path into the conference grounds was empty. I had passed the chapel building numerous times, but never noticed it until now. We slipped in the door and found a pew and sat down.

I thanked Mason for all his help. He was concerned that I was still shaky from my afternoon almost-disaster. I insisted I was fine, but then, out of nowhere, the strain of everything hit and I started to cry. I have to say Mason has always come through in a crisis, whether it's getting me a frozen lemonade to soothe my injuries after I confronted a murderer for the first time, or rescuing me when my mother turned my living room into a rehearsal hall when she was getting ready for her big audition. He came through again and put his arm around me in a reassuring manner and reminded me I was safe. Now that Sergeant French had taken over, I could just relax.

It might have worked if my cell phone hadn't started to play its musical flourish. I tried to swallow my tears as I answered in a whisper.

"Why are you talking so softly?" Barry asked. Without waiting for me to answer, he said, "Okay, what's wrong, babe?"

"Duck," Mason said suddenly, pointing toward the window. Two people were going by, and I recognized Spenser and his lady companion. Mason and I both slid onto the floor, and I held my breath while we waited to see if they came into the chapel.

"Was that Mason?" Barry said, his voice changing from concern to irritation. "How is it every time I call, you're with him? And why is he telling you to duck?"

"I guarantee we aren't having fun," I said.

"And you've been crying." Barry's voice changed back to concern. "What's wrong?"

I had been hoping to avoid talking to him until everything was settled, but no such luck. I told him the whole story. Almost the whole story. I left out the out-of-control car ride. I didn't think I could talk about it yet without falling apart. I could practically hear Barry hitting his forehead with the heel of his hand when I got to the part about the doll's head. I knew he was about to say something about me being really around the bend this time, so I got it in that we were hiding while Sergeant French tried to get the doll's face aged.

"Are you sure that cop is really doing that, and not just humoring you?" Barry said.

"I'm telling you, as we speak, he's calling in favors because he thinks my plan might work." Mason looked at me with a concerned shake of his head and gestured for me to hand him the phone.

"Our girl did good," Mason said into the phone. I wasn't sure if I liked being called "our girl," and I just bet Barry wasn't that thrilled with it, either. Though I did like the way Mason told Barry again how Sergeant French had actually listened to what I'd said. I wasn't quite as happy when Mason told Barry about the car ride. I could tell Barry interrupted.

"Yes, yes, she's really all right," Mason said. "I was on the beach when the car hit the sand. Just by chance I was there to do my tai chi. She was kind of shaken up, so the police officer suggested I stay with her." I just bet Barry didn't care for that last part, either. "But you know our girl, she bounces right back."

Mason handed the phone back to me, and Barry must have asked me five times if I was okay. Then he wanted to know why I'd left out that part of the story.

"I wasn't ready to talk about it. I wasn't sure —" My voice began to quaver, and I heard the frustration in Barry's breath.

"My God, Molly, what have you gotten involved with this time?" Then he caught himself and his voice softened. "I wish I was there to make it all right." I wished he was, too. After thinking I might never see him again, I wanted to throw my arms around him and tell him how much he meant to me. I could have done the last part, but it didn't feel comfortable with an audience. There were more frustrated-sounding breaths coming from Barry. "I'm just glad you're all right. I guess this isn't the best time to give the news I was calling about."

My stomach clenched. "What now?" I said a little too loudly and then repeated it in a whisper.

"Remember the things I mentioned that kept showing up in your house? This afternoon when I stopped over, there were some chairs and one of those climbing things for cats along with the boxes. I heard some noise and checked the house. Someone was sleeping in your son's room."

"Don't tell me it was Goldilocks," I said with a mirthless laugh.

"Wrong sex," Barry said. "It was Samuel, and when I questioned him about what was going on, he said he'd lost his place and moved back home. He was waiting for the right moment to tell you. I told him I didn't think that moment existed, and he should just call you, but . . . Well, neither of your sons exactly listens to me. And the cats. None of his roommates would take them, and Samuel didn't think you would mind."

I took it all in without comment. Barry finally added that he hadn't noticed a lot of hunks of fur around the house, which he took to mean the dogs and cats were okay with each other. This was the awkward part with Barry. He was in a circle separate from the one shared by my sons and me. Barry was trying to be protective, but my sons knew that my house was always their home, too. For now there was nothing I could do, anyway.

When I hung up the phone, I looked at my watch. I hoped Sergeant French would hurry; the workshops would be ending soon. We'd moved back up into the pew since the grounds seemed empty. Finally I couldn't take sitting anymore, and got up and started to pace.

After what seemed like eternity, but was probably around an hour, Sergeant French walked in the door, holding the book and a manila envelope.

I stared at it as he held it out. "It turned out better than your photo, though that isn't necessarily saying much." I opened the envelope and took out the print.

"That's who it is," I said, shoving it back. "C'mon, the whole group should be at the bonfire pit by now."

I walked on ahead, still holding the envelope. Commander and his workshop had set up a cheese tray arranged around a group of Japanese eggplants carved to look like penguins. He was circulating through the group holding a bottle of red and a bottle of white to refill their plastic cups. As I moved into the crowd, I noticed that Sergeant French stayed off in the shadow.

No doubt his plan was to move in at the right moment. Several tai chi enthusiasts immediately surrounded Mason.

Commander Blaine poured some red into Miss Lavender Pants's glass as I reached the center of the crowd. I pulled out the photo and Commander glanced over at it.

"Whoever took that doesn't have much of a future in photography," he said, shaking his head with dismay. "What a terrible picture. It barely looks like Nora Franklyn."

At the sound of her name, Nora looked up. "What picture?" she said, stepping away from Bennett and pushing through the people as she approached me.

I turned toward Sergeant French, expecting him to be moving in to question her, but he was still in the back.

"I never had that photograph taken. Where did you get it?" Nora demanded.

I took out the book and showed her the page with the doll model, and Nora's mouth fell open. She stared at the doll and then looked at the book's cover. "I don't understand. What was Izabelle Landers doing with that doll?"

"Are you sure you don't understand?" I said, watching her reactions. "You have the same doll, don't you?"

Nora just glared at me and didn't answer.

If Sergeant French wasn't going to take advantage of this opportunity, I certainly was. By now the whole group had stopped their conversations and were watching us.

"Izabelle Landers was your twin, wasn't she? You're the one who was on the beach with her. You knew about her peanut allergy and you got her to eat the peanut butter–laced s'more, and then you walked away and left her as the allergic reaction kicked in."

Nora's face had gone white and she appeared shocked. "Izabelle was Nina?" she said in a daze. She looked at the photograph on the back of the book. "We were identical twins. What did she do to herself?"

Miss Lavender Pants stared at Nora, studying her face. "I'm guessing she got her lips injected with that plump-up stuff. Probably some cheekbone implants, a nose job for sure." Her eyes moved to Nora's chest. "I guess both of you skipped the boob job."

Nora gave her a withering look as I continued. "I know you two didn't get along." I mentioned the memoir piece Izabelle had written about the orange soda incident.

Nora took a deep breath, and as she began to recover, she got defensive. "It wasn't my fault we didn't get along. She took the orange soda and everything else she could

313

from me. She didn't like being a twin and she blamed it on me. Not that it's any of your business, but our parents got a divorce right after those dolls were made. I think Nina blamed that on me, too. We went to live with our father, who never could keep us straight. Personally, I was relieved when she walked out of my life. I can't believe she was living in Tarzana all this time and I didn't know it." As Nora got more in charge of herself, she glared at me. "But kill Nina — are you out of your mind? She was mean as a snake to me, but she was still my sister." She glanced around at everyone staring at her. "And I can prove it. I'm allergic to peanuts, too. If I had handled something with peanut butter on it, I would have had an allergic reaction, too. Even if I'd shot myself with an EpiPen, I'd have needed follow-up emergency care. If you don't believe me, ask my husband."

Bennett came forward and said it was true, then started to describe Nora's attempt to get the airline employee to insist that nobody on the plane eat anything with peanuts. He looked at me with contempt.

Nora broke in. "The smell alone is enough to give me a sneezing attack. I need to know the ingredients of everything before I eat it or use it on my body." Now the scene at the airport all made sense.

"Wow, so I was right. This was a mystery weekend after all," the woman in the turquoise earrings said, starting to applaud. I ignored her comment, wondering how I could have been so wrong.

"But somebody sabotaged the car. Somebody didn't want this picture to surface." I looked toward the edge of the crowd and saw that Sergeant French had disappeared.

Adele burst through her group. "Pink, what did you do to my car?"

CHAPTER 24

"Pink, running isn't going to make it go away," Adele said, following me as I skulked to the administration building. No wonder Sergeant French had abandoned me. I had egg on my face and down to my shoes. Only the woman who still thought it was a mystery weekend had seemed satisfied. Nora had added that my accusations were heartless, and she threw in a few comments about how poorly the retreat had been run and said they were leaving. I was a little surprised when Bennett confronted her and said he could understand if she wanted to leave, but he wasn't going to abandon his actors. Everyone else had looked on with discomfort. Mason, in an effort to save the day, suggested an extra tai chi session. The crowd seemed anxious to get away from all the discord and abandoned their wineglasses, eagerly following him.

The lobbylike interior of the administration building was empty except for the person behind the registration desk. Someone had left the TV on and I glanced at the happy wedding scene on the screen, which seemed at complete odds with how I felt as I flopped into one of the overstuffed chairs.

"Well, Pink," Adele said, standing over me. "What are you going to do about my car?" Dinah came through the door and rushed over and hugged me with sympathy. She assured me that Mason's tai chi session would work wonders to smooth things over. That's the great thing about a good friend. She didn't sit and lecture me on my mistakes, but just stepped in to help.

I put my face in my hands, thinking what a mess things were. Maybe Sergeant French was right. Who would sabotage a car with bubblegum and yarn, or murder somebody with a s'more? The line kept going through my mind. I thought back to the tai chi group and felt my stomach clench as I pictured Adele's car stuck on the beach, surrounded by yellow tape. I started to get up. "Mason can't take them to the beach."

Dinah gestured for me to sit and said he was doing the session on the patio area outside of the Scripps building. I leaned back in the chair, and tried to forget about everything for a moment. It was useless; the background music on the TV swelled, and grabbed my attention. The happy music was annoying under the circumstances, and I got up to turn it off. Adele protested.

"This is my favorite part. Wait until they cut the first piece of wedding cake," Adele protested. After what had happened to her car, I figured it would be a good idea to humor her, so I stood with my hand over the power button as the bride and groom did a whole number with the piece of cake while the three of us watched. Dinah made a *yuck* sound as I stared at the screen.

All of a sudden the inflection of Sergeant French's line that kept going over in my mind changed. "I was wrong," I said.

"You can say that again," Adele said. "Mrs. Shedd is going to realize what a mistake she made giving you the rhinestone clipboard when she hears the mess you made. And you're still not dealing with my car."

"No, no, that's not what I meant," I said, turning off the TV. "I was wrong about Nora. I just figured out who was on the beach with Izabelle and what happened."

"Pink, haven't you made enough of a mess?" Adele shook her head and tsk-tsked a few times at me.

"Maybe, but I think I can fix it. But I need

318

your help." I nodded at Dinah and Adele. "I need both of your help."

Dinah was in right away, but Adele held back.

"I can't do it without you," I said to Adele. "You're the key."

"Me?" she said, standing a little taller. "Hmm, so I'm the key. Well, all I can say is it's about time you realized my importance. Okay, Nancy Jessica Drew Fletcher Pink, I'm in."

With the tai chi session over, our group headed for the dining hall. I watched from behind one of the tall Monterey pines as people began to congregate by the entrance, waiting for the dinner bell and the opening of the dining hall. I was relieved to see that the key players were all there. Dinah and Adele came down the stairs from the deck outside the administration building and walked toward the waiting group. The sound of their arguing got everyone's attention.

"I'm telling you, Pink is the one responsible for the mess in my car. It's her fault the floor mat stuck to the accelerator. I mean, if she was going to chew bubble gum, couldn't she have at least wrapped it in some paper before she threw it on the floor? She must have thrown some of the yarn down there, too," Adele said with a toss of her head.

Dinah bristled. "Molly doesn't even chew bubble gum, and if she did, she certainly wouldn't throw it on the floor. Adele, it's your car. The bubble gum and yarn on the floor were yours. Accept the responsibility."

"No way, Jose," Adele said. "And I'm going to prove it." She took on a huffy stance that was a little too convincing, and I began to wonder if she'd forgotten they weren't really arguing. Adele did have a habit of getting carried away.

"This ought to be good," Dinah said, throwing in an eye roll and a hand on her hip.

Adele took a defiant stance. "I'm going down to the beach before the tow truck comes, and I'm going to get that blob of bubble gum and yarn. Pink's saliva is on that gum, saliva with her DNA. A good friend of my boyfriend, the famous children's author, will be glad to do a test on it for me."

"So long as you send a sample of your DNA with it, so he can see that it was really you who chewed the gum," Dinah said, pretending not to be aware that the dinner waiters were watching.

"Don't worry, I'm going to send along samples from the other presenters, so when

Pink's DNA matches, she can't claim it was fixed. I got the plastic wineglasses and marked the names on them." Adele sounded extremely proud of herself, which I knew wasn't an act. I hoped nobody really thought about that last part, and realized it would have been impossible to do. There was more of an interchange between them, but I didn't hear it. I had slipped from behind the tree and was on my way to the beach.

I heard the dinner bell ring as I crouched on the passenger side of the car, away from view. The yellow tape had broken loose and was flapping in the breeze.

I felt the vibration of footsteps in the sand and swallowed hard as my body tensed. I could feel them getting closer and my heart rate kicked up. But when a hand touched my shoulder, my heart almost jumped out of my chest.

"I didn't mean to scare you," Dinah said, reading my panicked body language. "But I couldn't leave you here alone." I waved for her to get down and put my finger to my lips. She'd barely hit the sand when we began to feel the vibrations of footsteps. They quickly grew in intensity and then they stopped. We both swallowed hard. This was definitely it.

The car rocked as the driver's window

shattered. There was more noise and motion as something pushed through the glass and the door was unlocked. The two of us popped up like jack-in-the-boxes just as the car door opened. I knew who we were going to see. Sergeant French was probably right. Most people wouldn't think to use bubblegum and yarn to make an accelerator stick. But most people didn't work on a TV show where the hero's claim to fame was that he used everyday things in unusual ways. Bennett was already leaning over the seat toward the gas pedal. When he saw us, he jumped back.

"Ladies," he said, actually making it sound like he was glad to see us. He was certainly good on his feet. "I heard you talking up by the dining hall. I thought I'd come down and see if I could help," he said, as if we wouldn't notice the broken window.

"I don't think so," I said as I walked around to the other side of the car. "I know what you did. I know how you did it. I'm just not sure why you did it."

"I don't know what you're talking about." Then he leaned down and pulled out the wad of gum and yarn and threw it toward the water. It made a splash as it hit. "I'll be going now," he said, but Dinah ordered him to halt.

Bennett began to laugh. "What are you two going to do, tie me up with your shoe-laces?"

Dinah and I didn't say anything. Bennett thought he was home free, but he didn't know what was coming up behind him. We could see what was going to happen before he did. Suddenly a pouch bag slapped him in the cheek, swung out and came back and hit him again. "You? You're the one who wrecked my car," Adele yelled like a banshee, swinging the purple bag harder as Bennett tried to shield his face, yelping with pain. Adele kept swinging the bag, and no matter how he moved his hands, he couldn't avoid injury. When he tried to leave, she was on him like cream cheese on a bagel, and he couldn't get away. I had never realized Adele had such a good arm.

Bennett wasn't the only one who could use everyday things for extraordinary purposes. Dinah and I raided the backseat and took out a one-pound skein of burgundy worsted yarn and began winding it around and around his legs. Not giving up, he tried to hop away while still trying to get hold of the pouch bag. He didn't know who he was dealing with. Adele kept winding her arm and the bag kept eluding his grasp.

"You women are crazy! What are you doing now?" an angry voice said. When I looked up, Nora was jogging across the sand toward us.

Adele stopped swinging the pouch bag, but held it at the ready.

"What do you have in there, rocks?" Bennett asked, massaging his chin.

"As a matter of fact, I do," Adele said. "I found some pretty ones on the beach and there's my cell phone, too."

"Enough chit-chat. Is somebody going to tell me what's going on? And for heaven's sake unwrap his legs," Nora barked.

I looked at Bennett. "Are you going to tell her, or should I?"

He grunted. "I've got nothing to say."

"In that case," I said, getting my thoughts in order. But Adele beat me to the punch.

"He not only broke the window of my precious car, but it's his fault Pink ended up driving my car on the beach. Will you look at it? I wonder if it will ever work again." Adele went over and stroked her car.

Nora looked at Bennett strangely. "You didn't do that, did you?" Then she reconsidered. "Don't say anything."

"There's nothing to say. You can't prove that I did anything to the car, or that anybody else did, for that matter. The evidence is gone out to sea. And that ridiculous story about the s'more . . ." Bennett said.

"We saw you smash the car window," Dinah said.

This time Nora spoke. "We'll pay for the window. I'm sure it was just a mistake. We'll pay for several windows. Now undo him this instant, or I'm calling the police." She had her cell phone in her hand.

Dinah and I looked at each other. Before we could tell her to go ahead, I saw a police car park along Sunset, and a moment later Sergeant French trudged across the sand toward us.

Nora rushed over to him. "Thank heavens you're here. Those women tied up my husband." Bennett said something similar, and suggested we should be arrested. No one could say he didn't have nerve.

Sergeant French surprised me by asking me what was going on, then listening carefully as I told him the scenario with the s'more and Bennett breaking the window and tossing the wad of gum and yarn into the water to cover up what he'd done.

Bennett laughed it off and said, "I'm afraid Ms. Pink got carried away with her amateur sleuthing." He looked to Sergeant French, appearing to expect some kind of agreement. Instead, the police officer took out his handcuffs and slapped them on Bennett.

"What?" Bennett said in shock.

"Do you know who he is?" Nora demanded.

Sergeant French nodded. "I know exactly what name to put on the arrest report. For now, you're under arrest for vandalizing the Honda. But I'm confident you'll also be charged with attempted murder and murder."

"He got rid of the evidence," I said in a low voice. "Your people took samples before, right? Now they'll know whose DNA to match it with."

"Thanks for the suggestion, Ms. Pink. Don't worry, we're professionals." He pointed toward the flapping yellow tape on the car. "I had my forensic people go over the car thoroughly when I was here before. They took a sample of the glop under the accelerator along with everything else before they released the car."

This time Bennett didn't smile. I noticed Mason had joined our group on the beach, though he had stayed several steps back.

Even though Sergeant French made sure Bennett knew his rights, being handcuffed did something to him. He totally lost his cool and began to babble. "I did it for you," he said, looking at his wife. He turned to the rest of us. "All these years Nora has stayed by my side. She's managed my career and seen me as a star when I knew I was just a working actor who most people barely recognize. We've been through a lot together. I've had my lapses, and she's always forgiven me. I had to protect her."

Nora tried to silence him and when she noticed Mason, tried to secure his services on the spot, but Mason declined and Bennett kept talking.

"It was all a plan. When Izabelle asked for help with her presentation, it was just a reason to get me alone." He paused as if he expected understanding.

"You could have kept your pants on," Dinah said with disgust.

Bennett shrugged her comment off. "What can I say — I'm weak. When a woman offers herself up, I'm accommodating. When we met again the next morning, I saw the photo of the doll in her book and recognized it as the same doll Nora has. When I confronted her, she admitted she was my wife's twin. She said our relationship would be our own little secret, but I didn't buy it. I knew the cruel things she'd done to my wife when they were kids. She took everything my wife valued. You don't know how devious she was." He detailed how while his wife had not known where her sister was, Izabelle knew everything about Nora's life. He spoke directly to his wife. "It seemed to bother her that you had married your way into Hollywood and had stayed married for a long time. She'd been dumped by three husbands. To me our tryst was just a lapse, but she wanted it to be the beginning of something. At the very least I was sure she would throw it in your face. I couldn't let her devastate you that way."

He said he'd appeared to go along with her plan and arranged the meeting on the beach. He knew about Izabelle's peanut allergy.

I couldn't help myself as I interrupted. "And I know how you did it."

All eyes went from him to me. "I saw a snippet of a wedding on a TV show. The bride cut the first piece of wedding cake and fed it to the groom, and then they kissed and frosting got all over both of their faces as the cake traveled back and forth." A low hum of *yuck* went through the group. "That's how you got her to eat the s'more. Well, eat is the wrong word, isn't it? You got it into her system. You bit off a piece and then kissed her. Tongues and all."

Dinah muttered something about it really

being the kiss of death.

Bennett said nothing, but there was just a flicker in his expression that made it clear I'd hit on the truth. "You probably removed the pouch bag at the same time, or maybe even in advance, and then threw it out of sight. And then you cold-bloodedly walked away."

Tears were streaming down Nora's face. Bennett kept silent, but I talked on. "You knew about the doll in the photo and overheard what I was planning to do. You didn't want me to find out Izabelle was your wife's twin because you knew that I didn't believe Izabelle's death was an accident. And that once I knew your wife was her twin, suspicion would fall on her. But that wasn't your real concern, was it? She had the alibi of not being able to handle peanut butter without it being a problem. But you were afraid once suspicion was off her, it might go onto you. You were afraid I might figure it out. And I did," I said with a little pride in my voice.

One of Sergeant French's colleagues led Bennett off the beach toward the police car parked on the street. He told Adele he'd arranged to have her car towed to a repair shop. She told him to talk to me.

The sergeant turned to me, and I spoke

first. "Thanks for showing up. When I left the message, I knew it sounded kind of strange, and after the whole thing with the doll's head — well, I wasn't sure if —"

Sergeant French's face broke out in an understanding smile. "I would show up," he said, finishing my thought. "This has been one strange case. We don't get a lot of murders up here, and they're usually by gunshot or stabbing. Never by s'more." He paused as if considering what he was going to say. "The truth is, Ms. Pink, I wasn't going to come. Frankly, when I heard you had set up some kind of sting, I wanted to steer clear of it. But I got a call. Detective Greenberg said sometimes the things you did seemed off the wall, but more often than not, you turned out to be right. I take it he's a friend of yours?"

Barry was much more than a friend, though I was still working on his exact title. I couldn't believe what he'd done. It meant more than all the sweet talk in the world. After all his telling me to leave it to the professionals and to stay out of investigations, he'd vouched for my ability. I felt a blush rise. I had some heavy-duty thank-yous to give him when I got back.

CHAPTER 25

"See, the man who likes you isn't a murderer," I said to Dinah as we headed away from the beach. Adele was just behind and wrapped in the afterglow of her pouch bag swirling.

"Wow, that was really something," Adele said. "Did you see how I detained the perp with my bag?" She caught up and put an arm around each of us. "Hey, you guys, we're like the Three Musketeers."

The purple pouch bag was hung across her chest and bounced as we walked. I was amazed to see how well it had come through its new purpose. One of the petals on the chartreuse yarn flower appeared a little smashed, but other than that it looked no worse for wear.

Sheila walked toward us as we stepped onto the boardwalk. Dinah put an arm around her and she joined us.

"Okay, maybe we're the Four Musketeers," Adele said in a surprisingly generous gesture. As we continued on through the dunes to the Asilomar grounds, Adele was already planning our Musketeer future. "The pouch bags can be our insignia," she said in a happy voice. As we stepped into the peaceful grounds of the conference center, Adele stopped abruptly and threw her arms around me in a hug. "Pink, thanks for letting me be part of the action."

When she'd released me, she grabbed Sheila's hand. "C'mon, let's get ready for the party. We can do each other's hair."

Just before they walked away, Adele mentioned that now that her car was not functional, she and Sheila needed another way to get themselves home, along with all the things they'd carted up there for the retreat.

"Do the problems ever end?" Dinah said, giving me a sympathetic pat on the shoulder. "I've got to find my writers and make sure they're ready for their big moment at the gathering." Figuring they might still be at dinner, she took off for the dining hall.

I stopped into the administration building to pick up the rhinestone clipboard and took the moment alone to call Barry. I was disappointed to get his voice mail. What I had to say didn't work for a message, so I told him all was well and I'd try him again later. As I stepped out onto the deck, a cab pulled up below and CeeCee and Eduardo got out. With everything that had gone on, I'd forgotten she and the cover model crocheter had promised to come when their respective commitments were done. For a moment CeeCee glanced around, and it was hard to tell if she was taking in the untamed beauty of the tall pine trees and the wild growth underneath or if she was looking for paparazzi. Knowing the actress–reality host–Tarzana Hooker leader, it was most likely the photographers.

They both looked up as I started down the stairs. We exchanged greetings, and before I'd reached the last step, CeeCee had begun talking.

"I hope I packed the right things. Of course, it's only overnight, but I was expecting something different. This doesn't look like a heels sort of place." She glanced down at the small suitcase Eduardo was holding along with his. "As soon as the charity event was over, I met up with Eduardo and we came up here," CeeCee said. She apologized again for having to cancel out at the last minute, but assured me her presence at the fund-raiser had made a big difference. She looked like she had gone directly from the event to the airport. Her soft brown hair was freshly done, and she was dressed in a red pantsuit with gold trim and wearing heels. Eduardo looked extra tan, as if he'd been sprayed with something to make him appear to have been kissed by the sun for his photo shoot. It was a good bet the color extended under the soft green tee shirt he wore with the tan suede jacket. I'd seen some of the covers he'd done, and he was all rippling muscles and six-pack abs.

"I'm sure Bennett did fine in my place," she said.

"I think he did a lot more than you planned," I said, getting right to the point. I was too tired from all that had happened to ease into the story. "Bennett's under arrest and on his way to the police station right now. He's going to be charged with vandalizing Adele's car, trying to kill me, and killing Izabelle Landers."

CeeCee's mouth fell open. "Oh dear! What happened?" I tried to stick with the main points and began with the fog delaying everything and the fact Bennett's wife and Izabelle were twins. Izabelle recognized Nora, but due to all the changes in Izabelle's appearance, Nora hadn't recognized her. I recapped how Izabelle didn't want to be a twin and had taken out her anger on her sister from the time they were kids.

"Once Izabelle found out who was taking your place, she probably started planning what she thought was going to be the ultimate hurt to her sister — taking away her husband."

"Oh dear," CeeCee repeated when I got to the part about the peanut butter–laced s'more. "I suppose it figures some of the plot ideas would rub off on him after being on *Raf Gibraltar* for so many seasons. I did a couple of guest spots playing a sitcom actress. I was in show number thirty-two, and Raf passed the antidote pills to his love interest Valerie through a kiss. And my character showed up again in show number forty-nine when Buzz helped his younger brother Raf get rid of Bradley Rogers by arranging for him to sit near the kitchen of the Tidewater Inn. Bradley was allergic to shellfish, and the smell of the boiling lobsters got into his system and sent him into whatever that shock is called," CeeCee said. "That was one of Bennett's bigger roles, and I think he was the one who picked Bradley's pocket before the meal and lifted one of those tubes that has some kind of emergency treatment in it."

"You mean an EpiPen?" I said. I told her about the crocheted pouch bag and the glow-in-the-dark yarn before I moved on to

Adele's car and my wild ride. At the end, she sighed with despair.

"I'm so sorry, Molly. If only I'd done the workshop, none of this would have happened. Well, I couldn't have stopped the fog, but if Bennett hadn't stepped in . . ."

Out of curiosity, I asked her how she'd gotten him to agree to take her place for the weekend.

The story was still sinking in for CeeCee, and she had to think a moment to remember. "Bennett runs a small theater. He's the producer, director — the works and it's his real love. It's one of those Equity waiver places — under fifty seats, so nobody has to be paid scale, or anything, for that matter. I said I would do the lead in an upcoming production. It meant something, because my name would draw attention to the play — get reviewers to show up and a lot of press coverage." She stopped and swallowed. "I guess that's all in the past for him now."

"So, what happened to the schedule? Did you cancel all the workshops?" Eduardo said.

"Izabelle died before most of the retreat people got here," I explained. "And it was too late to cancel anything. Up until Bennett's arrest, the workshops had been going

336

along as planned. I don't think most of the attendees even understand what happened." Then the realization kicked in that the actors had lost their leader just before their big performances, and I muttered, "Oh no."

"What is it, dear?" CeeCee asked. "Is there something I can do? Please, let me help." Eduardo offered his services as well. I told CeeCee about the actors and she said as soon as she checked in, she'd find the group. I told Eduardo about the crocheters needing help with blocks for the blanket Mrs. Shedd had agreed to donate. He dittoed about checking in, and said he'd get out his hook and link up with the crocheters.

Finally, I headed back to my room to change for the party. Mason passed me on the stairs. He'd already transformed from tai chi master to the person I was used to by changing into well-fitting jeans and a black cashmere turtleneck.

"Are you all right?" he said with concern. "You've had a difficult afternoon, to put it mildly." He didn't say it, but I knew I probably looked pale and horrible. I hadn't seen a mirror since morning and had been in an out-of-control car, taken a bumpy ride on the beach, had an embarrassing confrontation with Nora and another one that was at least successful with Bennett. And that didn't even count being concerned with the retreaters and their good time. I supposed if I didn't look horrible, something would have been wrong.

"How did you happen to come to the beach?" I asked.

Mason chuckled. "I think your investigating business is rubbing off. I saw Nora headed toward the beach, and I decided to follow her and see what she was up to. And if you're wondering why I didn't agree to represent Bennett, first of all, I'm off duty this weekend, but even if I was in my attorney mode, there was too much conflict of interest." He tilted his head and gazed at me in a serious mode. "Any way you look at it, you're involved in this, and to defend him I might have to try to discredit you as a witness." His eyes caught mine. "Sunshine, there was no way that was going to happen." He touched my arm in a supportive manner. "You can relax now. The murder is solved and the retreat almost over."

"*Almost* is the key word there," I said. "I told Izabelle's ex I'd help him with her belongings tomorrow. And since I wrecked Adele's car, I have to figure out a way to get Sheila and Adele and all the stuff they hauled up here back to Tarzana, and I have no budget."

"I'm sure dealing with Izabelle's ex won't be a problem, and as for the other —" He was all upbeat now. "I can solve that in a few sentences. You and I have plane tickets. We transfer them to your Hookers, and then I drive you and all the stuff back in my rental SUV." I was surprised by the offer, and after asking him several times if he was sure he wanted to do it, and he kept insisting he did, I accepted.

I said something about getting a red-eye to recharge myself, and Mason offered an alternative. He led me to the patio area behind the Scripps building. Once he made sure it was deserted, he stood facing me.

"I'm going to teach you a few tai chi movements. We'll begin with Awaken the Chi," he said, holding his palms facing up. He inhaled and raised his hands almost to eye level, turned them over and let them float down as he exhaled. He repeated it a number of times and watched as I followed him. Next he bent his arm at the wrist and had me do the same, then placed his arm against mine and began to move his arm in a circle, taking mine with him. "This is called Push Hands," he said as the move became slow and meditative. Almost like magic, all that had happened to me in the day poured out and I felt refilled with calm energy — and maybe some heat from his closeness. I glanced at Mason's face. His eyes were half closed and he appeared to be in some peaceful place. Gradually he slowed his arm to a stop and stepped away. Together we did a few more Awaken the Chi moves and finally let our arms flow down to our sides.

"Better?" he said when we'd finished. I nodded and thanked him. "That should get you through the party tonight." He gave my arm a friendly squeeze before I took off toward my room to change for the party.

When I finally saw myself in the mirror, I understood why Mason had been concerned. My hair had that stuck-your-finger-in-a-light-socket look, and I can only imagine how stressed my eyes must have looked before the tai chi, because they seemed frozen in a stunned mode. I was about to start repairing the damage when there was an insistent knock at my door.

Now what?

Adele grabbed my hand when I opened the door. "You've got to come, Pink. There's something strange going on." Sheila was standing behind her. Adele barely gave me a chance to grab my key and shut the door before leading me toward the stairs. With

Sheila in tow, I followed Adele outside and down the path. As we passed the administration building, CeeCee, Eduardo, and some other retreaters joined the parade.

Adele came to an abrupt stop in front of the low, wood shingle–covered building called Viewpoint. A sandwich board sign sat out front with a notice written in wipe-off ink that read "Special Fusion Craft Workshop."

"Somebody mustn't have gotten the message about Izabelle," I said, noticing the lights were on and there appeared to be some people inside.

Adele gestured toward me. "You're the one with the rhinestone clipboard. You better do something."

I went up the small staircase with everyone close behind me. After everything I'd been through in the last couple of days, could anything surprise me? When I looked inside the open door, my mouth fell open. Yes, something could.

A table was set up with samples of clothing and handouts as if the workshop was a go. A dress form wearing a familiar-looking jacket stood next to the table. "What's going on?" I said to the couple in the front of the room.

"I didn't know if anyone would come.

Welcome," Spenser Futterman said. His female companion pulled out a single-lens reflex and started shooting photographs.

"I'd like an explanation," I said, blinking from the flash of the camera.

"I can imagine you do," Spenser said. "First, let me introduce Marni Pottinger, who isn't really either my niece or cousin." He explained that she was a regular contributor to *Craft World* magazine and that he'd sold her editor on having her meet him at Asilomar to do an undercover story.

"Sorry for the subterfuge," Marni said, lowering her camera.

"So that's why you were talking to me," Adele said. "Are you going to use what I told you?"

Marni nodded at Adele. "I heard you thought a stitch you created was stolen, but since there isn't any proof, I'm going to have to leave it out. I will include what you said about crocheters feeling like second-class crafters. I got a nice photo of you wearing some examples of your work." She glanced at all of us. "The angle of the article is the dark side of the craft world."

"The dark side of crafts, huh? What I told you was nothing. You want to know about the real dark side?" Adele said, her voice filling with emotion. "How about this —

you could write about a stepmother who ridicules you for your craft choice and goes to your father and tells him that knitting is the queen of yarn crafts and isn't it nice how her perfect daughters all know how to knit, while his own daughter insists on sticking with her hook. Fast-forward to his birthday and the father gets a knitted sweater and some argyle socks that he goes on and on about how superior they are to the blanket his own daughter crocheted with her ten-year-old fingers."

We all stood in stunned silence. I don't think Adele realized a tear had rolled down her cheek. I had never seen her cry, and she almost never let down her defenses. Now her crochet craziness made sense. It went along with her Cinderella-without-the-happy-ending life story. CeeCee, Eduardo, Sheila and I all looked at each other and moved around Adele, doing a group hug. She seemed suddenly embarrassed.

"You didn't think I was talking about me, did you?" She quickly wiped her eyes. "That's just what happened to some little girl who lives down the street from me." She looked at Marni. "Forget I even brought it up." She waved at Marni to proceed. After an awkward moment, Marni mentioned the real focus of her story — Izabelle Landers.

Spenser took the floor to explain. "I'm an accountant by profession, but my passion is crochet and I came up with an idea for a fusion craft." He explained he'd made notes and come up with patterns for a book. He'd met Izabelle at Commander Blaine's office and mailing center. Spenser knew she'd come out with a crochet book and thought she might have some advice on how to get a book on his new craft published. He had given her a rough idea of his book to look over, but she'd returned it and said there was nothing she could suggest, and discouraged him from proceeding. "When I heard she had a book coming out about a fusion craft, I got it. She'd ripped me off. I came here to confront her, but she kept avoiding me." He glanced at the floor. "I'm not proud of it, but I snuck in Izabelle's room to borrow a copy of her manuscript. I wanted to show it to Marni so she could compare it with what I'd written." He said he was going to get an attorney who handled plagiarism issues as soon as he got back to Tarzana. I looked at the jacket in the front of the room and realized why it looked familiar. It resembled the one in Izabelle's closet. No wonder Marni had photographed it. It was one more piece of proof that Izabelle had stolen Spenser's idea. I noticed that Spenser didn't mention his second trip to Izabelle's room. I just let it be.

I stepped closer to examine the jacket, but couldn't find any knitting on it and finally asked him why there was no knitting.

"Why would it have knitting?" he said, seeming perplexed. I mentioned the title of Izabelle's book, *The Needle and the Hook.* His face relaxed into a smile. "The hook is for crochet and the needle is for sewing. I called my book *The Hook and Eye,* as in eye of the needle. He took the jacket off the dress form and showed how the body of the jacket was fabric, but the sleeves and trim around the neck were crochet.

After that, everyone started talking. Adele wanted to make sure the photo of her was flattering. Eduardo wanted to tell Marni how tough it was being taken seriously as a crocheter. CeeCee wanted to make sure there was no mention of her in the article. She tried to avoid any negative press. And I looked at my watch and shrieked. I still had hair that looked like it had been electrified, and it was almost time for the grand finale of the weekend.

It turned out I wasn't the only one with some final preparations to do for the party, and after inviting Spenser and Marni to join the gathering, everyone quickly dispersed.

CHAPTER 26

No fog or misty sky this time as I stepped outside Lodge and headed for Merrill Hall. The sky was a brilliant orange and the trees had turned into silhouettes. I had done some quick work with a hairbrush, put on fresh makeup, and changed into the black jean outfit I had worn for my dinner with Mason. Now that the mystery of the fusion craft and just who Spenser and Marni were was settled, all the loose ends had been taken care of. I suddenly felt bittersweet that the upcoming party was the last official event of the weekend.

Merrill Hall was a meeting hall–auditorium and one of the original structures from the YWCA camp days. The building had the Arts and Crafts signature of dark wood and liberal use of local stones. But this time all the dark wood didn't seem moody or brooding. It was amazing what the warm color of the sunset could do.

Maybe the warmth of the people helped, too.

Our group was too small for the main area, so we were using the open space at the back of the building. As I walked inside, I let out an automatic *Wow!* Commander and his group had outdone themselves. I suppose if there was a theme to their work, it was what we did over the weekend.

Commander was hovering over the long table set up under the windows. He and his group were setting out the last of the decorations on the burgundy tablecloth. Napkins folded into swan shapes were lined up at the back of the table. Palm trees fashioned out of crookneck squash with fronds made from cucumber peels were scattered around the eggplant penguins and sheep made out of cauliflower, with black olive heads and grape stem legs. Was there supposed to be a theme to the decorations? The only thing they had in common was that they didn't belong together. But they were fun anyway. Small paper plates and plastic silverware had been artfully arranged to the side. Commander had taken a watermelon and cut the rind so it looked like a basket. The red interior had been scooped out and mixed with other fruit to make a colorful salad. There were trays of little cream puffs. Some trays were marked "Savory" and some were marked "Sweet." They smelled buttery and freshly made, and my stomach gurgled, reminding me I'd missed another meal, this time thanks to my sting on the beach.

A large punch bowl surrounded by handled cups sat at the end of the table. I hadn't seen punch with frozen strawberries and scoops of orange sherbet floating in ginger ale since I'd been a kid. A woman placed an index card attached to a piece of driftwood next to each food item, listing the ingredients. I guess after the whole peanut thing, they were being extra careful.

"Taste the cream puffs," Commander said, noticing me looking them over. He sounded a little nervous, but mostly excited. This get-together was the climax of his workshops. "They're so simple to make and such a crowd-pleaser." He waited while I tasted one from the Savory side. It was so delicious, I sighed. The filling was sour cream with a garnish of black caviar. He gestured toward the Sweet side, and I took one of those. The flavorful puff was filled with pieces of strawberry topped with whipped cream. Commander beamed with pride when I told him I wanted his recipe.

He left to join the rest of his team. They

were all wearing green Asilomar tee shirts and were arranging chairs, putting on music, adjusting the lighting and setting up areas so each of the groups could sit together.

Over the weekend, the groups had bonded, and already I'd heard e-mail lists had been circulated so they could get together again.

People were filtering in, and a number of them stopped to tell me how much they had enjoyed the workshops. The woman with the turquoise earrings waited until it was just the two of us. "My husband and I really enjoyed this weekend." She was in Dinah's group, and she indicated her husband, who was wearing one of the green tee shirts and working alongside Commander as they arranged chairs. She leaned close to me. "I should have guessed who did it. Of course, you'd hire an actor to play that part." She looked around. "Where is he? I'd like to compliment him on his performance."

I realized it was useless to tell her it wasn't an act. I wished it all *had* been an act, and that Izabelle and Bennett would come in now and take a bow, but that wasn't going to happen.

Jeen Wolf came in, followed by her knitters. She stopped and complimented me on how well I had dealt with catastrophes. Neither the fog nor a murder had ruined the weekend for the retreaters. The knitters, with their tote bags on their arms, marched toward some chairs. Jeen shook her head with frustration as she watched Jym working on something as he walked in. I almost choked when I saw what he was holding. He was in deep concentration as he moved his gold-toned hook through a strand of forest green yarn.

While I was trying to make out what he was working on, Adele brushed past him. Would she ever cease to surprise me? Instead of her usual wild fashions, Adele wore a long, shimmery, cream-colored shift with one of Sheila's famous scarves as an accent. The scarf had loose stitches with a mixture of yarn textures in shades of aqua, turquoise, and royal purple that had a gold thread running through it. The only Adele touch was the lavender pouch bag with white flowers. When she caught a glimpse of Jym, Adele's lips turned up in a triumphant smile and she nudged his arm, giving him a thumbs-up.

"How'd you get him to try crochet?" I said. "He seemed to be such a committed knitter."

Adele appeared proud of herself. "I have

my ways." Sheila had just caught up with her and watched as Jym stumbled over something because he was looking at his crocheting instead of where he was going.

"What's he making, anyway?"

"Well, Musketeers," Adele said, "all I had to do was appeal to his engineer's sensibility. I told him he could crochet a hyperbolic plane."

"A what?" Sheila said. Adele explained it was a geometric figure that expanded exponentially from any point on its surface, always curving away from itself. Sheila and I both looked confused by the definition.

Adele shrugged. "Ruffles. It's all about making ruffles, but it's math at the same time." We all looked at the long thing hanging off Jym's hook and got it. "I'll tell you guys all about it next time the Hookers get together."

Adele took Sheila and the other crocheters to a group of seats next to the knitters, and I was happy to see them all talking to each other. Mason came in and waved as Dinah and the writers arrived. The actors were clustered around CeeCee and seemed to move as one unit as they found some chairs. Everybody looked at Eduardo as he came in. He was used to getting that kind of attention and barely seemed to notice.

When you're very tall, with shoulder-length black hair, a face so perfect it looks like it was created by an artist and lots of muscles in all the right places, people tend to look at you. And when you sit with a bunch of yarn people and take out a hook and some crocheting, you're assured of more stares.

I felt my cell phone vibrate. I'd finally remembered to turn off the ringer. I knew the call was from Barry, and even though it wasn't the best time, I wanted to talk to him.

As I flipped the phone open, I stepped outside. It was completely dark now and the sky was filled with stars. In the distance I could hear the roar of the surf.

"Hi," I said, putting the phone to my ear. "I'm glad you called. There's something I really want to tell you."

"You do?" he said, his voice open and expectant.

"I can't thank you enough for the call to Sergeant French. And the things you said about me being right a lot of the time."

"Oh," he said, his voice deflating. "I was hoping more for something along the lines of how much you miss me and you're counting the hours until you come home."

"And that, too," I said with a smile. "I'm ready for this weekend to be over. At least if

I couldn't get through it without a dead body, the whodunit is solved." Barry wanted to know what time my plane arrived. I mentioned the change in plans. Adele had been quite happy about it. Barry didn't take it the same way.

"Just you and Mason?" he said with annoyance in his voice. I glanced in the window and realized everyone had gotten some of the food and it was time to begin the program.

"I'll tell you about everything tomorrow night when I get home. Miss you," I said before clicking off.

I stepped to the front of the room, holding the rhinestone clipboard with my notes on it.

I welcomed everyone to the gathering and smiled. "It's been quite a weekend." I paused as a smattering of comments like "You can say that again" and "That's an understatement," along with a few "Hear, hears," filled the room. "And true to being a creative event, it defied whatever plans had been made and became something different." I said I wanted to compliment all of them on how they adapted to the obstacles thrown in their way, and I had them give themselves a round of applause.

"Before we start, I'd like to have a moment of silence for Izabelle Landers." I took some time to explain who she was, since she had died before most of them had gotten there. "She'll live on in all the flowers and pouch purses her workshop group made." Everything stopped as everyone put their heads down for a few moments. Then I continued. I hadn't been quite sure how to talk about Bennett, but had to say something. "For any of you who don't know, Bennett Franklyn has been arrested and will no doubt be charged with causing Izabelle's death. Due to his legal troubles, he won't be attending the party. CeeCee Collins has generously stepped in to help the actors with their performance."

Mason came forward to begin the event. He demonstrated Awakening the Chi and had everyone do it a number of times before letting his arms float down to his sides.

I introduced the knitters next, and they filed up front with Jeen and Jym in the lead. On the count of three they all took out their baby-blankets-in-progress and showed them to the group. Although they were all a simple knit-and-purl combination, their yarns were all different colors. I noticed Jym had stowed his crochet project. Everyone applauded, and the knitters took a bow.

Adele was waving her group up before the

knitters were back to their chairs. I noticed that Sheila was holding her own with Adele and helping the group take out their projects. Everyone had completed one of the pouch purses, each with one or more six-petaled flower embellishments. Some had made additional flowers and wore them pinned to their clothes. One renegade was making an afghan. Adele nodded, and Commander flipped off the lights. The flowers took on a ghostly glow and seemed to be floating in space. There was more applause, but the crocheters didn't leave the front when the lights came back on and Adele nudged me over. As usual, I was finding out I wasn't in control of my own show.

Adele waved to Jym and Jeen and their group, then she motioned for Eduardo to come up. Jym and Jeen each carried a brown paper grocery bag. Adele described Mrs. Shedd's commitment of crocheted and knitted blankets to be donated to the local shelter.

"Our boss isn't a crafter, so she didn't get that a weekend wasn't long enough to make blankets in addition to the workshops," Adele said. My, but she loved the spotlight. She had no problem making eye contact with the crowd. "What to do, what to do?" She surveyed the crowd, trying to build up suspense. "First, I whittled it down from blankets to one blanket, but even that didn't seem possible until I came up with the perfect solution." Adele walked over to Jeen and Jym. "I reached out to my knitting sister and brother and offered a solution. A perfect solution, I might add."

Adele gestured for them to empty the paper bags while she continued on with a rising voice. "I forged an alliance, and we agreed to pool the blocks each of our groups had made and fashion them into one blanket that honored our yarn solidarity." Adele paused as a cornucopia of knitted and crocheted blocks in all different colors tumbled out and the audience cheered. She threw out her hand and pointed at Eduardo, who held a strip of blocks he'd just finished crocheting together. He gave a humble nod of his head and the audience cheered.

"Okay, Pink, I got them all worked up. I hope you can keep the momentum going," Adele said as the groups gathered up the blocks and exited the front.

I introduced Dinah and her writers. They'd all written fifty-word paragraphs about a summer memory and each read theirs. Because they were so limited by the word count, most of the pieces seemed to have a poetic quality. Dinah beamed with pride as they read.

CeeCee brought the actors to the front next, and they assumed their places. She stood off to the side, ready to prompt lines if needed, but in the short time Bennett had prepared them well. They knew their lines, and though they might have been a little too theatrical, the short play went well. Miss Lavender Pants stole the show by deciding to do her part with a Scottish accent.

Commander and his group came up last, and got applause for the evening's events and everything else they'd put on as well. Everyone descended on the food table, and the buzz of conversation got louder.

"Did you taste the puffs Commander made?" Dinah said, holding a paper plate with a selection of the sweet and savory. When I nodded, she handed me one of the savory ones anyway.

"Wow, that man is a prize," I said, checking for her reaction. Dinah's perception of Commander Blaine had changed when she thought he might be a murderer. As soon as she thought she couldn't have him, she seemed to say less about how finicky he was and more about his enthusiasm and ability to make everything into an occasion. I was afraid that now that he was out of the running to be a murderer, Dinah's interest might wane. It seems to be human nature to want something when it's unavailable and lose interest once it is. Dinah glanced over toward the table. Commander was putting out more food and encouraging everyone to help themselves. He beamed as compliments came from all directions. "Commander is a nickname he gave himself as a kid, and it stuck," Dinah said. "He told me about it this afternoon. His real name is Sylvester. I'm going to keep calling him Commander, though. Sylvester sounds like some kind of weird synthetic yarn."

I was going to comment that it seemed like they might have a future, but Commander got everyone's attention and said the evening was going to end with a sing-along and marshmallow roast at the fire circle.

I held on to the rhinestone clipboard and followed at the edge of the group. Leave it to Commander. He had tambourines, castanets, maracas and bongo drums available. He took out a guitar and began playing camp songs. Some of the people helped themselves to instruments and played along, and others just took wire forks and marshmallows. I noticed Dinah was sitting at Commander's side.

Mason found me and offered me a perfectly roasted marshmallow. "It'll be nice driving back. We can make a trip out of it. We can stop for a late lunch at the Madonna Inn and maybe at a winery in Paso Robles. There's always Solvang and Santa Barbara, too."

I laughed. "And we won't get back for a week."

Mason grinned. "What's so bad about that?"

CHAPTER 27

The morning was chilly and overcast, but the inside of the dining hall was bright with the buzz of conversation as the groups hung together for the last time. There was lots of hugging and promises to get something going back in Tarzana. Nobody seemed very interested in food. Commander Blaine had an envelope for each person that contained a coupon for his mailing center, the recipe for the puffs, and an e-mail list for the group.

I arrived late because I'd met Zak Landers in Izabelle's room. Originally, I was going to pack up her things and arrange to get them to her ex, but there were other things to deal with and he'd driven up and was staying at a motel in Monterey. I had told him about Nora, and he'd gotten in touch with her. She was in the room, too, when I arrived. I barely recognized the woman who'd made the fuss at the airport. Her face was drawn and her expression troubled as she looked over her sister's things.

She picked up a copy of her sister's book and thumbed through it. She stared at the photo on the back as if it was still hard for her to believe that Izabelle was her twin. "I don't want anything," she said finally and walked out.

It was a little more comfortable when she'd gone. All I could think to say to her was that I was sorry, which hardly covered both her losses.

Zak had begun to pack up Izabelle's things. He gestured toward the box I'd brought back from Adele's workshop when she suddenly got concerned about clutter. "Let's see what's in there," he said. I was going to tell him it was just samples of crocheted pieces, probably yarn, maybe some patterns and probably some hooks, but decided to go with the flow and just empty the box and show him the contents.

I dumped it on the bed, and sure enough some flowers fell out that had a double layer of petals, some more pouch bags with a slightly different design, some handouts with patterns for the bags. As I was separating the balls of yarn, I saw it. Izabelle must have thrown it in the box when she stopped in her room before she met Bennett. I held the white fuzzy choker. I could see Adele's point: the white puffs did look like marshmallows. And when I turned it over, just as Adele said, there was a small spot of pink nail polish.

Zak said I could have everything in that box and the ones we'd brought back late last night. He had no use for crochet supplies. He did want to keep the manuscript and anything related to her fusion craft. I suppose he thought it might bring in some money. I mentioned he might be hearing from Spenser Futterman and left it at that.

He thanked me for my assistance and helped me take the boxes to my room.

Back at breakfast, Adele was hugging all of her people. I stopped next to her and put the choker on the table. She stared at it for a moment before turning it over. When she saw the pink mark, her lips spread in a relieved smile. She held it up and waved it around before going off to find Marni.

Mason was all smiles and waved me over. He already had a cup of coffee poured for me. I saw him look toward the door, and his mouth twisted in displeasure. I turned to see what had inspired his change of mood. Barry Greenberg had just walked in and was looking around. I didn't care if I was working — I ran over and threw my arms around his tall frame.

"What are you doing here?" I said.

He seemed at a loss and just mumbled something about he'd decided to pick me up.

"You drove six hours to pick me up?"

"I missed you, what can I say?" He tried to shrug off his comment as if the long drive was no big deal, but his eyes gave him away. I told him I still had some things to do, and we arranged to meet later.

Breakfast ended and our people all went outside and hung around. Dinah's group had gone for a last walk to the beach. Everyone else seemed to be prolonging the last moments of being together in this picturesque spot.

I checked the administration building and made sure everyone was getting checked out okay. CeeCee was at the desk, making arrangements to extend her stay. She was glad to be away from the paparazzi and said she'd finish putting the blanket together and make sure it got delivered. She said it was the least she could do.

When I was sure everything was under control, I met Barry on the deck and he followed me up to my room. When he saw the narrow beds and Spartan surroundings, he laughed. "Maybe we couldn't have worked things out after all." I packed up my things and we loaded them, along with the boxes of crochet supplies, into his Tahoe. I stopped to pick up the registration stuff from the administration building and put it in the SUV, too.

Adele had all the supplies and things she'd brought up gathered together by the main driveway. Commander brought over some of the things he'd had shipped up, too. Dinah was with him. She winked at me when she saw Barry before getting into a cab for the airport with Adele, Sheila, and Commander.

We still didn't know what the prognosis would be for Adele's car. I'd called Mrs. Shedd to fill her in on the end of the weekend. Though I knew she was back from the cruise, I'd just gotten her voice mail. My message had been so long, it beeped off before I finished. With everything going on, I'd missed her call back. Her message was short and made my stomach churn.

"Molly, I've thought long and hard all during the weekend about the future of the bookstore. My decision isn't the kind of thing to be left as a message. We'll talk in person when you get back."

What did that mean?

Great, my list of things to deal with when

I got home had just gotten longer. On top of my son moving back home, and the two cats, there was now uncertainty about my job.

Mason came out pulling his duffle bag and saw the pile of stuff. "I guess you won't be needing a ride after all. What about all of this?"

I felt funny asking Mason to haul everything if I wasn't going in his car, so I looked at Barry and he shrugged a yes and started to load up the Tahoe.

Mason stepped close to me. "It was a memorable weekend."

I thanked him for everything, and hugged him. Barry was busy arranging all the extra stuff in the Tahoe as Mason went on to his rental Explorer.

Other retreaters were getting in their cars and leaving, or heading for the airport in cabs. I took one last look around the weathered buildings of Asilomar and climbed in the front seat of the Tahoe. Barry got in his side and started the motor, but before he could put the car in gear, Mason ran in front of the hood, waving his arms.

Barry stuck his head out the window. "Is something wrong?"

"The motor won't turn over on the Explorer," Mason said. "The rental place is coming to pick it up, but they can't guarantee when they can get me a replacement. So I'm kind of stranded. I was hoping I could hitch a ride back to Tarzana with you."

"What about flying back?"

"Not an option. All the flights are booked up." Did I detect the glint of a smile in Mason's eyes?

Barry was unmoved. "You could call another rental company."

Mason was unmoved, too. "I already tried. Would you believe there isn't a car available in the area?"

Barry blew his breath out, clearly not pleased with the way this was going, and I don't think he exactly believed Mason. "How about I try calling for you? I bet I can find an available car." Barry locked eyes with Mason. Mason pulled out his cell phone and reached out to hand it to Barry, calling his bluff.

"Never mind. Get in," Barry grunted in capitulation. Mason was definitely smiling as he went for his things.

"You must be tired from driving up here," Mason said after he loaded his duffel bag in the back. "I'd be happy to drive."

"No worries, pal, I have it covered," Barry said with gritted teeth as he put the SUV in gear.

As we drove out the gate of Asilomar, Mason leaned against my seat and showed me the hook and yarn he still had from Izabelle's workshop. "Maybe on the way back you could show me how to crochet," he said. "I'd like to make a dog sweater for Spike. Of course, I'll need your help."

I watched Barry clench his jaw and I knew what he was thinking. Mason fought dirty.

It was going to be a long ride home.

ALL-PURPOSE POUCH PURSE

Easy to make

Supplies:

J hook (6 mm), or size needed to obtain the gauge, for purse

H hook (5 mm), or size needed to obtain the gauge, for flower

Needle for finishing

Safety pin or stitch marker

1 skein Red Heart Designer Sport yarn (279 yards/255m) — makes two purses with leftover yarn

1 skein Bernat Glow in the Dark yarn (approx. 72 yards/66m) — makes multiple flowers

Stitches:

Single crochet, double crochet, triple crochet, picot (chain 3, single crochet in third chain from hook, single crochet in the next 2 single crochets)

Dimensions of body of the purse:
Approx 6 1/2 inches by 8 inches

Gauge for purse:
12 single crochet stitches = 4 inches
15 rows = 4 inches

Gauge for flower:
The diameter after the first round = 1 inch

Using the J hook and Red Heart Designer Sport yarn, chain 16.

Row 1: Single crochet in the second chain from the hook and across. 15 single crochet stitches made. Chain 1 and turn.

Row 2: Single crochet in the first stitch and across. 15 single crochet stitches made. Chain 1 and turn.

Repeat row 2 twenty-two more times. On the last row do not chain one or turn; instead, finish off.

Make two pieces with above directions. Place them together, right sides facing out. Join pieces by attaching yarn with a slip stitch on the top left side. Working through both thicknesses, do a single crochet in the same stitch and continue single crocheting down the side. At the corner do 3 single crochets and then continue single crocheting along the bottom. At the next corner do

3 single crochets, then continue single crocheting up the other side. Add an extra single crochet on the top stitch. Do not finish off. Chain 120 for the handle and, being careful not to twist the chains, connect to the other side with a slip stitch. Do not finish off.

Edging

Beginning with the first stitch of the body of the bag, start the picot stitch *(chain 3, single crochet in the third chain from the hook, single crochet in the next 2 single crochets)* Repeat from *to* around the body of the bag. Do not finish off; instead, continue and make a single crochet in each of the handle's chain stitches. End with slip stitch in the first stitch in the body. Finish off. Weave in ends.

Six-Petaled Flower

With the H hook and Bernat Glow in the Dark yarn chain 10 and join with a slip stitch.

Round 1: Chain 1 and do 18 single crochets in the ring. (Mark the first single crochet with safety pin or stitch marker.) Slip stitch to marked first single crochet.

Round 2: Chain 1, single crochet in the marked stitch from the previous round, * chain 3, skip the next two single crochets, and single crochet in the next single crochet. *Repeat *to* 4 times. Chain 3 and slip stitch into first single crochet.

Round 3: Slip stitch to move the yarn to the next chain 3 space *(single crochet, double crochet, double crochet. Triple crochet, double crochet, double crochet, single crochet).* Repeat *to* in the 5 chain 3 spaces for the petals. End with slip stitch to first single crochet. Fasten off. Weave in ends.

Tack flower or flowers to front of pouch purse.

Flowers can also be attached to pin backings and worn as a pin.

Note: Flower can also be made in Red Heart Designer Sport yarn.

ADELE'S MARSHMALLOW STITCH

Using a P hook (11.50 mm) and white Red Heart Baby Clouds yarn, yarn over and put hook through chain stitch, pull yarn back through, yarn over, go through 2 loops on the hook, which leaves 2 loops on the hook; yarn over, go through stitch, pull yarn back through, yarn over, go through 2 loops on hook; which leaves 3 loops on hook; yarn over, go through stitch, pull yarn through, yarn over, go through 2 loops on hook, which leaves 4 loops on hook; yarn over, go through stitch, pull yarn through, yarn over, go through 2 loops, which leaves 5 loops on hook; pull yarn through all 5 loops. Chain 1.

Note: Adele is still trying to figure what to do with the stitch.

COMMANDER BLAINE'S SAVORY AND SWEET MINI CREAM PUFFS

1/2 cup butter
1 cup milk
1 cup bread flour
4 large eggs at room temperature, unbeaten

Put butter and milk in a heavy saucepan and bring to boil. Add the flour all at once and stir vigorously with a wooden spoon until the mixture no longer sticks to the side of the pan. Remove from heat and cool ten minutes. Add eggs one at a time, beating with the wooden spoon until the egg is completely mixed in.

Drop by rounded teaspoons onto a buttered cookie sheet. Bake at 400 degrees for about 25 minutes, until the puffs are golden. Cool completely on a wire rack. Cut off tops, fill and replace tops. Makes about 30 appetizer-size puffs.

Filling

SAVORY

8 ounces of sour cream

3.5 ounce jar of black lumpfish caviar or 15
  kalamata olives, finely chopped

Place approximately 1 tablespoon sour cream in puffs and garnish with approximately 1/3 teaspoon caviar or 1 chopped olive. Replace the top of the puff. Makes about 15 savory cream puffs.

Other savory options: ham, cheese, lox and cream cheese, creamed spinach, crab salad, egg salad, chicken salad.

SWEET

8 ounces whipping cream, whipped

About 15 strawberries sliced thin

Place about 1 strawberry in puff with about 2 tablespoons of whipped cream on top. Replace the top of the puff. Makes about 15 sweet cream puffs.

Other sweet options: pudding or custard, other kinds of fruit, ice cream

CLASSIC S'MORES

For one s'more:

2 graham cracker halves

2 large marshmallows

2 blocks of milk chocolate about the size of
the graham cracker halves

Place chocolate on graham cracker halves.
Roast marshmallows so they are golden on
the outside and molten on the inside. Put
roasted marshmallows on the graham
cracker half and chocolate combination,
place the other graham cracker and chocolate on top. Squeeze gently so the heat of
the marshmallows melts the chocolate.

ABOUT THE AUTHOR

Betty Hechtman has a degree in fine arts and since college has studied everything from tap dancing to magic. When she isn't writing, reading, or crocheting, she's probably at the gym. She lives in Tarzana, California, with her family and terrier mix, Goldy.

We hope you have enjoyed this Large Print book. Other Thorndike, Wheeler, Kennebec, and Chivers Press Large Print books are available at your library or directly from the publishers.

For information about current and upcoming titles, please call or write, without obligation, to:

Publisher
Thorndike Press
295 Kennedy Memorial Drive
Waterville, ME 04901
Tel. (800) 223-1244

or visit our Web site at:

http://gale.cengage.com/thorndike

OR

Chivers Large Print
published by BBC Audiobooks Ltd
St James House, The Square
Lower Bristol Road
Bath BA2 3SB
England
Tel. +44(0) 800 136919
email: bbcaudiobooks@bbc.co.uk
www.bbcaudiobooks.co.uk

All our Large Print titles are designed for easy reading, and all our books are made to last.